Falling from Grace

by

Louise Burness

PAPERBACK ISBN: 978-0-9957631-2-8

Louise Burness asserts the right to be identified as the author of this work.

This book is a work of fiction. Any similarities to any person or organisation are entirely coincidental.

Published by Charpollo Publishing

Credits:
Cover illustration by Louise Burness
Cover design by David Spink
Editing by NVG

www.louiseburness.info

For Natasha
Without you, my ears would have walls.

Chapter One

'For the millionth time, it was an accident. A silly, irresponsible mistake. Most definitely not a suicide attempt. You can keep me locked up here forever and I will never change my story.'

'I notice your use of the word story,' Dr Peter gives me yet another of those condescending looks over his bifocals. I grip on to the edges of the oversized armchair and exhale my frustrations.

'I can't win, can I? If I tell you the truth you don't believe me, but if I lie and tell you that I did intentionally throw myself over the balcony, then you'll keep me in to safeguard me. Trust me, if I had meant to kill myself then I would have made it a bit more dramatic. From the first floor onto grass says concussion, not death to me. I may be mad but give me some credit.'

'Nobody has said that you're mad, Grace.'

'Oh, but I am. Clearly, stark raving bonkers. You insist that I'm not concussed, so I must be. How else would you say that I got here of my own accord if I can't remember consenting? I wouldn't voluntarily admit myself to a mental institute.'

I try to recall the events of last night, coming round in that curtained off cubicle in Accident and Emergency to see Mum and Dad by my bedside, their faces full of joy that I'd woken up. I managed to mumble an uttering of surprise at their presence.

'What the fuck?'

Mum's chair was close enough for her to stroke my brow. Her warm, brown face filled with concern. I felt five years old again as I listened to her lilting Caribbean tones.

'Shush, Gracie, you're safe now. We came as soon as we heard. Does your head still hurt? You're going to have a cracking bruise tomorrow.'

I'd rallied myself. You're a grown woman for goodness sake, get a grip. I'd spotted a member of staff and tried to attract her attention with a wave.

'Honey, they want to keep you in a while. Just until you're feeling better.' Dad leaned in to hold my hand, the remaining tufts of his blonde hair tousled from where he'd run his fingers through it. Something he always did when he was worried.

'I'm fine, I don't need to be here. I'm getting dressed and going home. Ask that nurse to call me a cab.' I'd tried to pull myself into a sitting position but the room whirled around me and I fell back onto the bed.

'It's in your own best interest, dear. Just stay in for a few days so they can monitor things and you'll be home before you know it.' Dad paused and glanced down the corridor. 'Oh, here comes Dr Peter now. You're in very safe hands, Gracie.'

'So, how's our patient?' The doctor's voice had echoed around the cubicle making my head throb. Mum answered for me, I zoned out and tried to piece together the events of the evening.

Firstly, what the hell gave those two the right to turn up unannounced? I've been fending for myself for years and they think they can show up now and tell me what's best for me? I think back to the last time I saw them; the night of the endless, screaming arguments. I was an embarrassment. I had brought shame on the family. I was only seventeen years old, for Christ's sake, and a hell of a lot tamer than most of the crowd I hung out with. All these years I've stood on my own two feet, proved to everyone that I can be self-sufficient and successful. Well, they're a day late and a dollar short, I don't need anyone's help.

I must have passed out then, as that's pretty much all I can recall about last night. I woke up in A&E and have been moved somewhere else, with this Dr Peter to look after me. I didn't agree to this nor to my parents frantically rushing to my bedside for that matter. It's been such a confusing few hours. I stare at this strange man opposite, watching me from his threadbare wingback chair, hoping for answers.

'How did my parents know I was in hospital? They don't even know where I live. Shit clearly got real for me in the past twenty-four hours so I suggest that I stop talking and you start.'

'It must be difficult to see your parents again after so long, maybe overwhelming?'

'Of course it is. We didn't exactly part on good terms.' I throw the doctor a withering look. 'Anyway, you know what I mean, of all the people in the world to show up at my bedside, they'd be the least expected. Actually, I take that back. As shocked as I was to see them, I think my idiot ex-boyfriend would be the last person I'd expect to have been there. Why on earth would you just throw away a ten year relationship? Now, he's one you want to hunt down and put in this place.'

'How did it make you feel when the relationship ended?' Dr Peter's voice is infuriatingly calm. I feel a ball of anger swell and burn furiously in my chest. I don't want to talk about Josh, nor do I want to think about him, but I know that refusing to answer will drag this out more than I need right now. I've seen enough *Dr Phil* episodes to know how these things work. I swoon back onto the chair, a shade over-dramatically.

'I've never felt such utter devastation in my life. He meant the world to me and I don't know how I'll ever love again now he's gone.'

Dr Peter raises an eyebrow at me. Maybe I took that too far, considering I don't give a flying one.

'Sorry, I'm prone to exaggeration; I must do it a hundred times a day.' I notice my clenched fists are shaking and attempt to regain some decorum by folding them into my lap. The doctor jots something down on his pad, I lean to the side to sneak a peek but he catches my eye and moves the pad a little closer to his chest. It's probably best that I don't know: bat-shit crazy, keep in indefinitely, don't get too close in case she bites. I chuckle to myself, something along those lines, I guess.

'I was justifiably fuming, of course. After a decade of being together, I thought the talk he had come round for meant he was finally making things permanent with us. Not to break the news that he was about to run off with some trollop after dumping me. When I saw the ring box it gave me a feeling of control. I could ruin that part of his life, since he had just devastated mine. Pathetic, I know. He didn't have to marry me; it just would have been nice that after all that time together he had considered it. Why her? Why after such a short time?' I explain with a forced sense of calm. 'Anyway, I don't intend to sit around like that Dickensian woman, jilted and eating wedding cake, in a white frock I bought off eBay. You know? What's-her-name?'

'Miss Havisham.'

'Yes, Miss Havisham. That's the one, thank you. I mean, it's not like I would allow anything in my past to scar me for life. I'm fine.'

'Tell me about your past, Grace. Do you feel it was a happy time?'

'It was average, I guess, if ducking flying crockery was your thing. We didn't have much money in our house. In winter, we'd all huddle around the fridge to keep warm.' I give a little snort at my humour. Dr Peter is less impressed, I can tell. 'It's probably the reason a successful career was so important to me, I never wanted to find myself struggling for money. My parents worked hard in menial, low-paid jobs that never got them out of the difficulties they faced. I didn't want my future to be living endlessly from hand to mouth without any luxuries like heating or electricity.'

'Do you find you reflect on the past often?'

I raise my eyes to the ceiling to show I'm trying to recollect my entire existence in just a few seconds.

'Nope, look, this all seems a bit one-sided. Is there anything you'd like to share with me?'

The doctor exhales slowly before speaking.

'OK, Grace, let's take a break for now. Have a rest before the group session with our other visitors later on this afternoon.'

'Visitors?' I frown.

'Yes, we prefer that term to residents as that would imply a long-term stay, or patients, as that would signify an illness. We'd like to see you back on your feet and out into your day-to-day lives again as soon as possible. Of course, we will always be here to support you, whenever you may need us.' Dr Peter presses the intercom button on his desk. 'Ariel, will you please see Grace to her room?' He snaps shut his notepad before observing me like a specimen in a jar. The door opens within seconds and a pretty, blonde woman appears in a haze of blue floral and a perfume that smells of summer.

'Follow me please, Grace,' she smiles warmly and extends a welcoming hand. 'I'll give you a tour of the facilities.'

She's making it sound like some deluxe spa, rather than the torture chamber I rather suspect it is. This grates on me, I'm far from being an idiot and I refuse to be treated like one. As we turn into the corridor, I take my chance to question Ariel. She's by far the friendliest face I've seen in here and I sense that she's a bit of a soft touch. The doctor's cool demeanour has unnerved me, as did that of the admission nurses last night. There was an air of superiority surrounding them that I didn't care for. I must have been knocked clean out by my fall as I don't even recall my trip to the hospital. Now, to be told that I'd be here for an indefinite period until I had dealt with my so-called issues, was terrifying. They had been officious in their check-up of me before settling me into a side room, where they looked in on me like suspicious parents at regular intervals throughout the night.

'What is this place?' I glance around, looking for clues to the identity of my new location. Ariel gives a musical laugh.

'I suppose you'd call Arcadia a retreat. It's a rehabilitation unit for people like yourself, in need of additional support. As soon as we knew that you were physically fit and healthy, we wanted to address your emotional wellbeing.' She stops abruptly and indicates to a door on the left. I peer through the window.

'This is our art therapy class; we like to encourage all of our visitors to rediscover any passions they have had.' We continue by the various rooms, with everything from baking to creative writing taking place.

'These are all activities that people may have enjoyed but forgotten about or let go,' Ariel continues. 'We find it the best way to recovery, along with extensive one to one sessions, like you just had with Dr Peter. We also have a variety of programmes available to encourage new skills, would there be anything you think you'd be keen to try, Grace?'

'Wine tasting?' I flash Ariel a hopeful smile.

'I'm afraid alcohol isn't allowed on the premises. We view it as unhelpful as it suppresses emotions. We prefer to keep feelings open to allow our visitors to deal with them, not bury them.' she finishes sternly. I roll my eyes to emphasise how unsurprised I am at this news. 'If you would like, I can give you a copy of the itinerary to look over in your room. I'm sure you'll find something interesting to take part in.' Ariel pats my arm apologetically.

Well, this is going to be a bundle of bloody laughs: twice daily therapy sessions, sharing a room for the first time in thirty-odd years, no booze and no chance of escape. Maybe they'll have happy pills, surely one could not expect to be caged like a zoo animal without some perks. We eventually come to a stop in the middle of the next corridor.

'Here's your room. Let's see if Kirsty is home.' Ariel gives a quick knock before walking in. 'Just you for now, she's probably in class. She's a keen writer is our wee, Scottish lassie,' she chuckles. I grimace as she attempts a shockingly bad, Glaswegian accent. 'Right, I shall leave you to settle in and give you a knock when group begins. Feel free to pop down to reception and see me if you need anything.'

I watch as she click-clacks her way down the hallway and disappears around the corner. I close the bedroom door and glance around. I'm finally alone. A sense of calm creeps over me for the first time today. Now I can attempt to gather my thoughts and make some sense of my situation. I touch the tender part on the back of my head and wince, it was quite a knock I gave myself. I could have hurt myself badly had I missed the small patch of grass in the back garden and landed on the paving stones, even from that fairly small drop. Strangely enough, I feel safe within these four purple walls with nobody around to interrogate me. No one to question my motives or try to second guess my intentions. In here I am just me. The completely normal, if not clumsy, head of department with a fancy-pants car and a North London flat. What could possibly make me want to end it all? Men come and go, hey-ho, I'm already over it. I wouldn't flatter Josh's ego by being even remotely suicidal over him. His bit of stuff is welcome to him. In fact, I quite pity her, she has no idea what an asshole he really is. I give the bedroom a furtive once over. Two single beds line the near and far sides, an unkempt one with a tartan blanket to the right, that I assume is Kirsty's, and an immaculately made one with a patchwork quilt to the left. Mine. I flop down onto it and pull the comforter over me. I need to think of a way to convince that bloody doctor that I'm not a risk to myself, or anyone else for that matter, and get out of here as soon as possible.

***

'Thompson, get your feet off the table, boy. You are not at home.'

'But Miss, I'm knackered from playing me Xbox all night, ain't I?'

I throw the teenager a look of exasperation and turn back to my register, predominantly filled with absentees.

'Jones?'

'Here, Miss.'

'Collins? Collins? Anyone know where Aria is today?'

'She ain't coming in; she's still not done last week's homework and you said not to come back till it's done, innit, Miss.'

'Fabulous, thank you, Chardonnay. It's reassuring to know my students take their education so seriously. Right, I guess that's it for today then. Twelve of you out of a possible twenty-seven, not a bad turnout compared to Monday. So, who can remember where we left off yesterday?' I look out at the sea of disinterested faces in front of me and it makes me sigh. They really could not care less about Biology, or in fact school in general. The movement of water particles from a high concentration to a low concentration through a semi-permeable membrane, is evidently not high on their list of learning outcomes, and I can appreciate this. Once upon a time I thought it mattered, back when I was a fresh-faced graduate, all wild black curls and broad smiles. I was excited for my career to begin and anticipated the difference I could make to London's inner city, disadvantaged youths. Actually, it's the reason I chose this school with its poor attendance and reports; I felt I could inspire and equip these children for their paths ahead.

I glance around at my class, even by the school's overall poor educational standards these are the great under-achievers of their year group. The scummy bits at bottom of the barrel was how the head had described them. No wonder they didn't try, with attitudes like that from people who should be fighting their corner. I had tried and failed over so many years now. I couldn't muster any enthusiasm for teaching them, and in predictable return, they had absolutely no intention of learning.

Take Darren Thompson for example: a string of DNA failure, encompassing every unfortunate feature his parents possess, including his father's sticky-out ears and his mother's buck teeth. He openly told me yesterday that he had taken my class purely in the hope that he could strike it rich with his own meth lab. After a few nods had confirmed the other pupils' agreement, I had frostily informed them that if they had paid attention to anything I said, then they would realise that what they needed was Mr McIntosh's chemistry class down the hall. I had to agree that a *Breaking Bad* style life was indeed a fantastic idea but in reality, their scrawny, acne-ridden bodies would be pumped full of bullets by the end of first week. So well 'ard were they, that any failure to hand in homework resulted in a phone call from mummy, informing me that their brat had been a bit poorly last night and just wasn't up to it. This particular boy had looked crestfallen at my insistence that we would absolutely not be covering the topics suited to furthering his career in the sale of methamphetamine.

'We got up to the bit where you said we were in the wrong class if we wanted to make crystal meth but were too stupid to understand chemistry,' he sulks.

This wasn't quite how I had put it, but as science subjects go, first level biology was considered a good starting block, before moving on to chemistry or physics. This was the education board's sociological experiment, to treat the children with educational challenges as if they could sail through a biology exam unscathed and maybe (just maybe) they would.

'Darren, trust me, if creating an illicit, methamphetamine hydrochloride laboratory in a recreational vehicle, in the wilderness of Albuquerque's wasteland was the easy option, I would not be standing in front of you apathetic bunch of reprobates in an attempt to impart on you how the imperative knowledge of photosynthesis and osmosis will impact upon your future.'

Darren stares at me panic-stricken, his oversized Adam's apple bobbing up and down as he gulps back his shock.

'Miss, I don't even know what that means...'

'It means if it was that fucking simple then *I would be doing it*.' My class stare at me mutely as I stand in front of them, red-faced and hyperventilating. I place my hands on the desk in front of me and close my eyes, taking slow, steady breaths. I glance anxiously at the clock, it's only 3pm. I seriously can't face a double period of this shit. I stare at them wild-eyed as they shrink in their chairs, the clock ticks to fill the ominous void for what feels like an eternity.

'Fuck it, class dismissed. If anyone asks why, say I've sent you out on a field trip to study examples of osmosis. Which, to exemplify, is how the copious amounts of sub-standard wine that I am about to consume will find its way into my bloodstream and numb me from this shitty, mundane excuse of a life.'

'Well, as meltdowns go that sounds pretty spectacular, Grace. Are we planning on a career rethink before we get fired or going straight in for instant dismissal, hmm?' Karen glances over her glass with a smirk.
'Thank you, my dear friend, for your unconditional support. It'll be fine, they got an afternoon off and in lieu of more, they're not going to dob me in. Besides, I'm just having a bad week. Josh changed the pass code on his phone again. Why would he keep doing that if he has nothing to hide?' I take a large gulp of wine and frown at my friend's mocking, green eyes.
'I wonder. Doesn't the fact that you searched his text messages, personal email, work email, Facebook, WhatsApp and Twitter accounts, and still found nothing not mean anything to you?' Karen tucks a stray red lock that has escaped from her impeccable up-do behind her ear. I always get no-holds-barred advice from her, we've known each other since year six and she's the only school friend I've really kept in touch with.
'I forgot to search his trash though and he may have deleted some messages. I never thought of that until now. You're the lawyer, why didn't you suggest it?'
Karen raises an amused eyebrow at my questioning.
'Ten years and seven months and not a whiff of a proposal. Then all of a sudden he's working loads of overtime and cuts our dates down to two a week, from five, and I can't even remember the last time he stayed over. You're not telling me that there isn't something funny going on,' I insist.
'I'm amazed you stuck around for so long. What is it you told me a few months back? If there is no ring on your finger in three years then cut him loose, you really need to start taking your own advice. Ten years, Grace, you were in your prime when you met him and now you're thirty-seven years old. Even thirty would have been fine, giving him his three years to propose plus a little courage time. Come on, Islington is awash with single, virile men. If you know where to look, of course,' she winks.
'God, I hate it when you're smug. So, what you're saying is it's all my own fault and I should have done something about it before I was past it?'
'Kind of,' Karen shrugs.
'Helpful, thank you.'

***

I sit bolt upright in bed with a violent intake of breath, disorientated for a moment before everything floods back to me.
'Shit, I'm still in this bloody place,' I groan.
'Aye, you are that, hen. You and me both. Bad dream?'

A peroxide blonde sits cross-legged on the bed opposite, staring curiously at me. A slash of red lipstick gives her mouth a mean appearance and a thick, black slug of liquid eyeliner almost covers her upper lids. She is impossibly thin and glamorous in a rough kind of way. Edgy. That's what they'd call her on *Next Top Model*.

'No, a really good dream actually,' I pull myself reluctantly into a sitting position. Part of me wants to go back to sleep, to be free of here, but the lure of finding out more about my room-mate has got the better of me. 'I was in the pub with my friend, drinking wine. Oh, I can almost taste it; a rich, oak-aged Rioja and a good year it was too. It was the one we had two weekends ago.'

The twenty-something woman opposite shrugs.

'I wouldn't know, I'm more of a vodka and shots kind of girl myself.'

'So, you're Kirsty, I assume?'

'The very one, and you're Grace. Ariel told me I was getting a new room-mate. I guess I did well having the space to myself all this time, I wonder why that was...' She trails off lost in thought momentarily, before snapping back to the present. 'So, tell me, what brought you in here? Well, obviously the same as everyone else but by what means?'

'Sorry? I don't know what you're talking about, means of what?'

'Killing yourself, numpty. This is a suicide clinic, not fucking Disneyland,' she snorts. 'What was your means of choice? An overdose? A wrist-slashing? We never see the more permanent ways in here. The no going back ones.' Kirsty points an imaginary gun to her head and mimics the sound of blowing her brains out, complete with the splat against the wall.

'That's sick,' I retort. 'You don't waste any time in interrogating people, do you? Actually, I didn't try to kill myself, I fell from my balcony trying to reach a ring that I'd dropped. OK, I actually threw it away, it landed on the edge of my next door neighbour's veranda and I thought I could reach it as they are only a couple of feet apart.'

'A normal person would have knocked on the door and retrieved it that way, not dangled over the edge. That, was never going to end well,' she scoffs.

'What is it with this bloody place? Nobody believes you when you say it was an accident. Trust me, I'd have been much more creative if I'd meant it. I didn't even leave a note, not that anyone would have cared anyway.'

'Aww, poor little Grace with nobody to love her. That makes you a prime candidate for suicide, FYI.' She raises an eyebrow challengingly at my glare.

'What about you then, what are you in for?'

'Same. Total freak accident,' she sighs. I stare in horror at Kirsty's outstretched arms. Long, angry scars run from her wrists to the inside of her elbows. 'I was minding my own business, walking along carrying a sharp kitchen knife when I accidently slipped and fell into a hot bath. They didn't believe it was an accident either, for what it's worth.'

'Holy shit, I'm amazed you're alive.'

'Yeah, well I am, thanks to my arsehole husband who forgot his phone and came back to collect it, before meeting his bitch on the side,' she smiles wickedly. 'I go through his messages and I knew he was screwing around. Anyhoo, I'd only just begun to lose consciousness and they managed to stitch me up and pump me full of someone else's blood to get me back. I wasn't impressed.'

'Bitch on the side, I like that. If it's any consolation, my ex was a dick too, we weren't married though. Ten years and nada, we didn't even live together. Now he's off to Brighton to be with the woman of his dreams.'

'Figures.' Kirsty states matter-of-factly. 'They all get bored eventually, I don't actually know why I'm surprised after my track record. My husband, Ty, never had a job but always inexplicably had money. I know there were dodgy goings on, drug dealing and theft mostly. I didn't question where the money came from and he didn't offer any kind of explanation. I was a bit of a mafia wife in that sense; ask no questions and take what's given. That worked well for us for a while but he got lazy. He started taking me for granted and not coming home, that's when things started to go tits up.'

I try to look impassive at my room-mate's questionable morals as she continues.

'I was only fifteen when I ran away from home, I guess I was seduced by an older man's attention and the seemingly glam lifestyle. I met him two weeks after my sixteenth birthday and I'd been on the streets for five months.'

A gentle knock interrupts us, Ariel pops her head around the door and gives us a warm smile.

'Hello, ladies, good to see you getting to know each other. Just thought I'd remind you that it's time for group therapy.'

'If we must,' shrugs Kirsty. She pulls on some scuffed, red patent heels and teeters to a standing position. Her attire looks more in keeping with a night out clubbing than a therapy session. I glance down at my beige jumper, blue jeans and Ugg boots. This will have to do, I have no change of clothes here and no idea of how to get more. We follow Ariel down the hallway like obedient puppies and I glance at some paintings on the walls by the art department. Water colours of meadows, seascapes and mountains, pretty good for supposed amateurs. My artistic attempts are limited to biology diagrams and even my best efforts end up barely resembling something recognisable, let alone the intended subject. We continue along the corridor and into a large room with plastic chairs set out in a circle. At the opposite end of the room, an elderly, slightly balding gentleman with a moustache, watches approvingly as the room fills up. He takes off his brown, tweed jacket and hangs it officiously on the back of his chair. I take a seat between Kirsty and a rather haughty, middle-aged woman, and take in the room. I try to second guess the reasons that may have brought these people here. I see a variety of ages around me, split almost equally between male and female. If this really is a suicide clinic, as Kirsty claims, then I reckon the well to do woman on my right screwed up a multi-million-pound deal in her important, city job. She took this way out in place of being fired and having to explain to her husband that they'd have to sell their seven-bed house, with views of Hampstead Heath, and pull their kids out of Eton and into the local comp. Yes, that's it, I congratulate myself. I've got her sussed for sure. Working out the reasons why a person has found themselves in here is much more interesting than the means used to kill oneself. Although Kirsty appears to favour the latter. I've always been much more intrigued by a good back-story. What journey has been taken for a person to end up in the place they're at now? My thoughts are interrupted as Ariel finishes her chat with the man opposite me, she takes a seat next to the group leader at the head of the circle. He clears his throat and glances around us with a smile.

'There are a few new faces here I see, so let me begin by introducing myself. My name is Gabe and I'm the group therapy leader here at Arcadia. In these sessions, no one is forced to contribute, you may simply listen if you prefer. We do not judge anyone for being here but we want to offer our support and care to all of you equally. If you'd like to say something, then please wait until the person before you has finished before you begin. Any volunteers to get the ball rolling?'

A florid man in a brown, woollen jumper glances cautiously around the room before slowly raising his hand.

'Oh, for fuck's sake!' Kirsty gives an exasperated sigh.

'Please, Kirsty. Jim is as entitled as anyone else to have his say. Perhaps you can go after him today. After all, you have been here for two months now and I'm sure we'd all love to hear something about you.'

Several nods confirm Gabe's request and Kirsty scowls her disapproval at the group. Jim gives an apologetic cough before beginning.

'Well, I know many of you are familiar with my story by now but we have some new people and I don't mind sharing it again. I find it somewhat...helps.' He pauses, glancing nervously in Kirsty's direction before continuing. 'My wife and I had many happy years together, she was my entire world,' he shakes his head in awe. 'We had two sons, William and Robert, and we raised them on our farm in the West Country. We'd looked forward to our retirement for many years and I had just handed over the reins to my boys. We were just two months into what should have been the time of our lives when my wife got sick.' Jim gives a dramatic pause and glances around the room. Kirsty gives the aggressive exhale of someone who has heard this story one too many times and Gabe responds by shooting another warning look in her direction. Jim ignores her obvious dissatisfaction and picks up his story again.

'We had planned the trip of a lifetime to start off our retirement, a Mediterranean cruise; ten ports, all inclusive. We were all packed and ready to go, when my wife suddenly took a turn for the worse and I had to call an ambulance.'

'I'll skip to the end for you so you can zone out, shall I?' Kirsty leans in to stage whisper to me. 'She died in the ambulance on the way to hospital and...'

'*Kirsty.*' Gabe's face has turned a terrifying shade of red, I shake my head violently to deny any association with the rude and insensitive person next to me.

'Well, I'm just saying what everyone else is too chicken-shit to admit. How many times do we have to hear this bloody story? I'm sick of it. In fact, I wish we'd known this irritating arse when we were trying to kill ourselves. Half an hour with him and we'd all have died of fucking boredom anyway.' An incensed Jim gets to his feet.

'Take that back, you little witch.'

'To think, I actually felt sorry for you the first time I heard that story, but after the gazillionth time, I think she was a lucky cow for getting away from you,' Kirsty retaliates.

'She didn't want to get away from me,' Jim barks. 'I know you find me boring but she didn't, we would chat for hours. I would do anything to speak to her right now.'

Gabe's small frame scurries across the room in preparation of separating the two, as Jim towers over Kirsty.

'And what would Jim say if he spoke to his wife right now...hmm? Let me see,' Kirsty taunts. 'Would it be, "sorry dear, I couldn't go on without you.

It was the final straw when you popped your clogs only one week after my beloved Neddy got turned into a Pritt stick?" I don't care, Jim. None of us do.' Kirsty turns to face me. 'Yes, that's the prequel to the beloved wife story, a dead fucking horse!'

'I thought I'd seen my fair share of cows but I have never met one quite as stupid as you.'

Kirsty pulls herself up to her full height but it makes no impact next to Jim's six foot four.

'Is that so? And I always thought farmers were supposed to spread shit on their fields, not spout it,' She spits. 'We're all sick of hearing your attention seeking drivel. She's *dead*. Get over it! You're not the only one with problems.'

I sit motionless with shock as two security guards bodily remove Kirsty from the room. She kicks out violently in anger at being restrained as Gabe directs a puce Jim back to his seat.

'Are you alright, Grace? You look a bit shaken.' Ariel sits herself down on Kirsty's empty seat.

'You can't make me share with her, she's unhinged. She'll frickin' kill me,' I manage to stammer out.

'Don't worry, she's just a little troubled and confused at the moment. I think you'll be a calming influence on her. You're a secondary school teacher, right?' I nod my confirmation as I watch the struggle make its way out of the door. 'Well, Dr Peter personally chose you to share a room with Kirsty as he thought you'd make a good impression on her. You're used to challenging behaviour and providing guidance, you'll be the positivity she need right now.' She pats my hand, a little too patronisingly for my liking. 'There are other paths to go down than suicide, like helping people more troubled than yourself. Talk to her, help her see that she needs to be more patient with other people and their circumstances.'

I silently grit my teeth as I stare at Ariel's hopeful smile. I can't bring myself to be mean to her but I couldn't be further from suicidal, not only that but she's so off the mark with her bumper sticker psychology. I'm only looking out for myself from now on, it's all anyone else does. I am aware that playing the game is my only ticket out of here; live by their rules, admit I've made mistakes and that I'm beginning to see how I can use my experiences to help others. I don't have to deny an attempted suicide but I certainly won't admit it. I can bullshit my way out of here better than my class can blag their way out of detention. I plaster the biggest smile I can muster onto my face and turn to face Ariel.

'You're so right and I think I'm beginning to see that now. I'll have a little chat to Kirsty once we get back to our room and I'll pop down to reception for a brochure on classes to take.' Her expression is one of rapt joy and I can't help but feel a little guilty. Who cares, my charm offensive has officially begun. It's five days until the weekend and I aim to be out of here and back in the pub by Friday night.

Chapter Two

'Jesus Christ, Grace. Stop being such a bloody nag. This promotion means I'm pretty much working around the clock. I'm sorry I haven't seen much of you but I'm absolutely shattered.' Josh runs a hand over his meticulously groomed hair. 'Look, there's no point in me staying over tonight, I need to be up at five to meet Steve.' His eyes seek approval that I'm not willing to give, I meet them with a defiant stare.

'Can you call it a promotion? It's only the two of you working on your own magazine?' I strain to keep the hint of sarcasm from my voice.

'Funny girl! Yes, I think you'll find I can. It's a much more responsible role that I've taken on. I'm now covering the property section of En-One, as well as entertainment, and I'm still overseeing half of the sales for ad space until we get someone on board for that.'

'I could do it, I'm always up for a new challenge,' I offer graciously.

'Outside of school hours, obviously.'

'No offence, but you're a science teacher, not a sales rep. Plus, I don't know that being a couple and working together is wise,' Josh sniggers. 'We'd be sick of each other by the end of week one.'

'Actually, I'm also head of department, and what's wrong with being a science teacher?' I bite. 'It's a bit soon to suggest it'll be any kind of success, so I wouldn't be stupid enough to give my job up for it.'

Josh's face flames momentarily at the implication that his project may flounder. So what? I couldn't care less. He's so dismissive of my achievements these days. When I had been promoted last month, I ended up celebrating on my own with a takeaway and a bottle of Prosecco. I hadn't, and probably never would, forget that. The reality is, that no matter how flippant of me he can be, I keep hanging on like some love-starved, Stepford wife.

To tell the truth, I noticed that Josh has been particularly distant this past week. I've barely seen him. I met Steve's wife, Elaine, outside the Angel tube a few days ago. She had been hesitant in discussing the new mag and how hard they were working. Elaine pushed the pram far more vigorously than necessary and made excuses about the baby needing a feed. I found it strange, because twenty minutes later I spotted her browsing through the sale rack in Oasis, looking like she hadn't a care in the world. I had raised my hand in a cheery wave as she ducked down from view. I wanted her to know that I'd seen her. Rude woman, but it did get me thinking. Why had she acted like that? What was she hiding?

'We'll make a fortune selling advertising space,' Josh is still warbling on about this mag. 'Grace? Are you listening? I'm not stupid, my entire career has been spent in journalism, I should think I know what I'm doing.'

I roll my eyes at the glamorisation of a role that had consisted of notifications in the back of the local newspaper; the hatches, matches and dispatches section. It wasn't exactly cutting edge—live from Afghanistan—kind of stuff, but Josh would big up its importance to everyone that he met.

'Did I tell you that Rachel from the English department got engaged?' I query. 'She only met Jacob six months ago, they're keen to get married as soon as possible. They can't wait to start a family.'

'That's nice. Just remember I don't do weddings, so if you get an invite tell them not to bother with the plus one.'

Josh once told me that even his own wedding day wasn't much fun. As he describes it, his ex-wife was the one that insisted on the hoopla. I give up on the conversation with an audible sigh and flick on the TV. I wriggle into my plush, chocolate sofa cushions and settle down to watch *Come Dine with Me*.

'Oh, not this shit,' Josh announces, grabbing the remote control from my lap. He aims it defiantly at the TV and the dramatic theme of the evening news booms out from the surround sound.

'Fine, suit yourself. I need to make dinner anyway.' I get halfway to the kitchen before pausing and turning back. 'Actually, why don't we go out tonight? There's that new Greek place that just opened up at the bottom of Theberton Street. Rachel and Jacob have been, they said it was fantastic.'

'I'm really going to have to make a move soon. Steve and I are interviewing a couple of sales candidates tomorrow and I really could do with composing some interview questions.' Josh reaches into his pocket and places two fifty pound notes on the coffee table, with a cheeky wink. 'Why don't you call Karen and take her out? She'll be far more fun than boring old me. I'm so knackered that one glass of wine would leave me snoring before the starters arrive. Sorry, Gracie.'

With a quick peck on the cheek, he picks up his coat and car keys, and slams his way out of my flat. I dash to the front window to watch him leave, staring blankly at a rain sodden Upper Street below me. The lights of Sainsbury's local illuminate the road, I watch as Josh walks over to his usual parking space, by the disused post office. He's on his phone and I'm already forgotten about. I watch enviously as the post-work crowd make their way to the pub; some braving the lousy weather with blown out umbrellas, others laughing as they huddle from the downpour in shop doorways and wait for the worst to pass. It's barely gone seven in the evening and the October sky has already darkened.

Autumn, my favourite season of the year. I love the change in the atmosphere from balmy, fragrant days, to crisp, drawing in nights. Somebody to giggle with over dinner and then cuddle up in front of a movie with, would have made tonight perfect. Josh and his delusions of grandeur have taken precedence over everything this past month. They haven't even filled half of the first magazine yet and he thinks he's Rupert Murdoch's more successful half-brother. I half-heartedly text Karen to see if she fancies the new restaurant, it's not quite the same as a date with my boyfriend, but it beats staying in. The school breaks always makes me antsy and crave some company. People say they would kill for the holidays that a teacher has, but in reality, it's boring when others are at work and the long days stretch in front of me like an endless abyss. My phone lights up with a hopeful buzz and I quickly type in the pass code. Karen's meeting a guy, I should have guessed. She has several dates a week since she joined that online site three months ago. She sends another message straight after, enquiring if I can I be her 'phone-a-friend' if he turns out to be a dork. We can meet for a drink if he's not worth wasting a few hours of her life on. It's the best offer I've got, so I agree.

I do have other friends, but they're all happily coupled up with their husbands and complacent in their roles as mothers. They're now more interested in having conservatories fitted than going out. It only occurs once a week in an attempt to keep their husbands happy, if it fits in with when their cleaners can babysit, of course. They have all become nanny-hunting, baby bores. I couldn't give a shit that darling Cornelius has already surpassed his Early Years Foundation Stage, or that little Magdalene is in the top one percentile for linguistic formation. I hate the smugness they have, as they smirk their way through a rummage in their bag for their phone. Which must be checked at regular intervals, in case of emergency. Or the wild panic in their eyes when they discover the latest binkie or boo-boo, followed by a frantic call home to check that the babysitter knows the location of the spare. Those smiles exchanged with other tables that say, 'kids, huh?' Whilst I sit there feigning patience with the other half of my conversation hanging in the air redundantly. I think I'd rather stay in by myself than endure an evening of baby talk.

The last time I'd called a mummy friend to go out it was far too short notice, at least a month was standard, to allow the allotted two hours off for a quick bite to eat. Instead of the night out I requested, I was invited round for bath time followed by dinner and drinks. I have no interest in having a seven month old baby kick bath water in my face, whilst Mummy tells her how clever she is. Followed by a dinner that was served at 10pm and consisted of some hastily defrosted leftovers from a batch cook a month ago. Never ever again.

By nine o' clock, I decide that Karen's date was clearly going so well that she didn't need rescuing, so I make myself some toast and peanut butter. I really can't see the point in cooking anything more elaborate just for me. It's more hassle than it's worth. I check my phone again, my text to Josh remains unanswered. Typical. Resigning myself to an early night I switch off the bedside lamp and put on the news. It may be full of disaster and suffering, but at least it makes my life seem charmed in comparison.

***

'Oi, Grace, it's time to get up. They stop serving breakfast at nine and get the arse if you don't show up. You'll get the bog-standard lecture on the importance of routine, and trust me, it's so not worth it.'

I roll over from my position of facing the wall and blink sleepily at Kirsty. 'I'll get up in a minute. Hey, remember we had that little chat last night if they ask.'

I had informed Kirsty that the staff had asked me to promote a good influence over her but I had absolutely no intention of patronising a grown woman by sitting her down to have a talk about her behaviour. I sit up and shake the dream from my head. It angers me that Josh can still haunt me while I sleep, I prefer to forget things but therapy drags it all to the surface. Some find that cathartic but I'm not one of them.

I'm not a morning person and never have been. A cup of coffee and a smoke was all the breakfast I needed, and although I did quit at Josh's insistence last month, I'd give anything for a cigarette right now. I'm sure it would get me out of this major grump I'm in. Perhaps suicide central has a shop, I haven't got anything else to lose and I'm beyond caring. With the promise of a nicotine hit giving me new resolve, I swing my legs out of bed and walk over to the mirror. Pushing my black curls to one side, I inspect the damage. The bruising looks somewhat worse today as bruises do when the yellow and purple starts to kick in, even on my brown skin it's evident. The most serious knock by far had been the one to the back of my head on landing, but I had caught the side of my face on the neighbour's balcony too. The angry blotch covers almost a quarter of my face and has crept over one of my eyes. I need to try and find a way to style my hair to cover it. I don't know why it bothers me what the others would think, but I don't like the thought that they may assume the harm caused would be intentional on my part. I pad down to the shower cubicle with my towel and some clean, asylum type clothing that Ariel had helpfully left on the chair by my bed last night. I carefully place them on a dry patch of bench. The shower room is painted in a shade that I could only describe as institutional grey. I shiver as the cold breeze seeps under a gap in the window, waiting for the water to warm up. After checking it several times, I realise that lukewarm is the best I'm going to get and step bravely under the flow. My breath catches, I wash as quickly as I can with the multi-use shampoo and body soap. The yellow liquid in the pump dispenser on the wall smells vaguely of cheap washing up liquid. I definitely need to find a shop: fags, chocolate and some decent toiletries must be purchased, along with some underwear that doesn't belong to some random of unknown hygiene standards.

'Good morning, Grace. Did you sleep well?' Ariel greets me at the door of the canteen. 'Wow, I do love that dress on you, although it is a little big on your slim figure. The orange really brings out the brown in your eyes.'
I frown at her statement and wonder if it goes well with my bruising too. It would be quite difficult to match yellow, purple and burnt orange, I'd have imagined. I muster a smile from the very core of my being.
'Yeah, fine thanks. Hey, is there a shop around here? I need to pick up a few essentials.'
'Not on site, I'm afraid, but the staff are always happy to pop into town to get things for you. What is it that you need?'
'Just some toiletries, chocolate and cigarettes,' I shrug apologetically. 'I did quit but I'm feeling pretty stressed about everything and I think it may help.'
Ariel gives a pretty, rosebud pout and shakes her head.
'I can get you the first two but I'm afraid we're a no-smoking centre. You really don't need it. I know what will help you, Angie's yoga class, it really shows you how to focus and harness positive energy whilst releasing all that negative.' Ariel beams and gives me a gentle poke in the stomach to show me just where I'm storing my negativity. I resist the urge to inform her that I'd be happy to release it all by screaming in her perfect face until she fetches me some smokes. Instead, I sigh and take the tray that she has offered me. Walking along in the shuffling line of inmates, I give a cursory glance over what's on offer. All around I can feel eyes burning into me,

waiting for me to slip up and not eat, or show any sign of being less than ecstatically happy. I smart a little at feeling this way because I'm not like the others in here, the Joes and the Kirstys. I'm perfectly well. Not a risk to myself in any way. Bloody do-gooders, what right do they have to intervene in my life anyway? I half-heartedly throw a croissant onto my tray, skip the queue waiting for hot food and go straight in for the coffee. It's the one vice I'm allowed and I can barely wait for the kick to whizz around my body. As I walk towards the rows of tables and benches, I spot Kirsty waving frantically at me and manoeuvre my way through them towards her.

'Grace, take a seat and meet some other non-suicidal people. Just like you,' my room-mate snorts derisively. I shake hands with the three in front of me and feign interest in their names, Alison, Jane and Laura? I may have already forgotten. I'm not here to make friends, my sole mission is to get out as soon as I can. I highly doubt any of them would want to be friends if they met me on the outside. I pick up my coffee and take a long sip of the lukewarm, murky liquid. It tastes nothing remotely like coffee and I spit it back into the cup in a most unladylike fashion.

'Decaf,' smirks Kirsty. 'They get you all ways in here.'

'You've got to be fucking kidding me. This has been the only thing I've actually looked forward to since I found out I wasn't allowed to smoke. I'm absolutely gasping for one. Kirsty, you've been here ages, you must know someone that can get me some? A bent screw or such like.'

'Oh, hark at this one acting like something out of *Orange is the New Black*,' Kirsty clutches her stomach in mirth. 'It's not prison, hen, it's way worse than that. We're not even allowed visitors. You have no chance of getting anything in or out of these four walls, yourself included, until you are no longer deemed at risk.'

I slump forward defeated in my chair. A sympathetic glance from the next table catches my eye, the hoity-toity woman from yesterday's group session looks quickly away from my gaze. She's sat completely alone, staring sadly at her runny scrambled eggs and burnt toast.

'Who's that lady? She always looks so lonely. We should invite her over to sit with us.'

'Who, Brioche? Get to Falkirk, Grace,' Kirsty snorts. 'That one's too snooty to sit with the likes of us. She hasn't spoken to anyone at all, not even the staff.'

'You don't know what happened to her, maybe she's had a really tough time of it.' Kirsty rolls her eyes but I press on. 'She hardly going to be in here if things are going well for her, is she? Anyway, what would Ariel say about that, Miss judgey-pants? I bet you she'd talk to me; you're just not giving her a chance. I'm going over there.'

'Seriously, don't waste your time. I've seen people try and she totally blanks them,' Kirsty warns.

'I'll see you after lunch.' I pick up my tray and carry it over to the next table, sitting opposite the woman I know only as Brioche.

'Hello, I'm Grace. It's nice to meet you,' I smile. I'm immediately stonewalled by the woman opposite, so powerful that it feels like a force field.

'I'm in because I fell off my balcony, but they think I was trying to top myself because my boyfriend of almost ten years ran off with another woman. He had just finished his break-up speech to me when I noticed the ring box on the floor, it must have fallen out of his coat pocket when he chucked it down in temper. So, one month with her and he was about to propose but I wasn't good enough after ten years? I decided to chuck the ring—not myself—over the edge. Then I realised it was probably worth a fair bit, and I wasn't leaving it on the verge of my neighbour's veranda so that he could sell it to buy weed, and that's when I fell. Anyway, that's my story, what did they get you in for?'

Brioche's chair scrapes back abruptly and she walks quickly away with her tray. I glance back at Kirsty who shrugs at my failed attempts of friendship. I push my half eaten croissant away and pass by Kirsty's table as I leave.

'Yeah, you don't need to say you told me so. I'll see you back in the room later, I'm off to my morning therapy session.'

Ariel appears from nowhere and pulls me aside as I leave the dining room.

'Good try, Grace. I think if anyone can get through to her it'll be you.'

'I'm not sure about that, but it was worth a shot. What's her real name? I can hardly call her Brioche; it doesn't seem right.' I cringe at mentioning the cruel moniker that Kirsty has allocated the woman but Ariel seems unfazed.

'Let her tell you in her own time, she needs to be receptive to your trust and friendship. You can do it. I have faith in you. Just remember that nobody is in here because they're in a particularly happy place and you'll be halfway to understanding her.'

I'm about to argue that I'm in a perfectly happy place but I can't be bothered. They don't believe me and I'll never get out of here if I don't at least pretend to be mending my ways. I'll get to the bottom of what's bugging Brioche, at least it'll make this dull existence a little more bearable in the meantime.

Chapter Three

I turn my key in the lock and push my way into the apartment block. The howling wind catches the door and swings it violently against the wall with a loud bang. Oh bugger, any second now she will be out here brandishing her mop at me. I shift my carrier bags to the opposite wrist and wrestle to close the door as quickly as I can. How many times have I intended to put a stopper behind it to prevent banging? My heart leaps as I hear the familiar click-squeak of my neighbour's front door. Four-foot-two of terrifying, elderly woman appears in the frame, illuminated menacingly in the dark hallway by the one hundred watt bulb behind her. 'Girl, how many times I'm telling you not to kick my door?' She scolds me in her, rather endearing, broken English.

'I'm sorry, Mrs Malik, the wind blew in the entry and hit it against the wall. I promise I would never kick your door.'

Mop in hand, my neighbour blocks my path defiantly, ready to launch into a tirade of whatever wrong-doings I have committed this past week.

'I'm seeing that boy here again last night. I tell you one week ago he should not be in your home without a chaperone. You have given your parents my note? Is not right, I'm telling you.'

'Mrs Malik, I'm almost forty, I don't need a chaperone. Now, I don't mean to be rude but this shopping is heavy and...'

'Your ginger cat, he's shitting in my flowerbeds again.'

'I told you last week, I haven't got a cat.'

'I'm telling your landlord, he throw you out for having animal,' she waggles a small, brown forefinger at me. I put down my bags and lean against the wall with a sigh.

'Mrs Malik, I own the property. I don't have a landlord, nor do I have a cat, for that matter. I'm sorry that I accidently banged the entry door. I will endeavour not to let it happen again. I'm truly apologetic that you're offended by my gentleman caller but I can assure you, he mostly talks about himself, eats my food and then leaves.'

The elderly lady gives a dissatisfied grunt, I smile graciously and attempt to gently squeeze past her. She moves a couple of inches before placing the mop across my path once more.

'I just remembering, I haven't shown you new pictures of baby Sanjeev. Come, come.'

I dump my bags in her front hall and trail obediently behind into the vibrantly coloured and overwhelmingly hot front room. The delicious aroma of curry comes from a bubbling pot in the kitchen. My West Indian mother practically weaned me on the stuff and it can be torture passing by my neighbour's front door. Often I'm not even hungry until I smell her latest creation.

'Sit, girl.'

'It's Grace, Mrs Malik.' I take the thick wallet of photographs she holds out and begin to leaf through them. 'Oh, what a gorgeous little boy, just look at those big, brown eyes. You must be so proud.'

My neighbour shifts contentedly in her armchair and settles in to watch my reaction. Mrs Malik does have a beautiful family. Some of the pictures of her daughter's wedding have crept into the latest pile; a stunning girl in red and gold. We chat about her only girl, Preet, who has a top job as a consultant at the Queen Elizabeth hospital in Birmingham. Her son, Aakash, is a hotshot lawyer up in Edinburgh. Such a bright family of whom she is rightfully proud. They have a smattering of beautiful, almost identical, children between them. I glance over to the dresser, where Mrs Malik's own wedding picture takes pride of place. If it wasn't for the fact it was in faded black and white, she could easily have been mistaken for Preet. She catches me gazing at her photo.

'That was the day I meet my Adi. Our parents would not let us see each other until the marriage but I was happy. For me it was love at first sight and he tell me the same,' she smiles with pride. 'Such a handsome man, to the day he die.'

I watch my neighbour lost in her reverie and feel awful about having to leave. I do enjoy her company but I have frozen goods in my carriers and the thought of them rapidly defrosting makes me restless. I wait until there's a natural lull in the conversation and stand to indicate my intention to go, mumbling my excuse of needing to refrigerate my perishables. It can take a good fifteen minutes to escape from this point, and sure enough, Mrs Malik picks up her conversation again. I slump back down onto the sunken sofa once more. I know she's lonely since her family moved up north. They've tried to get her to join them but she won't budge from the home she first had when she moved over from Mumbai, or Bombay as she still refers to it as. She moved to London back in the early 70s as a newlywed, Adi died ten years ago after a long battle with Dementia, but her family are too busy to visit more than twice a year at best.

'Such a pity you let yourself get old before you marry, girl. No good Asian man will want you now. Why your parents not organise wedding before now, I do not know.'

My sympathy dissipates like an ice cube in boiling water.

'My family aren't Asian, Mrs Malik,' I explain patiently for the umpteenth time. 'I'm mixed race, my mother's family are from the Caribbean, and my father is English. My parents' culture tends to encourage people to find partners for themselves. Although I must admit, I haven't done a particularly good job of that, so perhaps your way would have been better.'

She leans forward in her armchair and peers curiously at me.

'Those dark eyes and all that black hair? You look Asian.'

Each time we meet we have a variation of the same conversation. I know the bottom of my carrier bag will be swimming in water and my flat always feels Baltic after I leave here. I stand to go, preparing myself to be blunt now. My neighbour scurries to the kitchen on fur lined slippers and begins to rummage through a cupboard full of Tupperware. She ladles a generous amount of curry and rice into a container and seals it all round with a series of clicks. She pops a chapatti on top and puts it into an ancient, Safeway bag. This woman has a collection of antique carriers from stores that were bought over or shut up shop years ago. I thank her with a hug which makes her tut and blush, she waves me off with a dismissive hand and closes the door behind me. What a bonus to have a homemade takeaway, even if it does come with a side order of guilt. I hear a combination of bolts and locks being put in place as I climb the last row of stairs. I really should pop in for a longer chat when I have the time.

**

'Grace, you've made progress today.' I snap out of my reverie to see Dr Peter's smile.

'Completely irrelevant conversation alert. I have no idea why I told you all that. I guess I don't know what you want to hear.'

'Everything we discuss has a relevance.'

'My neighbour's curry making skills and her hatred over the fact that I have a less than favourable gentleman caller?'

'Why do you think you chose to talk about her today?'

'She's lonely and has nobody else to look out for her. Maybe I'm just worried about her being there alone in that flat where I can't hear her comings and goings. It's a subconscious way of looking out for her, I guess. She was right too; Josh was no good for me. I don't know what my outlook is for the future, maybe I should forget about men altogether.'

'Would you like to explore this further in your next session, Grace?'

'I guess,' I shrug. 'I suppose I best go get some lunch. No offence, but the canteen food isn't a patch on my neighbour's. I think that has more to do

with thinking about her above anything else. Did you hand pick mediocre kitchen staff specifically to give us an incentive to get out of here?'
A knowing smile is my reply. It hasn't escaped my notice that no staff dine in the canteen.

'Oi Grace, we're over here.' I carry my tray of congealed mac and cheese, watered down orange juice and fruit jelly over to Kirsty's table. As usual, her adoring public hang on her every word, desperate to be one of the cool kids after not making the cut first time around. There really is very little difference between my school canteen and this one. As the women around the table bitch about their ex-husbands and bratty teens, my mind wanders back to Josh. He told me years ago that he split with his ex-wife because she wanted kids and hinted that he'd had an affair around that time. He really hadn't been keen to get married and settle down. Come to think of it, hadn't he actually used the word settle on its own? I should have sniffed out the commitment phobia a mile off. I silently chide myself; so you thought you could tame the wild boy, did you? How has that worked out for you? Got yourself institutionalised, you idiot.
I watch with interest as Brioche enters the room, she points to what she wants to eat and ignores the greetings of others. This woman is an enigma, there has to be something else going on. She surely can't be so stuck up that she would refuse to even acknowledge the person serving her food. I wonder how she gets on in her therapy sessions, do her and Dr Peter just sit and stare at each other for an hour?
'Day two of trying to get Brioche to talk. I'll see you guys later.'
'You're wasting your time, Grace. She won't speak to the likes of you,' Kirsty shouts to my retreating back. I lurk by the cutlery tray and wait until she takes her seat before sliding into place opposite.
'Hello, there,' I smile across the table at the woman. 'I hope you don't mind me joining you again, that lot are a bit rowdy for me. OK, I'm going to play a game. You won't tell me anything about you so I'm going to try and guess, and if I'm right, I want you to tap your nose. That way we can communicate without you having to say anything at all.'
Brioche stares blankly at the untouched tray in front of her. To me she seems sad rather than aloof and having Kirsty and co on her case with their snob-bashing jokes would hardly be conducive to opening up. They can be pretty intimidating, with a pack instinct that wolves would be envious of. I look carefully at the woman opposite.
'So, I think your name is Barbara,' I pause, waiting for a nose tap. She definitely looks like a Barbara but possibly a Maureen or a Liz.

'You're married and have two teenage children.' Nothing, not even a flicker of recognition that I'm talking to her. 'You work in the financial sector and lost a multi-million pound deal and that is why you felt you had to take the way out that landed you in here.'

The woman's face stiffens but her expression is unreadable.

'All right, more about me. I'm a Science teacher at Holly Berry High but I'm pissed off with my job. The kids just aren't interested and it's become a chore just to go in. You know, not enough to make me suicidal, but enough to make me want to walk out and never go back. Teenagers are such a pain. If I never saw any of them again for a hundred years, it'd be too soon.'

Brioche takes rabbit sized nibbles of her sandwich, everything about her demeanour screams defeat. It's almost like she's doing the bare minimum to survive and I can see that she could be in here for an excruciatingly long time. An awkward silence hangs over us as I struggle to fill the void. I glance over to Kirsty's table where the raucous laughter continues. Who cares, I'm missing nothing by not by being part of their group. It had once been so important to me, that sense of belonging. I had compromised my own self-worth by trying to be one of those girls in high school and it had taken me down a path from which I never could return. A familiar ball of anger fires up in my stomach, I look quickly away and turn my attention back to Brioche. She gazes vacantly at her tray with the catatonic stare of someone deeply disturbed. I break her trance with my outburst.

'Look at those bloody idiots, acting like they're so perfect. They're no different from you, me, or anyone else in here. I'd love to see you stand up to them when they give you abuse. Get some fight, lady! I know you have it in you.'

Just like yesterday, Brioche's chair scrapes back abruptly. She walks away with her barely touched tray, dumping the contents in the bin, and pushes her way through the swing doors. I admit defeat. I feel horribly guilty for coming on so strong when she's too fragile to fight back. I need to work on building her up before she can take on anyone else. Clearly she has a hard enough time coping with her own problems. Why not talk then? It's the fastest route to escape after all. She could be stuck in here forever if she doesn't open up. I make my way reluctantly back to Kirsty's table, where the others are now openly mocking Laura over her comments on her parents' divorce.

'They didn't use you as a prawn in their relationship, you were a *pawn*,' Alison slaps the table with glee.

'Stop trying to make me look stupid,' Laura's face flames. 'I'm only going on what my brother told me at the time.'

'Oh trust me, I'm not making you look stupid, you're managing that all by yourself.' Alison clings to Kirsty for support as they dissolve into a fresh bout of giggles.

'If you want to know real stupid then you should meet my sister. She named her twins Ruby and Blue after the West End nightclub she conceived them in.' Even I have to chuckle at that. 'She's not even sure which of her two late-night dalliances in the loo is the father. Now, this is how stupid she is, she asked me if she could be having one from each.'

'You know what they say: two's company, three's an orgy,' Kirsty smirks.

'Actually, that is completely scientifically possible...' my comment is ignored.

'She was known as Duke around our way,' Laura muses. 'As in, The Grand Old Duke of York, she'd also had ten thousand men.'

'Those were the days,' Alison sighs. 'I remember so many nights out where I'd have missed the last tube home. I'd look at the guy chatting me up and wonder if he appealed to me slightly more than the night bus did. Two rowdy hours on a tour of London in a top deck smelling of booze, kebabs and vomit? There weren't many guys that escaped an overnight stay with me.'

'Those words that fill the heart of any Londoner with dread: night bus and rail replacement service.' Kirsty shudders. 'Mind you, it still beats a walk home in the pissing rain and howling gales of Glasgow. I don't miss the shite weather back home one bit. In fact, I had to laugh when our local council tried to persuade everyone in our street to use greener energy. Solar panels in Scotland? That's about as much use as a hosepipe ban in Venice.'

'I used to enjoy my sunrise walk home after nights out,' Jane muses. 'Well, until I got run over by a milk float that is.'

'We have a winner!' Kirsty chortles. 'Jane takes the dunce's hat. How the fuck did you manage to get run over by a milk float? Don't they go like...four miles per hour? That's like saying you were chased by a snail.'

'No wonder you're in a failed suicide clinic,' Laura deadpans. 'How did you attempt to kill yourself? With a butter knife?'

'Yes, I tried to spread myself to death,' Jane throws Laura a superior look.

'My ex, Barry, used to drive a milk float,' Kirsty smiles nostalgically. 'He was gorgeous: built like a brick shit-house, with a boner you could hang a wet duffel coat off of.' We cackle like a coven at Kirsty's description of her ex. 'I wonder if he's married. I may have to look him up on Facebook. Right you ugly bunch, as much as I'm enjoying all of your banter, the joy that is group therapy looms.' Kirsty's troops rally around at her command. 'I wonder who'll be getting a slagging off in writing class today? I'm bored of writing about Jim.'

As we walk into the meeting room, I note with disappointment that Brioche hasn't joined us for group, and fret that I may have upset her too much to attend. A girl named Lisa is talking for the first time today. She's only twenty-one and it saddens me that she can find herself in so much pain that she would want to kill herself at such a young age. I nod furiously in agreement when she expresses her anger towards her boyfriend of three years for dumping her for someone else, in this case, her best friend. Once she has finished and we've all given the usual slightly patronising applause at her bravery, Gabe gives Kirsty an enquiring smile.

'Kirsty, how are you today?'

'Oh, you know, living the dream. Yourself, Gabe?'

'Fantastic, Kirsty. Thank you for asking. Would you care to take the stage? We would love to hear of the journey that brought you to us.'

Kirsty gives a dramatic sigh before wobbling to her feet in those four inch, tacky heels.

'Oh, why not, it has been two months. I think I've built enough suspense by now,' my room-mate announces drolly to the curious room.

Much speculation had been occurring in the sub-groups about Kirsty's story, everything from drug addiction to prostitution. She puffs up her tiny frame, self-importantly and begins her tale.

'Hi, my name is Kirsty and I'm a suicidal, bi-polar, Catholic, bi-sexual, hermaphrodite.' Gabe narrows his eyes as he tries to recall these distinctive details from my room-mate's admission file. Kirsty pauses to allow us all to digest this information. 'I am here because I had a nasty accident with a kitchen knife and a hot bath but I'm now totally cured and ready to leave. The only thing that would be any good to me now would be a twenty pack of fags and a bottle of vodka. I imagine my ex is happily shacked up with his bitch on the side, therefore I have absolutely nothing to want to kill myself over, other than being stuck in here with you losers.' The room is so silent after Kirsty's speech that I have to waggle a finger in my ear to check that I haven't in fact gone deaf. Finally, a male voice pops up.

'You're a *hermaphrodite*?' Jim asks in amazement.

'Contrary to what you think, Jim, that is not a breed of Highland cow. Yes, I am indeed a hermaphrodite. I figured that out based on the fact that my ex told me to go and fuck myself on an almost daily basis.'

A ripple of laughter fills the room and Gabe beams proudly at this rather unconventional form of sharing.

'Actually, my soon to be ex-husband cheated on me. I'd like to say that was the reason I tried to top myself but I don't think it was. I think I was bored and wanted to create a bit of a drama. Dr Peter is having a field day with me in therapy and I'm proud to say he can't seem to figure me out. I'm a mystery, even to myself. I don't know if I need a shite or a haircut most days, but that's just me. When I work out what the issue is I'll be the first to stand up and talk to you again. But hey, what doesn't kill you makes you a ball-breaking bitch...I mean stronger.' Kirsty gives a tiny bow and plonks herself back on the chair. We all applaud her, despite being virtually none the wiser about her emotional state. To find the humour in the darkness of her situation is quite a gift, and to come out and say she has no clue what's wrong with her or why she did it, well that takes guts. Especially in a place where finding the answers will set you free.

Evening activity time comes around and I decide to head along to Kirsty's writing class. I could do with a good laugh and the movie they're showing tonight I've seen a hundred times before. I had chuckled at the irony of showing *One Flew over the Cuckoo's Nest*, in this glorified asylum. I also want to watch Kirsty in action, as the best essay from the class is going to be made into a script for the end of the month stage show. My room-mate was already tipped to be the winner. The pen hovers over the sheet of A4, my head full of nothing. Has my existence been so boring that I can't think of a single thing to say? What about my kids at school? They're enough to put you off ever having any. People ask me all the time what I love about not having kids and I have to say...it's not having kids. I warm to my subject and start with a title to give me inspiration.

The Birthing Hypothesis,' by Grace Ellis. The real reason why I'm not part of the troops sitting outside cafes, chatting over lattes, and picking snot and raisins from my unwashed hair. If Kirsty can manage to find a sunbeam of humour in an otherwise dark world, then you can bet your sweet ass that I'm going to try. I give a deep inhalation and begin my outline.

How would you go about experiencing pregnancy, birth and the early months of being a new parent, without having to go through with it for real? Once one is embroiled in such a scenario, it's too late to disengage. Using my scientific knowledge, I have prepared and experienced, first hand, an educational experiment for you to gain imperative insight to the flip side before experiencing it for real. Are you missing out in your non-participation of the procreation game?

One must begin by giving up much loved indulgences: cigarettes, alcohol, blue cheese and medium rare steaks, amongst other things. Basically, all the good stuff that makes life worth living. This alone was enough to give me the mood swings of any pregnant woman to the point of borderline insanity, no offence to anyone here in Arcadia. Next, I required a craving so I opened the kitchen cupboard and decided that this random aspect of growing another human being would involve the first three items that I saw. After devouring my creation, a concoction featuring cornflakes in gravy and garnished with pineapple chunks I discovered that, all by itself, my morning sickness had kicked in.

I give a soft chuckle and Kirsty lifts her head to give me a curious glance. 'Let me see,' she whispers.

'Fuck off and stop trying to copy me.' I loop my arm around my sheet of paper, the way I had in junior school, and lay my head down to concentrate. I hear Kirsty snigger at my infantile pose and smile into the dark space between my face and the desk. This is easy, I become so engrossed in my subject that my pen soars across the lines almost by itself.

For months I recreated the discomfort of trying to adopt a comfortable sleeping position by placing footballs of increasing sizes into my pyjama bottoms. I recreated the agony of haemorrhoids by microwaving a bunch of grapes before shoving them into the back of my knickers.

My pen hovers, is that taking things too far? No, bugger it, this is pure fiction and although I hate to blow my own trumpet, it's actually quite funny. I never have to see any of these people once I get out of here, so who cares what they think of me.

I spent several months wishing I hadn't put myself in this situation but forced myself to continue for research reasons, not only because I'm a scientist, but in real life there would be no turning back at this point. To emulate an actual labour and birth at forty weeks, I bought a box of Imodium and took the maximum dosage allowed (see, I told you I wasn't suicidal) then ate a half dozen eggs consecutively, drank a pint of prune juice followed by the hottest curry I could find. A Vindaloo, I recall. As a side note, never trust a curry with the word loo in it, there's a very good reason for its presence. So why did I do this? The reason being that I could enjoy the full effect of something wanting to detach itself violently from my body, whilst being in so much excruciating pain that I couldn't even consider passing it. It was the best I had to work with and I was stunned by the similarities to real life experiences that friends had told me about. After around twenty hours of intense agony, things finally hurried themselves along. Thankfully, before I'd carried out my promise of taking myself into A&E, admitting my folly and begging for medical intervention. After the simulated birth, I set my phone to waken me every two hours from my nightmarish, feverish sleep. During this arduous time—or what others may call the new-born experience—I'd wander blearily into the spare bedroom and set off my personal alarm, usually reserved for the late night dash from supermarket to car in the underground parking lot. I'd allow the piercing sound to go on relentlessly for forty-five minutes, whilst pacing the room holding a large watermelon in a blanket.

I glance up from my essay to see Kirsty's narrowed eyes, she peers at me curiously before glancing down at her own four lines. I give a cursory smirk and go back to my page.

Next, I needed to experience the agonising mastitis that my friends had described. My method of choice: a ten-mile jog in a woollen jumper and no bra, followed by a liberal application of deep heat to the nipples.

I frown at this and tap the pen agitatedly against my teeth. I'm surrounded by suicidal people and could actually be giving them ideas on how to self-harm. None of this is true but I'll still have to start with a disclaimer in a, 'don't try this at home, kids,' style.

But how can you show yourself the cost of having little people in your lives? Children aren't cheap. I gave this grim acknowledgment as I withdrew three quarters of my monthly wage and headed towards the nearest drain. Now, don't look so shocked, I realised what good my money could do and made a generous donation to my local children's respite home instead.

This latter comment is true, I do make a regular donation to those poppets and their relentlessly working carers. I read back through what

I've written and smooth out the crumples that have appeared on the sheet in my haste. I turn over the page and start on the other side.

Despite friends telling me that having children can be the most rewarding thing you'll ever do, people also tell me slamming your fingers in a car door hurts. Neither of these do I feel the need to check out, for accuracy. Therefore, my research has concluded that I'm not suited to parenthood. Staying sober at all times in case one's child wants a lift somewhere? You don't want to get into the habit of not drinking wine every day. Snap! before you know it, you'll be a gnat's knacker away from a dry sherry at Christmas...it's a slippery slope.
I was done with the soccer mum bit after forcing myself to stand at the edge of an empty football pitch in the rain. Forty-five minutes I managed, before crawling my chilblained body back into bed that Sunday morning in January. With regards to the teenage years, I decided that if I wanted to have a door slammed in my face I could simply become a member of the God Squad or an energy salesperson.
So, to summarise, thus endeth my experience and whilst I take my hat off to those who do, this is why children are not—and never will be—for me.

I read back over my scrambled notes and wonder where this had all come from. The class leader's voice interrupts me, and I raise my head to see the elderly lady smile approvingly at her silently engrossed class. Kirsty had told me earlier that Teresa was a retired nun who had penned a couple of inspirational quote books. She was now devoted to helping people like us develop our writing skills, in order to improve our self-esteem and create a catharsis for our troubled pasts and suicidal tendencies. Load of old bollocks if you ask me; the ramblings on my piece of paper shows nothing about any inner turmoil I may harbour. I could spend the rest of my life holed up in this joint and they'd never be able to show me this angst they talk of. I'm strong, I'm independent, and the only therapy I need is a bloody good night out.
'Now ladies and gents, I'd like you to swap your work with the person seated next to you and have a read through. I want you to give feedback, nothing nasty, just some observations and thoughts on what they've written,' Teresa gives the room a beatific smile. Kirsty holds her hand out to me, triumphantly. I hadn't counted on sharing this today and it's far from polished.
'Give. It's not like the whole class gets to see it and I'll be kind,' Kirsty gives me a knowing look that says she'll be anything but, should she think

my offering is crap. I reluctantly hand over my page and take Kirsty's in return. She has written a comedy sketch about Glasgow life from a child's point of view. It's only half a page but I gaze in awe of her talent and humour. It's to a much higher standard than my meagre attempt. In fact, it's far superior than anything I could ever hope to write. I lay Kirsty's page down and study her profile as she reads. Her face gives nothing away and for some reason this unsettles me. It had taken a lot of courage for me to join this class and I probably would have been more in my comfort zone with the cookery group. I'm not a really a creative type. Scientists like cold, hard facts; tangible, proven things. Recipes suit that methodical side of me nicely. My stomach sinks as realisation dawns on me that half term ended yesterday.

'Grace, this is fuckin' brilliant,' Kirsty beams at me with pride. 'I had no idea you were so funny. What's up? You look like you've seen a ghost.'

'This is Monday, right? I have no idea if my work has been told that I had an accident. I could lose my job. I'll probably lose it anyway if they find out I've been in a suicide clinic.'

'Chill, Grace, I'm sure Ariel has taken care of it. Won't your family have contacted them?'

'No, most definitely not. Only a few friends and my ex-dickhead know where I work anyway. Not that they'll even notice or care that I'm missing. I need to check what's going on. Can you cover for me, please.'

'OK,' Kirsty gives me a cautious glance. 'Don't do anything stupid though, just go to reception and come straight back.'

'Teresa, please excuse me. I need to use the restroom.' The tutor smiles as I scurry past her desk. I make my way down the long corridor, glancing in at the other groups as I pass and giving an unreciprocated wave to Brioche in her baking class. I round the corner and stare in turn at the empty reception desk and the front door. It has an alarm but by the time they realise I've gone it'll be too late. The thought of ordering a takeaway and sinking into my sofa with a large Rioja is all I can think about. It's that, versus tasteless food, group therapy and no end to this nightmare. There's no competition. Before I can change my mind, I've made a run for it. The security alarm screams in my ears as I dash outside. With adrenaline pumping in my veins, I look frantically left and right until I spot a train station in the distance. With a backwards glance, I see two guards sprinting down the corridor at full pelt. Proving that my years of being the fastest runner in high school would pay off, I take off over the grass towards the fence, which I know I can easily scale.

Bye Arcadia. Bye crazy people. Grace Ellis is going home.

Chapter Four

I sit in my local bar on Upper Street and stare across at my darkened flat. Underneath, I can see the warm, flickering lights of Mrs Malik's front room as she watches Emmerdale. I've been staking out my own home for over two hours now to see if anyone would turn up. I had made it from Arcadia to the main road and hid in the overgrown grass until I was confident the guards had given up. In the distance I could see the train station but a bit further along was a bus stop. Of course, it would have made sense to them that I would have headed to one of those. Instead, I had hidden for an hour or so then ran a little way along the road to a petrol station, where I climbed into the passenger seat of a white van and hitched a ride to Dalston. The man driving wasn't the chatty sort, so I filled the silence by talking about my car breaking down. My mechanic husband would pick it up later for me. It was the best excuse I could come up with to distract from the fact we were so close to an institution. I didn't want him getting any ideas that I may be a potential runaway.

John, the barman, didn't give more than a cursory glance in my direction when I asked him if I could help myself to a wine and bum a smoke. I often helped him serve through the busier times and this was payback. Silly Grace had left her keys at work and rather than trail back through the traffic, she had to wait for Josh to arrive and let her in. John had no idea that Josh and I had split. I hadn't felt like explaining the situation to anyone and this had served me well, now that I needed to concoct this story. I'd be back over later with money, as promised. In reality, my handbag, purse and keys were left back in the flat. I guess it hadn't occurred to the paramedics to grab them after my fall when their priority would have been to get me straight to hospital. I smile at the thought of my spare key under the plant pot in the corridor. Everything I need is back home. Other than the outfit I was wearing that night, which is undoubtedly currently rotating in an industrial size washing machine back at Arcadia. It wasn't a favourite outfit, designer, of course, but it was last season and probably headed for the Oxfam shop soon. I bask in the pride of my own efficiency and take another large sip of wine. All I need to do now is to be honest with school about my head injury and being unable to contact them. As far as I'm aware, nobody in my everyday life knows anything about this. A few days away to get over the break up with Josh is all Karen needs to know, if she even noticed that I'd gone.
My thoughts wander back to Josh and his increasing distance from me.

When had it started? Maybe as far back as last Christmas. Ten months ago? Yes, probably around then. He complained about me showing him up at his work's Christmas do. He said I was common, that I had drunk too much and was making a fool of myself. Up until that point I'd had one of the best nights of my life. His CEO and I had been doubled over with laughter at the sense of occasion. Jeff, a thrice married man of rosaceous complexion, had the kind of laugh that made you concerned for his health. He cackled as I told him a story about Karen's latest man of the moment, who had taken to hiding out in her bathroom and tying a piece of holly to the string of each of her tampons. He told her it was for her festive period. Jeff and I clung to each other, sloshing wine over the pristine, white table cloth in our mirth. Josh had apologised loudly to the entire table, exclaiming that you couldn't polish a turd. I retorted that this was true, but you could roll it in glitter, and the laughter from Jeff started up again. After another hour of japes, Josh had decided I'd taken things too far. Admittedly, I probably had. I inwardly cringe at the words that blurted out of my mouth.

Hey, Jeff, do you know that Josh has renamed his secretary Miss Thrush, because she's an irritating...'

I never finished my sentence. I was pulled ungraciously backwards in my chair, my wine glass tipped and a third of a bottle of quality Pinot Noir seeped through my specially bought for the occasion, Dior dress. The table watched on as Josh threw me over his shoulder, grabbed my bag and coat with his free hand and dumped me unceremoniously outside, on a bus stop seat.

'Spoilsport,' I'd muttered. 'Refreshingly working class, that's how you describe me, is it? Your boss told me that tonight. I'm not common, I'm just having a good time. You're nothing but a snob.'

He had remained silent but I felt the rage through my drunken state. He had put me in a taxi, handed the driver a tenner and told him where I lived. I wiped the condensation from the cab window and scowled as I saw him walk back into the party.

I smile at the memory of that night, despite my ultimate humiliation. I think it may have been the last time I felt truly content; people laughing with me and rooting for me to stay and be part of their group. Maybe that was why he hadn't been interested in taking a more permanent step with me. He was the type who liked to keep his woman in her place. Being the life and soul of a party didn't fit the stereotypical image he had of a partner. It was clear he thought he was destined for special things, but not whilst being in a relationship with a lowly science teacher, in a school full of poor kids. Well stuff him. I don't need a man in my life. How many single women of my age can say that they're fast on their way to becoming mortgage free, have a head of department role, and a brand new car? Not that many, I'm guessing. I really haven't given myself the credit I deserved in the past. I've been more focused on where my friends were in their lives than what I'd achieved in my own. Well, no more, I'm taking my power back. People only have an advantage over you if you allow them to. Happiness is a choice. I sink the last of the dregs in my glass and decide I have enough Dutch courage to head home. With a cheery wave to John, I remind him I'll be back over soon to pay my bar bill. I dodge the cars and buses on Upper Street, huddling the threadbare, donated cardigan around me like a wrap. I'm hardly dressed for the weather but I wasn't wearing a coat when I fell and I assume it wasn't a priority to put one on me when the ambulance arrived. I push the entry door to my flat and grab the handle to stop the wind from carrying it. A slight rattle against the wall causes me to whisper swear words into the dark hallway. Still no replacement bulb fitted in the communal hall, I see. The work-shy lout opposite Mrs Malik had happily taken a bulb from her and promptly did nothing with it, after pilfering the original one for his front room. I lurk by the door for a moment or so, to check that I've arrived unnoticed. There's no familiar click-squeak of my elderly neighbour's door so I creep forward, taking cartoon-like, tiptoe steps. I almost reach the staircase when my heart sinks. Mrs Malik, in curlers and slippers, clutching two milk bottles to her bosom, freezes as she sees me standing there.

'Girl, what you doing? You shouldn't be here,' she screeches. 'I had to call ambulance, I thinking you was dead, for sure.'

'I'm fine, Mrs Malik. Look, I'm perfectly well so they said I can go home.' She eyes me with suspicion.

'I was telling ambulance peoples I mind pussy cat for you.' She pushes her door open to reveal a ginger tom, curled contentedly on an armchair. The cat gives a sleepy yawn and stretches out a paw, before starting in fright. He springs up with a hiss and shoots underneath the coffee table.

'Oh dear, he is angry that you leave him,' she laughs.

'Mrs Malik, that is *not* my cat. You must let him out, someone could be looking for him.'

'I been letting him out, he come back. He like old Mrs Malik. You no want him? I keep?' she glances at me hopefully.

'Well, if he keeps coming back to you then you're probably just as well to. He's likely homeless.'

My neighbour gives a tiny jump and claps her hands.

'Girl, you must go rest peacefully now.'

'Don't worry, I will. Take good care of Ginger.'

'He name is Turmeric, like Indian spice. You know it?'

'I do, Mrs Malik. It's a wonderful name and he's exactly the same colour. Now, please excuse me but I need to get to bed.'

My neighbour for once doesn't argue. I hear the soft click of her door closing and her voice rings out from her kitchen.

'Turmeric, shishu,' which I recognise as Hindi for baby. She shouts some words that I don't understand but the tapping of a bowl makes me think she's calling him for his supper. Bless Mrs Malik, she didn't even ask me in now she has someone else to fuss over and feed up. Pity, I could have done with a good curry after days of prison food. Never mind, I'll phone for a takeaway after a long, hot shower. I can't wait to get this hospital smell from my hair. I have no idea what I have in the house, a few ready meals in the freezer at a guess. Not good enough for my first celebratory meal home. My lovely neighbour, always looking out for me, had called the ambulance after my nasty spill. Nosy neighbours can be as much a Godsend as a curse. I fetch my key from under the plant pot and let myself in. There's a slight smell from the bin I'd been meaning to empty all week, and it's bitterly cold. These old Victorian buildings take hours to heat up again. Who cares, I'm home. With a sigh of relief, I hit the hall light. A familiar voice rings out from the kitchen.

'Hello, Grace. You really must find a better hiding place for your key, it was the first place we tried before putting it back for you to use.'

I turn quickly back down the hall and out into the corridor.

'Not a good idea, love, you need help. We're taking you back to Arcadia.' The security guard I dodged earlier steps out from the stairwell and blocks my path.

'Why don't we collect some of your belongings while we're here? Perhaps you'll feel more comfortable with your own things.' Ariel steps into the entry and gives my hand a squeeze.

'Or, I could come in for my counselling sessions and stay here at home instead?' I suggest, hopefully.

'Grace, you're not well, dear. We need to help you. You've been through an extremely traumatic event. You'll be back to your old life soon, I promise. The school is aware of your situation, they know you'll be off for

a while but only due to the accident, nothing else has been said. Kirsty mentioned that you were worried about losing your job.'
I walk reluctantly to my closet and pull out a few outfits.
'Well done, Grace,' Ariel beams. 'I knew you'd see sense.'
'Actually, what I did see is that other security guard hiding in my kitchen. I could probably take you two out, but not him.'
Ariel gives her musical laugh but the look on my face shuts her up.

I look out as London passes me by in a blur, feeling my freedom disappearing. The green spaces get bigger, buildings get fewer. I can't quite gather my bearings; I hadn't paid too much attention on my journey home in the white van. Is this Hertfordshire? I'm not a countryside kind of person. My hay fever flares up just walking over Highbury fields to my favourite gastropub. The lack of food mixed with the wine makes my head spin. At this point I'm too tired to care where they're taking me, I just want to sleep. I come around to Ariel patting me on the shoulder and instantly regret dozing off. My head thumps as I make my way from the car to the retreat. Ariel sees me to my room and offers to bring me tea and toast. Any thoughts I had of crawling into bed dissipate, as Kirsty bounds into the room, kicks off those garish heels and makes herself comfortable on her bed.
'Well? What's happening on the outside?' She demands.
'Not a lot. I went to my local for a bit to make sure I hadn't been followed, my neighbour stole a cat that she knows fine well doesn't belong to me, then I got busted by this lot. They let themselves into my home, cornered me and brought me back to this shit hole.'
'Was the telly on in the pub? Do you know how Arsenal are doing? I'd love my ex to be pissed off if they've dropped down the league.'
'I have no idea. What happened when I left?'
'Oh, my God, the place went *ballistic*. Teresa had a complete meltdown and totally blames herself for what happened. They were really worried about you, so I decided I'd cheer them up by reading out your paper.'
I stare at my room-mate in horror. How humiliating to have the entire class know what I'd written. I'm just about to go off on a rant when a knock at the door interrupts my thoughts.
'Here we are, some lovely tea and toast,' Ariel smiles benevolently.
'Teresa just showed me what you wrote in class and I have to say it, you're a funny woman, Grace. Don't keep it so hidden. Gabe even had tears streaming down his cheeks.'

I pick up a piece of toast and see that Ariel has spread it thickly with butter and jam.

'This is exactly how I used to have my supper when I was little,' I smile.

'Well, there you go, a little blast from the past to tuck you in tonight. I'll leave you ladies to chat. Keep on with the writing class, you're doing so well at it.' Ariel shuts the door softly.

'Do you like teaching, Grace?' Kirsty gives me a sly smile.

'I used to.' I hold my plate out towards Kirsty and she takes a half slice of toast. 'The kids don't want to learn and I spend most of the time wanting to bang my head off my desk. The walls close in on me in that school now.'

'So, you hate your job, your boyfriend dumped you, and you have no friends that you speak of. I can see why you wanted to off yourself.'

'I didn't, I told you it was an accident. Why will nobody listen to me?' I'm exasperated that nobody believes me, not even Kirsty. 'Anyway, I do have friends, I just can't be arsed with any of them.'

'Isolating yourself from others, that's text book behaviour.'

I glower at Kirsty from under my blanket. She continues, oblivious.

'Anyhoo, the reason I ask is that I want us to hook up and write scripts together once we, you know, get out of here. How about we make a pact to fast track leaving, by opening up and giving this twat-brigade exactly what they want?'

Now she has my full intention. I pull myself into a sitting position. 'Keep talking...'

'Well, you're in Islington and I'm in Hackney, it's so close it almost feels like fate. I need to find a new place to live but I like the north London area. Me and you could pitch comedy scripts to the TV stations and make some serious money. Fuck Josh, fuck Tyrone, we'll show them. Who needs men anyway?'

'You could come and stay with me until you get your own place,' I'm feeling inspired by her positivity. 'I have a spare room and we could work every night over wine...or vodka, for you. Can we really do this? It feels right, doesn't it?'

'Aye, it sure does. It's good to have something to look forward to for the first time in ages. Right, I want us to get into the zone by telling each other everything. If I can tell you, then I can stand up in class, tell this lot and get my arse out of this place.'

Chapter Five

The therapy group fills up as I watch an improved version of Kirsty saunter into the room. With a renewed sense of self-worth, she smiles sweetly at Brioche and takes a seat next to me.

'I'm glad we decided that I'm going first, you look bloody terrified.'

'I'm not an opening up kind of person,' I admit. 'I'm coming out in a cold sweat just thinking about you spilling all.'

'No need, I'll be fine. Think about the future, when we get out of here we'll be minted with our combined talent.' Kirsty hugs her oversized sweater to her tiny frame, radiating positivity.

Gabe makes his way to the centre of the circle, he places his jacket on the back of the seat and beams around the room.

'We have a new person joining us today, please say hello to Jess.'

'Hello, Jess,' we chorus. Her eyes dart around suspiciously as she shrinks into her chair.

'Would anyone like to volunteer to talk today?' Gabe looks around hopefully.

Jim gives a small cough from the chair opposite me, but Kirsty's hand shoots up. The room stares at her in surprise.

'Well, this *is* an honour, Kirsty. Twice in one week? I can see your one-to-one sessions are starting to pay off.'

My room-mate smiles warmly at the room before her eyes settle on a dejected Jim.

'I'd like to begin with a few apologies, there have been some people in here that I've been less than kind to. First of all, Jim. I'm truly sorry about the loss of your wife. She was beautiful. I did look at your photos although I may have seemed disinterested. I'm also sorry for the death of your horse, I had a cat when I was little and I know how heart-breaking it is to lose a pet. You're a lovely man and always go out of your way to make people feel better about themselves.' Kirsty makes her way towards a shocked, but elated, Jim. He stumbles to his feet and she wraps her arms as far around his waist as they will stretch. Jim finally finds his voice.

'You have no idea how much that means to me, Kirsty. You're such a talented girl and I can see you going far. Thank you, my dear. Thank you so much,' he chokes.

The room breaks into applause and Gabe almost bursts with pride. Kirsty waits patiently until we quieten.

'Number two on my list, a lady whose real name I don't even know,' she indicates across the room to Brioche. 'I've made a standing joke of you and that is unforgivable. I don't know your circumstances, it's none of my business anyway, but I'm very sorry for what you've been through and I wish you well in your recovery.' Kirsty makes her way cautiously towards the woman and extends a hand. 'I don't know if you're a hugger but I'd like to at least shake your hand.'

The room holds its breath as one, as we wait for a response from Brioche. She stands, and for a split second I fear she's going to lamp Kirsty one, as she herself would so eloquently put it. Instead, she grabs my friend by both shoulders and pulls her to her bosom. The room erupts even louder this time. Gabe looks beside himself and I fear for his safety. Kirsty makes her way back to her seat but stays standing as the room calms down.

'Thank you, everyone. I don't mean to cause upset to others, I think it's self-preservation that makes me act that way. I make jokes or pretend that I don't care, to keep people at a safe distance. I've been that way for most of my life.'

I now know the full story about Kirsty and it's a horrific one. Jim gives her an indulgent smile. We could all do with being a little more tolerant of each other, especially in here. As Ariel says, nobody has arrived at Arcadia from being in a happy place. Kirsty picks up her life story once more.

'I never had a conventional upbringing. My mother was an alcoholic prostitute, it's probably where I get my fashion sense from.' A smattering of laughter circles the room but it's borne of affection, not malice.

'My mum had a string of men around every evening, many asking how much she'd charge for a then fourteen-year-old me. Rather than be on my side, she'd thump me for attracting custom away from her.'

Several women in the room gasp, as I did, at Kirsty's revelation.

'Things changed when my step-dad came on the scene and not for the better. He was a drug dealer and made big bucks, enough for Mum to give up the game. He's also the father of the kid that I gave up for adoption, at the age of fifteen. My Mum had threatened to kick me out, I couldn't even consider looking after both of us from the streets so he went to live with people who could. I also didn't want the reminder of that horrible, violent man, which was not the wean's fault, but hey-ho. I was homeless until I met my husband, and for the first time in my life I had a stable base, until he cheated. I did say earlier in the week that I just wanted to create a bit of drama by killing myself but I've done a bit of soul-searching since then. The truth, I think, is that I knew I had to make a choice. Live on the streets again or die. I chose to die.'

Even hearing this for the second time doesn't make it any less shocking. Many people, including Jim, are now visibly upset. Ariel swoops around sympathetically with a box of tissues. Gabe thanks everyone for their contribution and ends the session early. Many other people in the room are now admitting that their issues pale in comparison to Kirsty's, but pain is pain, regardless. There have been serious breakthroughs today and Gabe looks thrilled, not only that Kirsty had come out with her real story for the first time, but that she'd evoked some kind of response from Brioche. Maybe this could be the beginning of a new start for her too.

Good news travels fast around Arcadia and thanks to Gabe, teatime sees some celebratory goodies. We have sandwiches, sausage rolls and cake. All the tables are pushed together to create a party atmosphere and Ariel puts on some music for us to dine to. I take a seat next to Brioche and we eat in amicable silence. I don't want to push things with her, she's come a long way today. My aim is to get her used to my presence and infuse her with positive energy. Kirsty is the centre of attention and has chosen to sit next to Jim. Arcadia's heroine of the hour laps up the attention from her adoring fans. She will be out of here in no time at this rate. I desperately want to join her but I'm terrified of standing up in group and sharing my story. I also want to crack the Da Vinci code that is Brioche before I get out. In the meantime, Kirsty can make herself at home in my flat and get to know Mrs Malik, and the stowaway Turmeric. We can both start working on a script independently, and chose the best parts from both to combine, once I get home. Tomorrow is my day to talk in class and I'm dreading it. The fact that I know there is absolutely nothing wrong with me makes me rather indignant about sharing. My past is nobody's business, but I have no chance of escape unless I tell the truth. Kirsty has been through the most horrific time yet she had the guts to stand up and tell a bunch of strangers what had happened. If I'm going to move forward in life then I have to match her bravery, starting with my therapy session with Dr Peter tomorrow.

After dinner, the others head down to watch a movie. I need an early night to mentally prepare myself for tomorrow. Knowing that there is no way Kirsty will let me off the hook, I sit a few seats away from her and sneak out once the others are engrossed in the action thriller. It's not my sort of movie anyway, all gun-toting men in vests and lots of explosions. I stand in the brightly lit hall and heave a sigh from the core of my being. My heart pounds in my chest and nausea washes over me just thinking about tomorrow. A flash of tan and white catches my eye down the corridor. I narrow my eyes to draw focus after the darkness of the TV room. A tiny, Jack Russell puppy sniffs around the bottom of the cookery class door. I didn't know they allowed pets in here, I wonder who he belongs to. I turn the corner into the next long hallway, but he's gone. I pick up my pace and make it halfway down the corridor when Ariel pops out of Dr Peter's office.

'Where are you off to in such a hurry?' She gives me a suspicious once over.

'I'm looking for the puppy, who does he belong to? He's adorable, I was just trying to catch him up.'

She stares at me, bemused.

'We don't have any dogs in here. Are you feeling all right, Grace?'

'Yes, I'm fine. I guess my eyes were just adjusting to the bright light after the TV room. I was just heading off for an early night.'

'OK, sleep well. I'll see you at breakfast.' She watches me until I get to my room and disappear through the door.

I pull my blanket over me and stare at the purple wall. How can I stand up in front of an entire group and tell everyone what happened when I was fifteen? The shame burns in my stomach as I think back to the bad crowd I had hung around. They'd bullied me for months, this popular group of teenage girls. Teasing me about my unruly, dark curls that were so different from their sleek, blonde locks. They didn't care about grades, they were all aspiring models and singers anyway. I already knew I wanted to teach and absorbed everything in class. I can still hear their snide hisses and feel the scrunched up balls of paper bounce off my head, when the teacher's back was turned. Dis-Grace, that's what they called me. Dis-Grace with the ugly face, wonky teeth and a stupid brace. When I finally lost it with them, and slapped the ringleader's face in the lunch hall, I was pulled into the Head's office and shouted at for a good half hour. After that I became Dis-Grace, basket-case. I started to care less about my studies and spent my Saturdays in the mall, nicking clothes from Chelsea Girl instead of studying in the library. I started to flout the school rules: short skirts, high heels and I back-chatted the teachers. The popular girls' respect for me grew, starting with uproarious laughter at my cheek in class. Before long, there was a seat for me at their table in the dining hall. My grades dropped. The teachers were flummoxed by my sudden, wild behaviour and my parents were at their wits end. I slipped down the classes into the middle groups and gained a lot of interest from the boys now surrounding me. That's when I met Cal and things took a turn for the worse.

'Grace, wake up. Today's your big day.' Kirsty's heavily lined, blue eyes stare down at me from a corner of pulled back blanket. I scowl from the inside of my cosy nest.

'Fuck off.' I curl myself into a foetal ball and seal myself off from the cold draught.

'I knew you'd sneak out of the movie, you unsociable cow. We were supposed to go over your story but I got back to find you snoring most unattractively. I thought I'd wake you early so you could practice it.'

'I'll practice it with Dr P.' My muffled reply is met with a tut.

'That's hardly fucking fair, I'm itching to know.'

'I think you'll find the itch came from your ex-husband, not me.' I titter into the dark as Kirsty's pillow hits me with a soft thump.

'Bitch! Right, I'm off to get some watery scrambled eggs and peely-wally toast. I'll be sure to lick every croissant in the basket to make sure I get yours. Enjoy your cold shower.'

I peer at Kirsty's retreating back with a smirk, as she leaves the room. There he is again. Just as the door closes, the little dog dashes past. I pull back the covers, shivering as the cold seeps through my pyjamas. I rush into the hall but he's nowhere to be seen.

'Kirsty,' I call out as she nears the corner. 'Who does the dog belong to? The one that just ran past you.'

'What dog?'

'The little Jack Russel, he scooted past you as you opened the door.' She raises a sarcastic eyebrow.

'Aye, you're definitely in the right place, hen.'

I stare in puzzlement as she walks away. Have I injured myself worse than we originally thought in my fall? Perhaps I actually have gone insane. My therapy session with Dr P is in just over an hour and I think I need to suggest that I be re-tested. I grab my clothes and scurry down the corridor. My heart gives a little leap as I observe a tiny, furry face peering at me from the corner.

'You're not there. My imagination is playing tricks on me. Go on, *scoot.*' He runs off and guilt immediately creeps over me. I close the cubicle door and step under the cold water, with a mental note to also talk to Dr Peter about the grossly inadequate plumbing. What I wouldn't do for a hot bath and a decent meal right now. It'll happen soon enough, today I have to take the first step in getting out of this dive.

'So from what I can gather, and stop me if I am wrong, is that you feel that this event was unresolved. Even though it was an accident, you still carry the guilt to this day. Is Scamp here at Arcadia, Grace?' Dr Peter stares seriously at me over his glasses.

'I only said he that he looked like Scamp, not that it was him. I haven't seen him since I was ten years old, I can't recall everything about him. I'm not saying he is *actually* here. It's just this dog...well, I'm the only one who can see him.'

'This must be a painful memory. You say that it was your fault that he was off the leash and ran into the road. Do you still believe that it is your fault?'

'I guess so. How do I move on? You're the shrink.'

'What do *you* feel you need to do? You are the expert in you. Sometimes when we think we see something, it is our brain trying to tell us things, it happens to people all the time. Some call it Deja Vu, others call them visions. But when we are in a heightened emotional state these visual ideas can be stronger than in our day-to-day lives. Do you think this is what is happening? You're not alone in experiencing this. It's not unusual.'

'Like Tom Jones syndrome?'

'You're very funny, Grace,' Dr Peter smiles. 'Do you find an escape in humour?'

'Why do you ask?'

'Sometimes we cover our true feelings of pain behind a mask, say humour for example, do you think this is something that you might do, Grace?'

'Erm, probably. I've never really thought about it,' I lie. It's exactly what I do.

'Let's think back to Scamp. Did anything else painful happen to you in your past? Explore in your own time, Grace.'

I take a deep breath. I've promised Kirsty I'll do this but I'm regretting it now.

'I don't remember everything, in fact, I don't remember very much. I never really wanted kids anyway so it's not like it was a disaster on that front.'

'You say it wasn't a disaster.'

'I didn't necessarily want to keep the baby, but it's my body, and they weren't giving me a choice. I most definitely didn't want to do what they were suggesting, but I may have considered adoption. Cal was no support, he dropped me like a hot shit after my so-called friends told him I was pregnant. Come to think of it, so did they.'

Dr Peter looks at me impassively, occasionally jotting something down on his pad.

'We were in the car and I remember my little brother had his ears covered to block out the shouting. We were heading towards the clinic and we'd stopped at some lights. Dad was just about to drive off again when I got out. I was just about to close the rear door when it hit me.'

'What hit you, Grace?'

'The bus.' I narrow my eyes at the doctor. He knows this, I know it's all in my medical notes. 'I was knocked clean out and when I came round they told me the baby was dead. My internal injuries and emergency surgery meant I'd never be able to have kids. My parents got their wish, albeit in a roundabout way. As I'm sure you already know, I never stayed in that house again. I moved on and made a new life for myself and I've never looked back. It doesn't affect me in the slightest. They actually thought I was going to die but I didn't. I'm way tougher than I look and that, doctor, is why I don't need anyone. I'm strong enough to stand up for myself. Do you really think after all I've been through that I would end my life because some idiot walks out on me? I don't *need* anybody and I certainly do not need therapy.'

'You're shaking, Grace. Would you like some water?' The doctor enquires. I hold the glass that he passes me firmly and focus on controlling my breathing.

'I have never talked about this and I never want to again. I'm bloody furious at you for making me dredge it all up.'

'Facing the past must be painful for you. I understand how cross you must be but you have shared a lot today, please see this as positive.'

Something about his calm demeanour fans the flames of anger inside me. It's all very well saying it will help me but he's not the one having to face the horror of what happened.

'Bullshit! I'm calling an end to this session right now,' I slam my glass down onto the table. 'Find some other way of treating me that doesn't involve raking over old ground.'

I slam the door behind me and take off down the corridor back to my room. No matter what Kirsty and I have planned for when we get out of here, I'm not sharing any of this in group today. Sod the lot of them in this happy-clappy dive. They can keep their hugs and positive affirmations. The only therapy I need is a bloody good drink.

Chapter Six

'What do you mean you're not standing up in group? We had a deal and I held my end of it.' Kirsty pulls herself to her full height and glares up menacingly at me.

'I'm just not, so let it go, all sharing does is make me feel like shit. I do not need to resolve anything, what's done is done.'

'You're never getting out of here with that attitude. What about our plan? For what it's worth, I know this is all a load of shite too but we have to look like we're trying.' Kirsty sits back down and pushes her plate away in disgust. 'What is it with this dump? Even I couldn't fuck up pasta this badly. I ate better when I raked bins on the streets.'

The group hushes, unsure how to respond to their ringleader's outburst.

'I'm off to sit with Brioche, I don't need this crap today.' I pick up my tray and push back the chair with my foot.

'Yeah, go fix someone else's problems instead of your own. You're in denial, Grace, deal with it,' she shouts after me.

I pass by Ariel, watching me curiously, and take a seat opposite my silent inmate. She momentarily catches my eye and I smile resignedly.

'Why is talking such a big deal in here? I prefer to sit with you, if that's OK. You're the only one who doesn't give me dull, open questions and then ask me every minute detail about what I've just said. At least Ariel takes the shit sandwich approach so you can cut through the bull.'

Brioche gives a barely discernible eyebrow raise.

'You never heard of a shit sandwich? It means starting with a positive, put the negative in the middle, which is always what the real point is, and then ending on another positive. For example: Grace, you are a great teacher, it's clear that you can't be arsed most of the time, but your students look up to and respect you.'

A tiny flicker of a smile crosses Brioche's lips.

'Actually, they don't. The kids probably wouldn't notice if a Bunsen burner caught my lab coat and I burst into flames, but you get the idea.'

For the first time I notice the panic in the woman opposite me, fear fills her eyes and I grasp across the table for her hand. She pulls it quickly away.

'My goodness, I'm so sorry. Is that what happened to you? Did you lose people you care about in a fire?'

Her chair scrapes across the floor and she hurries from the room. I stare sadly at her half eaten sandwich and untouched apple. Poor Brioche, I clearly hit a raw nerve there. A chill grips my heart, what a horrific thing to experience. Was it her husband? Her children? Maybe both. No wonder she can't speak about it. Kirsty breaks my train of thought.

'Anyone looking to lose weight in here should go and sit next to Grace. She can put you off the food quicker than the taste can.'

Kirsty's posse laugh raucously like cruel, high school girls. Ruth, the red-faced cook, glares at Kirsty from behind the counter, but it barely registers with me. The ones who can't open up are trapped in here, and that's me and Brioche for sure. As rude and blunt as she is, Kirsty is right. I'll never get out. I can't share and there is no other way forward, but in my opinion, old wounds are never meant to be re-opened. The torture of revisiting the past can't be the only way to advance. I have done fine all this time with a vault at the back of my mind bearing a flashing sign saying, 'Do Not Enter.' I push my tray away and run down the corridor to my room. Think about Brioche, I repeat in my head. How can you help her overcome what's happened? If I can fix it for her then maybe (just maybe) I can fix myself.

Group time rolls around again. Our day is punctuated by routine, something I've never been a fan of. We take our seats, Kirsty has got over her earlier strop and I sense that she's up to something. She nudges me urgently.

'Ten o'clock to you, cute new guy. Not my type but you'll be all over that like a rash.'

I glance over, to the left of me is an extremely easy on the eye Johnny Depp lookalike, in his early thirties. I'm not alone in the staring, many other women in the room have clocked him too.

'You don't fancy him?' I gape.

'Wrong shade for me, hen. You like white dudes though and you're by far the prettiest in here. After me, of course.'

Gabe draws our gaze from this God-like creature by clearing his throat to alert us of his presence.

'I see most of you have noticed we have a new visitor with us today. Please say hello to Mark.'

'Well, hello there, Mark,' Jane announces in a flirtatious manner. A few wolf whistles echo around the room, Mark blushes slightly and gives an awkward smile.

'Right, calm down, ladies,' Gabe scorns. 'There's no need to overwhelm the poor lad. Any volunteers to start us off today?'

Before I can stop her, Kirsty grabs my arm and pulls it into the air. Gabe doesn't notice her do it but sees me quickly put my hand back down.

'Grace! We'd be delighted to hear of your journey. Thank you so much for offering.'

I stare like a deer in headlights at his beaming smile, he looks so delighted that I feel an obligation to at least say something.

'I'm going to fucking kill you,' I whisper to Kirsty's smug, sidelong glance.

'Take centre stage and get Mark's attention. Make shit up, I don't care,' she laughs.

I reluctantly get to my feet.

'Hi, I'm Grace. I haven't stood up in group before so please forgive me, I'm not big on sharing. I...I've been seeing a dog. A little Jack Russell puppy that looks like my old dog, Scamp. I was only a kid when he died. Around ten, maybe, I don't quite remember. My parents told me to keep him on the leash but he was desperate to explore. Dr Peter thinks talking about my past may help me to open up,' I shrug. 'Anyway, I took Scamp out on my own one day, not long after we got him. We spent a lovely ten minutes fetching sticks and his favourite blue ball.' I pause and take a deep breath as I recollect the day. 'I remember thinking I'd see how fast he could run and threw his ball a long way off. Too long.' I glare at Kirsty before continuing, I never wanted to think of this again. 'Basically, he ran on the road and was hit by a car. It was all my fault.'

A few soothing sounds fill my ears.

'It most definitely wasn't your doing, dear.'

'You were only little.'

Gabe looks at me with sympathy. I knew this wouldn't be easy, guilt fills up inside me and my heart feels leaden. They wait patiently for me to continue and my voice comes out as a croak.

'Of course, there have been other low points in my life but I'm not ready to talk about those yet.'

'That's OK, Grace,' Gabe smiles. 'Would you like to tell us anything else about Scamp?'

I think about running home to my parents with the man who accidently hit Scamp following me in his car, with my puppy wrapped in a blanket. I had thrown myself onto my bed and cried for hours. Scamp's patchwork, quilted blanket had been in its usual spot on the end of my bed. I inhaled his doggy smell and willed the awful truth of the situation away. I would have happily traded places with him at that moment. I was utterly heartbroken and filled with remorse. I slept with that blanket for years, and looking back, I think it was a way to punish myself for what I'd done. A kind of self-imposed torture. My parents had refused to get another pet after that. I couldn't be trusted. My brother had been distraught, he didn't speak to me for almost a year after it happened.

'No Gabe, I'm done.' I say quietly, sheepishly taking my seat again. The undeserved applause fills my ears and I burn with shame. See, this has done nothing to aid my so-called recovery. All I've achieved is to feel like shit, all over again. I fix my gaze straight ahead and zone the awful moment out again.

'Well done on your improvisation,' Kirsty giggles. 'You are one bloody creative person, half of the room is in tears.'

'Unfortunately, it's true,' I barely whisper. Kirsty doesn't hear, she's too busy whooping along as the others clap. The rest of group therapy passes in a blur, Jim speaks again and I zone out of Kirsty's sighs. She's smart enough to keep them almost inaudible, she's publicly made her peace with Jim but I can tell she still can't be arsed hearing his story for the hundredth time.

A group of giggling, middle-aged women follow Mark down the hall after the meeting finishes but he heads straight towards me. Kirsty gives me a gentle push to the side and speeds off down the corridor.

'Hey, Grace. I just had to come over and say that I'm really sorry about your dog. I had a tortoise once, I found her dead in the hutch and buried her myself. I wasn't far off the age that you were when you had Scamp, actually. It wasn't until years later that I found out they hibernate...I feel really bad about that still.'

'You buried your tortoise *alive*?'

'I'm afraid I did,' he sighs. 'Shelley was like a sister to me, she even ate all the leftover veg I snuck off of my plate. My mum would check the bin but she never checked the hutch.'

I clasp my hand to my mouth.

'Mark, I'm so sorry. I'm not laughing, it's just the shock.'

'You bloody well *are*. I sat there listening to your story about Scamp with my heart breaking and you think my tortoise's untimely death is hilarious? Well, thank you. I shall take my sympathy and fuck right off.' Mark raises a sarcastic eyebrow at me. I choke back a snort at the choice of name for his pet.

'I don't have animals now. I also lost a budgie to a ceiling fan and a hamster down the back of the sofa. There comes a time when you realise that living in harmony with creatures means never going near one again. I've been carrying this guilt for years, it's the reason I'm here.'

'You tried to do yourself in over a few dead pets?'

'That's my story and I'm sticking to it,' Mark gives me an enigmatic smile.

'You have got to come to our script-writing class, you're obviously a natural story-teller.'

'What, you don't believe me? How very rude,' he laughs. 'OK, count me in, I'll catch you later.' He disappears into his room with a cheeky wink.

Kirsty and I spend the afternoon sat cross-legged on our respective beds, talking about our future careers in script writing. We write down a few possible subjects, and the television channels that we consider suitable to our style. We then devise a plan for Kirsty, who is clearly leaving before I am. She will wait until 7pm on the day she gets out, before letting herself into her former home. From around 6.30, Ty will be out on his rounds. He doesn't reappear until the early hours of the morning, around 2am. This should give Kirsty around seven and a half hours to get into her old flat, pack her things and get to mine. Once there, she will make herself at home and get to work on the writing and research required. The fake it till you make it approach seems to have worked for my friend. Even though she's only acting the role of this loving, joyous creature who has seen the light, it seems to have worked. She's positively glowing with enthusiasm and excitement for our future. The angry woman I first met has calmed down several notches. I feel on the edge of something exciting too, it's just finding a solution to getting out that is problematic.

Now I couldn't care less that Josh has gone, any man that easy to lose isn't worth having in the first place. He held me back and I can see that for the first time. This spell in Arcadia has got me to stop and reflect on what makes me truly happy. I could have muddled along teaching the unwilling to learn until I retired, but money isn't everything. Financial security had been my aim all those years ago at graduation and I've achieved that now. With a minimal mortgage and good savings, maybe it's time to chill and enjoy life a bit more. I visualise nights full of wine and laughter as Kirsty and I work. Someone to cook for would be an added bonus too. I love nothing more than an afternoon spent in the kitchen with appreciative guests ready to sample my cuisine.

Kirsty has most definitely been handed the shittiest of lives: neglect, abuse, homelessness, and just when she started to feel secure, her husband starts playing away from home. I intend to show her what true loyalty and friendship can be like. We will have each other's backs and I aim to be the one who will stick by her, no matter what. I had left Kirsty to her adoring public this dinner time and sat in amiable silence opposite Brioche, who seemed relieved that I hadn't tried to make small talk. For the first time ever, she had finished her food. I was trying to breathe positivity and support into her, I sent thoughts her way to let her know that if and when she was ready to talk, I'd be happy to listen. I even received a tiny flicker of a smile as she stood up to leave. I smiled back, wishing I knew what to do to help her.

Kirsty and I walk together from the dining room to our writing class. We take our seats and I stare blankly at the sheet of paper in front of me, willing some ideas to spring to mind. I had harboured concerns over my last piece of work but everyone loved it. I have always been a fan of telling it like it is, they had all said my bluntness was refreshing. Maybe I should write about that? How people don't always say what they mean? I imagine an echo-type conversation between a Brioche character and a Kirsty sort. Brioche says her version and Kirsty translates what she really means. The creative juices begin to flow and my hand itches to pick up the pen. I barely notice the class filling up around me. This is a cathartic way to let out my feelings, this is real therapy. Mark gives me a friendly nudge to the arm on his way past. He takes a seat alone at the back of the class. Kirsty watches him pass by with an amused smile playing on her lips.
'Know what you're writing about today?' She enquires.
'Yes, and mind your own business, I'm not giving you any ideas.'
'Don't flatter yourself, I'm streets ahead of you. I'll be out before the end of the month anyway. I have bigger fish to fry than performing in front of you nut-jobs. I aim to hunt down and schmooze some fit TV producer, I'm even willing to go white if need be. I take my responsibilities to our future success very seriously.'
Kirsty has the morals of an alley cat; she complements my more reserved approach perfectly. I watch as Teresa walks into the room, giving us a welcoming smile.
'Hello, ladies and gents, thank you for joining us today.' She takes a seat at the front of the group. 'Good evening, Mark. I'm delighted you chose to come along.'
Kirsty throws me a sidelong glance.
'You're a sly, old dog, aren't you? You don't let the grass grow under your feet. I know you asked him to come.'
'I said it was a fun class. Big deal, he's really not my type.'
'Bullshit! I know you fancy him; I saw you chatting in the corridor. I bet you're not gonna leave until he does, are you?' Her eyes narrow as she awaits my response.
'Don't worry, there are some good takeaways around my bit. I'm sure you

can fend for yourself until I get home. Are you going to have enough money to live on until we start making some?'

'Ty puts an allowance in my account every month. Well, he calls it an allowance, I call it laundering,' she snorts. 'I haven't really needed to touch it in a while so I should have a few grand in there. Most of his cash is stashed away at his mum's house, that way if he gets busted dealing, they won't find loads in the bank or our place. He thinks I don't know that he keeps it under a loose floorboard beneath her sofa.'

'You weren't lying when you said you were a mafia wife. I couldn't live with all that insecurity.'

'I love living life on the edge,' Kirsty winks. 'I can't think of anything duller than teaching brats that don't want to learn.'

I smart a little at Kirsty's comment. Lessons are only dull if you allow them to be. I had tried, but lately I couldn't muster any interest. I rally myself from my thoughts before I lose my chosen subject to write about.

'Right, shush now and let me write this down while it's still fresh in my mind.'

I pick up my pen and embrace the silence of the class. I start with my title: *'Grace Ellis tells it like it is.'* I stare Kirsty down until she stops looking at me and goes back to her own sheet.

People never mean what they say and never say what they mean. I have created this handy guide so you can cut through the crap and see what's really going on in someone's head. For the purpose of this exercise, I'm setting the scene of two friends meeting for lunch. Above is the comment made and in the brackets below, lies the real meaning.

'Oh, my goodness, I'm so pleased you could meet up today, this catch-up is long overdue.'
(Six months really isn't long enough. I'd rather stick pins in my eyes than spend the next two hours with you, but it's always good to have babysitters on tap so I decided to squeeze you in.)

'You're looking well! I love your curves in that outfit. You're so lucky you can go short, I hate my thighs.'
(Did you eat for the whole six months I haven't seen you? You're rocking that elasticated waist but perhaps showing bits best reserved for your gynaecologist.)

'How's your job going? I heard on the grapevine that you got that

promotion. Well done.'
(I bloody knew you were shagging your boss.)

'Yes, I moved house, you must pop over and see it sometime.'
(Don't darken my doorway. You're about as welcome as herpes.)

'So, no ring on your finger yet, I see?'
(He's screwing that bird at work, the pope has more chance of getting married than you do.)

'Such a shame you haven't had kids yet. You'd better get a wriggle on now you're almost forty.'
(The Sahara Desert is more likely to sprout a forest than you popping out a sprog now.)

'Did you notice the new diamond earrings that my darling man bought me?'
(My other half got pissed and didn't come home last week. Still, at least he earns more than yours.)

'I'm loving that new style on you, I wish I could be so brave with my hair.'
(OMG, were you run over by a lawnmower?)

'Can you believe I've been married ten years now? I really thought he was out of my league.'
(Some us have a Mulberry handbag, some us have a Lidl bag for life.)

'You're so lucky you have a successful career, I don't know when I'd find time for a job now.'
(I work twenty-four hours a day, seven days a week, for no appreciation and shit all pay. My husband thinks I'm fat and my kids hate me. This is why I hit the wine by 5pm.)

'Such a shame about Jack and Emily splitting up, isn't it?'
(It's clear you've always fancied Jack. We have a sweepstake on how long it'll take for you to be all over him, I have 2 weeks.)

'Gosh, where does the time go? Let's not leave it so long next time.'
(I'll see you in a year...unless I need a babysitter.)

I close my pen with a satisfied click and glance over at the top of Kirsty's head. I can read a little of what she's written. *'Clean Living, by Kirsty MacDonald.'* The first line says that she's always wanted to grow a herb garden but hasn't had the thyme. I give a soft chuckle and smooth out my sheet of paper. We're going to make a great team.

Chapter Seven

'It really is commendable the commitment you've shown to our school and students, Grace. We feel that you're perfect to fill the role. It really was a one horse race.' The headmaster

beams warmly at me as the panel nod their agreement. Mr Wilson, a rather smug and misogynistic member of the PTA, holds out a clammy hand for me to shake. He refuses to allow anyone to use his first name, in fact, I have no idea what it is. Despite his son no longer being in my class, he spends a disproportionate amount of time in my lab asking questions about the science department's curriculum, when that was clearly the Head of Department's job. I'll never be bloody shot of him now, with my new position. I always got the feeling he was mentally undressing me as I answered his questions with limited patience.

I had been aware that Mick Brown, the current HoD, was due to retire in the next couple of weeks, but it hadn't occurred to me that they'd given me any consideration. My frustration expressed in the staff room had been mistaken for aggravation at being too long in the same role, and not for the apathy I felt towards teaching in general, these days.

'I'm thrilled you think so highly of me, John. It's an honour and a privilege to teach the children of Holly Berry High. I gratefully accept your offer and hope to be as successful as my predecessor. We've seen great results with Mick in charge and I'll be sorry to see him go.'

'I know you will, Grace,' John smiles. 'I haven't forgotten that passion you showed back when I first interviewed you. I had you earmarked for the post, from that day. You're more than ready and I have every confidence in your ability to do just as fantastic a job as Mick has.'

'How about we take Grace out for a celebratory drink? I think she's earned it,' Wilson smarms. I can barely disguise my disgust at the thought of spending any social time with this lecherous git. John sucks air through his teeth with a grimace.

'You all go ahead without me, I have a meeting later and best not be reeking of booze,' he gives a small chuckle at the very thought.

'Gosh, that's very generous, Mr Wilson. I'm so sorry but I have dinner plans...with my partner,' I add the latter part for emphasis. He looks crestfallen and I quickly avert my eyes from his pitiful gaze.

'Well, make sure you order the champagne tonight, Grace. You most certainly deserve it.' John gives me a fatherly squeeze of the shoulder as we stand to leave.

I can barely contain my excitement as I rush down the corridor to my lab. I hit call on Josh's name and pull on my coat with my free hand. Yet again, it goes straight to his voicemail. It's funny how he answers on the first ring to everyone else, other than me and his mother. I cancel the call without leaving a message and try Karen instead. She can do a quick dinner but she has a date at seven. There's hardly any point, I generally spend over an hour ploughing through the rush hour of London traffic. She says she will make time for me over the weekend, it's a huge achievement and a long time coming. She's clearly not thrilled enough to blow out a guy she's chatted to online only three times. I don't seem to hold much importance to my so-called nearest and dearest, these days.

The pressure of taking on such a position was a big deal, Mick had muddled through it for almost five years before taking early retirement. The financial rewards are huge, which is why he had taken on the role in the first place, but he had commented more than once on how he had started the job with a full head of hair. At least with the extra hours put in every evening I would miss the bulk of the traffic. Plus, leaving the building with the cleaners would mean that Mrs Malik would be too engrossed in Emmerdale to come out and interrogate me each night. I wouldn't miss Josh or my friends at weekends as this was when I would catch up with some neglected marking.

***

'When I began the new job, my work-load tripled. I'd work from home on a Saturday until 6pm, make dinner, have a glass of wine, and generally fall asleep before the end of Casualty. I've been known to work the occasional Sunday too. It was all far more overwhelming than I ever anticipated,' I rant away and Dr Peter listens calmly to my complaining. 'Karen's weekend celebratory dinner never materialised but she did squeeze me in the following Wednesday, when she had a last minute date cancellation. In a way, the timing of this new job was perfect. Everyone else was so busy and now I could say the same. The holidays still dragged, but I've never been one to go away by myself and would pity those people dining alone, or sat in the pubs trying to make conversation with the barman. Instead, I'd go to the gym, take spa treatments, and wine and dine alone at home, where nobody could see what a sad loser I was. It's around this time that I started to check Josh's phone. I hated myself for doing it, but I needed to know and felt I had nothing to lose. By this point it was pretty much a non-relationship anyway, the new magazine consumed all of his time and he'd get irate if I brought up how little I saw of him.'

'Being promoted is an achievement that is based on merit. Don't you think they chose you for a reason, Grace?'

I shrug away the doctor's compliment.

'They have a way of sniffing out the ones with no life, I guess he knew I'd commit to the stupidly long hours without complaint. I've been more financially motivated than career driven for years now. At some point, I stopped caring about making a difference to the kids and focused on making a difference to my bank balance. Nothing to be proud of there.'

'From what you've said, and correct me if I am wrong, but he selected you for the job because you were passionate about making a change. Do you not believe that to be true?'

'Maybe. I just feel like a fraud. I don't care anymore because the kids don't give a stuff about their education, they just want a quick buck and celebrity status. Why work your ass off in a long-term career when one topless shot, or a stint on *Big Brother*, could drop a ten-year salary straight into your lap? I know I sound cynical but it's true. There's no allowance made for discipline now either. I told one lad off a few weeks ago for back-chatting me, within hours the mother was up to school in her onesie with a fag hanging out of her mouth, slagging me off to the head. I just find it difficult to be motivated or to trust people now. Everyone is out for themselves, so why shouldn't I be?'

'You say you can't trust people,' Dr Peter muses. 'Is that the case in every aspect of your life?'

'Probably, it's not like Josh was any more trustworthy, is it?' I snort obnoxiously.

'Do you think you are a trustworthy person, Grace?'

'I have nothing to hide.' I meet his eyes defiantly. I know he's referring to me going through Josh's phone. I'm not claiming to have the moral high ground here, but what he did behind my back was way worse than me forewarning myself.

'I'm sure you don't. Let's go back to the plans you mentioned that you've made and explore this further. Are you intending to give up teaching?'

'I just want to have more fun in life, I constantly feel like a hamster on a wheel. Kirsty and I have a plan, if I tell you, you won't say anything, will you?'

'As you know, all our time together is confidential. As long as it isn't considered a harm to yourself or others, I have no reason to say anything to anyone.' He smiles warmly at me.

'Well, we're going to live as flatmates and write scripts to submit for TV shows. It's funny but I feel I've made a lifelong friend in Kirsty. She's a little more unorthodox than my usual mates, but in a good way, I find her attitude to life rather refreshing.'

'It sounds like you have some goals you are working towards, and it's great that you will both have ongoing support when you leave us. I read your latest offering in writing class, your talent is clear. You're on the right track for your future and I can see us parting ways, perhaps sooner than you think.' I look up sharply at the doctor's words.

'Really? That's the best news I've had in a long time. No offence to you all, I just can't wait to get home and start my new life. I feel like I have a second chance. I know Kirsty will be out first but she's going to be staying over at mine. We plan to get started on some work independently, we'll choose a few subjects and take the best parts from both of our contributions. How long do you think? A couple of weeks?'

'It's hard to say, Grace, your recovery dictates your time here, not us. We want you to leave here feeling whole again, so you don't have any need to come back to us.'

'I haven't felt this positive in years. Josh did me a favour removing himself from my life, I feel like I've been in a stagnant pond for a very long time. I was thrilled to get my promotion but it's funny how what you want and what you need can be entirely separate entities.'

'It sounds like we are singing from the same hymn sheet. You know yourself best, but sometimes we can't see the light in our darkest days. Let's stop here, it's nice finish on a positive. I'm looking forward to reading your next piece this evening.'

I take my usual seat opposite Brioche and eye the unappetising chicken dish in front of me with suspicion. It's a colour that I have never seen in a curry; a kind of egg yolk yellow with mushy veg of unidentifiable sort. Brioche gives the faintest flicker of a smile at my expression and glances down at her equally inedible, pasta dish.

'Do you think we'd get away with hijacking reception and ordering a takeaway? I think I could take out Dr Peter, do you think you could handle Ariel and Gabe? Come to think of it, Kirsty would manage all three and we could take a look through the Yellow Pages.' I brace myself for the first bite, Brioche raises her fork in unity and we take the first taste together. The lukewarm concoction makes me gag and Brioche gives a soft chuckle. I try to hide my delight that I caused this tiny reaction.

'My neighbour would go ballistic at someone deigning to call this a curry. What I wouldn't do right now for Mrs Malik's Biryani. Mind you, she has Turmeric now, so I imagine she won't need me for company anymore.' Brioche raises an eyebrow in question.

'Turmeric is a cat. Mrs Malik thought he was mine and told the paramedics who brought me in that she'd look after him. She's effectively stolen someone's pet. I did tell her on numerous occasions that he didn't belong to me but the woman is a law unto herself. I know she's lonely since her family all moved up north. He makes her feel needed, I suppose.' Brioche's eyes fill with sympathy. 'Mind you, I'm in the same boat and I'm lucky she looks out for me. I should make more of an effort to pop in and see her but you know how life is. I'll try harder when I get home.'

Brioche glances wordlessly at my fading bruises. She has no obvious marks herself, maybe her route was an overdose, after losing her family to the fire. I'm not asking again, her trust in me is building and I won't undo her progress.

'How are you enjoying the baking class?' I enquire. She wrinkles her nose with a shrug. 'Have you ever fancied writing? You could even just sit in and hear our mediocre offerings. I will warn you though, if you do participate, you have to share what you've written with the person next to you. I can say to Teresa that you want to come along and see what it's about, if you wish.'

Brioche looks at me intently. It would be good for her to come along as this could be a possibility as an outlet for her emotions. The non-verbal communication is a huge achievement and if she's ready to interact with me in this way, then maybe she can take the next step and write her feelings down.

'Have a think, there's no pressure. I'll say to Teresa that I've invited you as a spectator and leave it at that.'

Brioche gives me an almost imperceptible smile and picks up her tray to leave. I buzz inwardly as I watch her, my hard work is finally starting to pay off. Ariel manoeuvres her way through the tables as I stand to go, she grabs my arm with a girlish squeal.

'Well done, Grace. Finally, we have some response. Most people have left her to her own devices. She's been here for such a long time and this progress has only happened because of you.'

'Maybe she's just ready now. Whatever she went through she clearly needed that time to heal. But to not utter a word? Poor woman. I'll keep trying to crack the code. I'd be delighted if she talked, even if it was only to tell me to bugger off.'

I spend the early afternoon jotting down some suggestions for Kirsty and I to work on. I sit cross-legged on my bed, absorbed in the ideas swimming around my head. Every day occurrences seem to be a popular choice, those things that go unmentioned in society but everyone acknowledges that we all experience. I think I'm onto a winner with my subject of what people say versus what people mean, and I set to work on the first one. *'Social Media: my perfect life versus attention seeking drivel.'* I give a small chuckle at the endless writing possibilities on this subject. I start with my own personal pet hate. That vague, sad face emoji on a status, followed by a comment of, 'what's up, hun?' Then the original poster states enigmatically, 'I'll direct message you.'

Why bother? I have deleted these types purely for their pity parties. Pick up the phone and call a friend or relative. Don't tell two hundred people, half of whom are probably virtual strangers and another quarter, at least, who couldn't give a flying fuck that your goldfish is sick. Also on my hit list are, 'I love you, my honey bunny, you are my world,' types. I can feel the surge of irritation as I write and try to laugh it off. These energy suckers receive so many comments in response to this nonsense and I got only two for the post I put up about my promotion.

The door to the bedroom swings open and Kirsty launches herself onto her bed, a smug grin on her face.

'Guess who's getting out next week?'

'No way! How exciting, you must be thrilled.'

'My cup runneth over. Even better than that, guess who's leaving tomorrow?'

I hold my breath, daring to hope that she may have overheard something in the office, and it's me.

'Spill.' I demand.

'Only one pain in the arse with a dead wife and a PVA horse,' Kirsty gives a triumphant air punch. 'Just think, I never have to hear that fucking story again for as long as I live. I met him in the corridor, looking even redder than usual. His sons are coming by tomorrow at ten to take him home.'

'Bugger, I had hoped it would be me. Oh well, at least you're blazing the trail.'

'Open up, it's the only way. Make up a load of shit about why you tried to sky-dive from your balcony. Nobody has any clue if my story is even real or not, give them what they want and join me on the outside where the fags and booze are aplenty.'

'You didn't make all that up, did you? They have access to your medical records, they *know* stuff and we have no idea what's in those files.'

'Of course I didn't make it up,' Kirsty glances around shiftily. 'Why on earth would I do that? God, I thought I was happy about getting out but to have no Jim for my final week, that's the bloody cherry on the cake.' Kirsty does a little dance around the room. I frown at this woman, twirling around in front of me. I have no idea what is going on inside her head, she *could* be making it all up, even to me. It's entirely possible that she's created a scenario that even she believes. The staff here aren't stupid; they will have verified that she did have a child at fifteen that she gave up for adoption.

'You really are a mystery, aren't you?' I voice my thoughts out loud.

'Not really,' she plonks herself back onto her bed. 'I want the same as you and everyone else, just to be happy. Loaded too would be a bonus.'

One week and my friend will be leaving, does that mean I get notice of a week too? I'll bring it up in my next session. Dr Peter has said it won't be long but only if I stay on track. Maybe Kirsty's right, it's time that I change tact and face my past.

Brioche is a no-show in class, I think I expected too much of her too soon. I won't mention it but I may invite her again in a few days. I could always go along to her baking class, maybe the answer lies in being on her playing field. God knows I need all the help I can get in that department. I can cook pretty well, but baking has never been a strong point. I may as well use this time to develop a few skills. Kirsty had offered to give up her seat if she came along which was quite impressive of her, I thought. This time last week she wouldn't have given up her seat for anyone, let alone her silent nemesis.

'I bloody knew she was up herself and this just proves it,' she whispers as we take our seats.

'She's not, I think you've got her all wrong. There's a story there and it's not a pretty one.'

'Whatever, I think you're mistaken, but I'm good Kirsty now and if I can't say anything nice, then I won't say anything at all.'

I give a small eyebrow raise at this comment. She has hugged it out with two of the Arcadia inmates, but I know her well enough now, she's did all this to fast-track her ass out of here and not to make friends or amends.

I stare blankly at my piece of paper, nothing comes to mind that's worth writing about. All I can think about is Kirsty leaving me, and Brioche, with her tiny but impressive breakthroughs. Maybe they'd let me into the baking class right now. There's no point wasting an hour staring at the empty sheet in front of me. The ideas I had earlier are not for sharing yet. They will be previewed only when we pitch and I don't want anyone but Kirsty and I to know what's in them.

'Kirsty, I need to go, there's something I have to do.'

'Oh, not this shit again. You know they'll find you. Suck it up, buttercup. You're in this for the long haul.'

'No, not that. I'll explain later.' I walk purposefully to the front of the class and whisper my intentions to Teresa. To my annoyance, she tells the class that she's popping out for five minutes and walks me down the corridor to the baking group. I smart indignantly as she announces to the class leader that I'd like to take part. My school kids are given more trust than this.

'I'm sorry, dear, but you do have previous.' Teresa gives an apologetic shrug and wanders back off down the hall. I search the class for Brioche. She's right at the back, concentrating on her recipe book.

'Shall I just...' I indicate to the space next to her.

'Yes, please do. You're Grace, aren't you? I'm Mary, it's lovely to meet you.'

Brioche's head shoots up on hearing my name but I avoid her gaze.

'Yes, I am. Lovely to meet you too, Mary.' I pull my hair back into the supplied hairnet and pop on my apron.

'What are we making,' I smile at Brioche. She gives me a cautious once over and pushes the recipe book towards me. 'I hope you don't mind me being here. I decided I needed to develop a new skill and you look like a good teacher. I had writer's block in the other class so I thought I'd try this one out.'

I pick up the bag of flour between us and begin ladling it onto the scale. Once I have my four ounces, I dump the whole lot into the bowl. Brioche gives a tiny sigh and tips the flour back onto the scale. She places a sieve over the bowl and gives me a stern look.

'Sift the flour. See, I've learned something new already.'

We work away in amicable silence for the next hour, with Brioche occasionally correcting my mistakes. By the time we've cleaned our counters and washed up, our cupcakes are ready. I note with disappointment that mine haven't risen and Brioche gives a small chuckle at this. She's obviously not too squeaky clean and I like this edge to her. I watch closely as she whips up a pink, butter icing and places the bowl to one side. She begins to shape tiny, ornate flowers and leaves from pieces of royal icing. My eyes widen at her exceptional skills. She hands me a few pieces to practice on but nothing I make is a patch on hers. At the end of the class, Brioche hands me one of her cakes. It's possibly the loveliest thing I've tasted, in ages. I offer her one of my efforts, which she declines with a sarcastic smirk. I scrape my tray into the bin and Mary gives me a smile of consolation.

'Good attempt, Grace. You'll get the hang of it, just like everyone else has.'

I bid Brioche goodnight and head off down the corridor. I'm not going to question her on anything tonight.

'Grace, wait up. Why weren't you in class tonight?' Mark puffs as he catches me up in the corridor.

'I'm on a mission to make Brioche talk to me, I had block anyway. What did you write about?'

He pulls out a neatly folded sheet from his pocket and I sit down cross-legged in the hall to read it. He joins me on the floor and watches me closely.

The Ex-Directory, by Mark Green.' Oh, this will be interesting. I read through an account of his first ever date, with a girl named Chloe. He was fourteen years old, she was the ripe, old age of fifteen and the coolest girl in the year. Mark had taken her swimming, I assume purely for perversion reasons, and had decided to impress her by dive-bombing from the side of the pool. Unfortunately, the borrowed trunks from his elder brother had been a bit on the loose side and had slid down mid-bomb to reveal his puny, white arse, as he had put it. I chortle as I read through his experiences.

'Mark, this is hilarious. You really have a talent for comedy. Maybe Kirsty and I need to get you on board for our little project.'

'Do you really think it's good? I've never done anything like this before.'

'Of course, can't you see the tears of laughter streaming down my cheeks? Did you really climb down this next girl's drainpipe to find her father standing at the bottom?'

'Yes, he was super-strict and I was only helping her choose a hairstyle for the prom from some beauty magazines.'

'Sure you were,' I give a cynical laugh.

'Cross my heart and hope to die, I'm telling the truth.'

'Don't say you hope to die in this joint, Mark. The walls have ears, I swear. I thought I had relationship issues but yours have cheered me up no end.'

'Probably explains why I'm the way I am.'

'True, you see the funny side of everything, but that's a good way to be.' I give him a smile and a nudge. Mark looks like he's about to say something but hesitates. I can tell he's like me when it comes to opening up.

'Are you going to watch the movie tonight? It's a scary one. As if life in here wasn't enough of a horror movie,' he smiles.

'Yeah, why not. Get your coat, you've pulled, mate.'

Mark chats and cackles through the movie, much to the annoyance of those in front of us. I try to keep him quiet but it's impossible not to laugh at his silly voice-overs. There's an age-old formula to horrors, he explains. The popular blonde goes first, followed the black dude, and anyone who says, 'I'll be right back.' The culprit always turns out to be the joker of the group.

We leave halfway through the film, after one too many tuts from those trying to watch. We decide to head down to the empty canteen in search of some proper coffee. I don't risk putting the lights on as we try each walk-in cupboard door. Mark whispers through the dark for me to join him at the other end of the kitchen, where he has had success with an unlocked one. We rummage around in the dark, banging into each other occasionally. I give a tin a hopeful shake and pull of the lid. A quick root around inside reveals biscuits. Mark and I sit on the floor and stuff our faces, chatting quietly in the dark, cramped space. Now, why couldn't Josh have been as fun and spontaneous as this? I won't lie, I do fancy Mark. I hope we will at least keep in touch when we get out of here, if not more. He's single, I'm single, and we most definitely get on. Neither of us have had any luck in the relationship department and he loves to write as much as I do. It's strange how we've all been plucked from our everyday lives and thrown together haphazardly in this odd place. I would probably have never crossed paths with any of these people on the outside. I may be desperate to leave but I will be doing so with some great, new friends.

'Last one, Grace, you can have it.'

'No, you go ahead. I feel a bit queasy with all the sugar.'

Mark snaps the biscuit in half and we share it.

'I bloody love a jammy dodger, sod your poncey biscuits, this is as good as it gets,' he exclaims.

We freeze as we see the kitchen light go on, my eyes adjust to the brightness and I stare at Mark in horror.

'Ruth, can I just grab you for a second, please. Dr Peter wants a word about the menu plan for next week,' Ariel's voice sings out from the canteen door.

'Just a minute, Ariel. I forgot to lock a cupboard door,' Ruth tuts.

My hand shoots up to my mouth as I stare wide-eyed at a grinning Mark. 'Where 'av I put me bloody keys,' she mutters, just inches from us. 'They're behind reception, Ruth. I thought you were done so I hung them back up.'

'Blimmin' do-gooder. Me old legs can't 'andle the five-mile walk back down there,' Ruth's voice gains distance and I crawl, commando style to the cupboard door.

'Come on, hurry,' I hiss. Mark stands and pushes the door open, sauntering casually out into the brightly lit canteen. Feeling a little ridiculous on the floor, I dust myself off and we run to the exit. We peer Scooby-Doo style round the corner to where the cook lumbers heavily down towards reception. We take off down the corridor at full pelt until we reach my room. Mark pulls me into a hug and plants a crumby kiss on my cheek, before turning back and heading to his own room. I give a tiny, inward squeal as I watch him go. He feels the same, I just know it. I creep past a sleeping Kirsty and change into my pyjamas. I slide beneath the sheets and hug my knees to my chest. Things will be different from now on. I just know it. In Mark and Kirsty, I finally have *real* friends.

Maybe it was a sugar high or perhaps it was Mark getting so close, but I lay wide awake for most of the night, planning our lives outside of Arcadia and all the fun things we can do. My mind turns back to my breakthrough with Brioche. It's been a huge achievement having some communication but it's baby steps all the way with her. I turn restlessly in bed, picking out darkened shapes in the room, as Kirsty snores gently opposite me. Brioche isn't as daft as she looks, she's sussing me out to see if she can trust me before opening up. My mind buzzes as I toss and turn, trying to get a comfortable position. I finally feel like I'm about to doze off when a pressure on the bed makes me start. I lie frozen in the darkness as I feel something make its way up towards me. The heavy breathing and a distinctive, familiar smell. The pressure settles on my legs and I hear a soft whimper in the dark. For a second the relief washes over me when I realise it's only the little dog I've seen running around, then terror grips my heart as my conscious mind takes over and I realise that he exists only in my imagination. I gently lift my legs up and slide them towards the edge of the mattress. I feel the small bundle shift its weight and I pull myself out of bed, pinching my cheek to make sure I'm properly awake. I squint into the darkness before pulling the curtain to one side. A lamppost outside illuminates my bed; there's nothing there. I can still smell the slight warm dampness of dog but when I pat down my bed there's only the blanket. I sit down heavily. I thought I was getting better. I stare at Kirsty's back as she takes soft, shallow breaths. She's coming on leaps and bounds but I don't feel like I'll ever get out of here. I pull on my dressing gown and slippers and head down the hallway to the toilet and shower block, all the way looking out for this puppy that nobody can see but me. I push open the door to the bathroom and start at the sound of running water. It must be gone three, who in their right mind would taking a shower at this time of the morning? The water stops and I'm just about to head into a cubicle, when an arm reaches out from the shower for a towel. Long burn scars line her skin, all the way from the wrist to the shoulder and across her back. She steps out of the shower, facing away from me. Brioche? I sneak into the toilet cubicle and stand quietly, waiting for her to finish. A long sigh breaks the silence. She must shower at this time so that no one can see her. Poor woman, I imagine those scars will be nothing compared to the mental ones she carries. I feel terrible for having seen her, she clearly wanted the privacy that this time of the morning offers. I stand stock still for the ten minutes she takes leaves, my bladder aching at the sight of a toilet that I can't use for fear of being heard. Finally, I feel the rush of air as the bathroom door closes, I hang off for a few more seconds until I hear her footsteps moving down the hallway. Now I'm certain she's lost someone in a fire, her face gave that away when I asked her. Did she try to save them? Perhaps she was rescued and someone she loved wasn't, survivor guilt made her want to take her own life. So many puzzle pieces to put together, she just needs the right kind of support and I know I'm the one who can give it to her.

Chapter Eight

The low, winter sun streams through a crack in the curtains and directly into my eyes. I had the most vivid dream in which Kirsty, Mark and I were pitching our scripts to a producer in Television Centre. We stormed it and they signed us for a pilot on the spot. Despite this scenario being a product of my imagination, it lightens my mood as I traipse down the hall to the shower block. I needed an incentive to remove my writer's block and now I have a clear head. Not even an icy shower can dampen my enthusiasm, as I sing tunelessly and wash my hair. What a difference having my own things has made, the asylum standard wash had made my skin itch and only served to make me even more miserable than I already was. I just make breakfast before the canteen closes, Brioche has already been and gone, Kirsty and the others are just about to leave. Mark follows me in. I'm pleased to see him but I'm also glad not to be the last one potentially getting a bollocking for holding up the kitchen staff. Ruth stares at us mutely, radiating her disgust for us late-comers from every pore. I guess it's a bit unfair, she has been in here since five and we can barely make it in for nine. We ignore her glare and head down to the cooked breakfasts. I need nourishing today to nurture my ideas. We take our seats and I tell Mark about my dream, his look is slightly mocking as I speak but he listens quietly as I tell of the producer's awe at our talents.

'So, what was this hilarious script that landed us an instant deal? It's got to be a sign that you're onto a winner.'

'I have no idea, how annoying is that? Maybe it'll come back to me. Still, I think it's a good omen. I'm going to speak to Kirsty today about bringing you on board. If you want to, that is?' I give Mark a hopeful glance. He would be a great asset, but it also guarantees that we will meet up on the outside.

'I'm not sure Kirsty will share your enthusiasm, but go ahead, she can only say no. I had an idea for a script to write about later, I wonder if Teresa will let us team up.'

'I don't see why not. What's it about?' I pull a face at the bland scrambled egg I've just shovelled into my mouth.

'It's for a sketch called, 'it's not me, it's you.' I can't count the times I've heard that phrase the other way round. So I thought it fitting to pay homage to the ritual. It involves a break-up, with either you or Kirsty, and I run off with the other one.'

'Sounds intriguing; I look forward to hearing more in class. I have to try and catch Kirsty before therapy. She's always in a shitty mood after speaking to that poke-nosed bastard, as she refers to Dr Peter as. Anyway, I can't stomach this dog food, how you can simultaneously burn and undercook eggs is beyond me.'

'It sounds like a laugh, I suppose we could give it a try, but only if I can be the crazy ex. I do it so well.' Kirsty was just leaving the room when I raced down the hall. Ariel had intercepted me in my haste to catch my room-mate up and I had almost missed her. Everyone treats me with suspicion since my runner. Now anything faster than a stroll has one of them sticking their nose out of a door to stop me in my tracks.
'I'm glad you want that role, it's a bit close to home for me right now,' I sigh.
'I'm used to being the bat-shit one. Ty once said that all Scots were violent alcoholics. He never said it again after I threw my double vodka across the bar at him.' Kirsty turns on her scuffed heel and leaves me grinning after her. She has no idea how hilarious she is, coming out with these dark quips. I glance at my watch, I have an hour until therapy and I want to do a bit more writing. I head down to reception for some more paper to jot down my ideas. Ariel isn't in reception so I take a seat in the side room to the office and wait for her return. Just through the wall is Dr Peter's office and I accidentally tune into Kirsty's therapy session. I clasp my hands to my ears and prepare to leave, when something holds me back. Kirsty is getting home. I know I shouldn't listen in but I really need some tips on what are the right things to say to the staff. They watch us like hawks, everything seems to have an undertone or hidden meaning to them. I also need to know if she is telling me the truth or could be a potential danger to herself. I don't want to come home and find her in the bath with the knife block. Convincing myself that I have her best interests at heart, I press my ear to the wall.

'I always thought that talking therapies were a load of crap, but I do feel better for being in here. I know you've probably never met anyone like me, Dr P. Even I don't know why I do half the shit I do. I doubt I ever will.'
'That's ok, Kirsty, we don't always have all the answers immediately. It is helpful to admit that sometimes we are bound by uncertainty.' He pauses, as if he is recalling or reading through notes. 'Last session we ended by saying that you felt you would like to visit the effects your family had on your life, would you like to tell me about them?'
'Well, I don't know who my dad is. My ma said she could probably narrow the daddy odds down to around ten of her punters. I used to see most of

them around town. One guy down the local would buy me crisps and a lemonade. I used to think it was him 'cause he was nice to me. Another of them tried to hit on me when I was fifteen so I kinda ruled him out. Now I've stopped caring who it is.'

'Growing up without knowing must have been difficult. Did it make you feel like you lacked a parental figure?'

'Not really, I had Uncle Marion, she was like a two-for-one deal. She was my mum's first pimp and had a sex-change op when I was wee. She used to be Uncle Marcus but it was confusing for me to start saying auntie so we just stuck with uncle and changed the name. She was like a mum and dad to me, we would bake cookies and do normal kiddy shit but she would also batter any wee scrote that gave me arse-ache. We lost touch when I ran off to the streets.'

'Uncle Marion couldn't help you during that difficult time?'

'Possibly, but she was running some kind of unofficial knocking shop and wanted to protect me from all that. She called it The Cosy Inn, a play on words, obviously,' Kirsty gives a throaty laugh. 'I thought taking up a room that she could make money out of was a waste of resources. If there's one thing I've always been made aware of, it's the importance of cold, hard cash. Anyways, it was a hot summer, and I quite fancied the drama of being a runaway.'

'Please, go on.'

'It wasn't as bad as I expected. I found a bakery and slept in the back doorway there for most of the time. It was warm through the night and the dude who made the pies would bring me one out with a cup of tea for breakfast. I think he felt sorry for me. That worked well until he was off on holiday and the boss took over. He told me to piss off and threatened the nice guy with the sack if he let me back. After that it was the doorway of Woolies on the high road and a disused shed I found by an empty house. Yeah it was shite at times, but to be honest, doc, it doesn't come close to how I felt after Ty's escapades.'

'How did you feel when you found out about Ty's affair?'

'I was fucking livid. You really ask some stupid questions, don't you? I never doubted that he would stray eventually. I used to wonder why people bothered trying to hunt down their happy ever after in life? My attitude was that we're all dead eventually, so we may as well shut up and enjoy the ride.'

'I worry that your feelings have a lot of finality to them still, Kirsty, we are trying to look for the positives. Remember this was the objective you set yourself last week.'

'I know this isn't Champneys, I ain't here because I see the bright side in life, but I do feel like I may have dealt with whatever was bugging me now. Uncle Marion always wanted a better life for me. She said I would make something of myself and I wasn't like my ma. I honestly thought that achieving anything in life was impossible for someone like me.'

'Sometimes, when we feel low, seeing that there is light at the end of the tunnel can be that much harder.'

'I've see the light, doc. It's right behind that fairy, riding a unicorn down the yellow, brick road.'

I give a chortle at Kirsty's expression. He can't quite work her out and I love that. Who wants to be predictable and normal, what a yawn-fest. The only thing I ever prided myself on was my individuality, but Kirsty makes me look boring and average. She continues with her story.

'I actually got a street mate to call my ma when I was first in London, that was the worst waste of a twenty pence ever. She said she didn't know anyone called Kirsty and sounded out of it on something. I knew then that I'd made the right choice and would never go back. I'd practically dragged myself up until Uncle Marion came along, but by then it was just nice to have the company, I didn't really need guidance at that point. I hadn't followed my mother into prostitution like everyone expected, although she once told me that I put it about so much that I was stupid not to charge.'

'The reason we're letting you go home is due to all the positive steps you have taken. We can see that you have worked really hard to move forward. We don't expect anyone to have all the answers when they leave us but you are on the right path now. You know you can always talk to us if you feel like you are in a dark place again, don't you?' Dr Peter says gently.

'Aye, but I'll no be bothering with that now me and Grace are pitching our scripts. I actually have a friend, doc. I thought at first she was a bit posh for my liking but she's got a kind heart and seems to like me. Only Uncle Marion ever had my back but I'll get used to having someone else care if I live or die.'

'You seem to have a lot of friends in here.'

'Flies are attracted to shite. I know that it's my own self-esteem that's the problem, I never think I'm good enough. Brioche is clearly a classy bird and Jim was a successful businessman before he retired. What am I? A hooker's daughter with no talent and no qualifications. I've never even had a job.'

'I think it's important that we be kind to ourselves, Kirsty. Yourself and

Grace have formed a wonderful friendship and I am sure you will both look after each other when you leave here. I hope you can look forward to your script writing and all the positive things you are doing now,' the doctor says warmly.

'I never had much to look forward to in life but I do now. I may even look for Uncle Marion when I get out.'

'That's great news, Kirsty. Well, that's all for today. I'll see you tomorrow to start your discharge programme.'

I hear the therapy room door open and immediately I'm filled with shame. That was unfair, I would hate it if anyone listened in on one of my sessions. I do need tips but I also need to know the signs to look out for in case Kirsty nose-dives back down into her suicidal ways. I'm just about to leave when I hear Ariel's voice. I hurry from my hiding place and wait by the reception desk.

'Hi, Ariel, I'm out of paper. Do you have a notepad and pen I may borrow, please?' I flush with guilt that I've been eavesdropping and Ariel picks up on my harassed look.

'Of course, Grace. Look at you getting yourself all in a tizzy. Anyone would think you've been up to something.' She gives me a pointed look. I swear this lot are mind readers, I'm pretty sure she knows exactly what I've done.

'Of course I haven't,' I lie. Ariel follows my gaze towards Kirsty, walking down the hall, oblivious to us. She gives me a knowing smile.

'Sometimes we may feel we've done the wrong thing but if we do it with a kind heart and good intentions, to help or be there for someone, then can it really be wrong?'

I can feel my face getting hot and hope I'm not blushing. I take the pad and pen, with an awkward thank you, and head off to my therapy. Now at least I know the things I should be saying in my sessions. A good dose of honesty and admissions of not being perfect. It has worked for Kirsty; she's off home next week. It's all for the greater good, I repeat this like a mantra as I give a quick knock on Dr Peter's door. It's all for the greater good.

Chapter Nine

Kirsty, Mark and I sit at the back of the class and I can't help but feel like one of the naughty kids at school. The script is going well so far, I play the other woman and although I've no actual experience of being one, I have endless anecdotes to chuck into the mix. We huddle together, poring over our pooled one-liners and chuckling quietly. Teresa had been thrilled with our team-building exercise and asked that if we were finished before the end of class, would we consider reading some of it out. No pressure! Kirsty had warmed to her role of psycho ex frighteningly well. I could see this was a great outlet for her anger at Ty's bitch on the side. I glance at the clock on the wall; twenty minutes until we wrap for the evening and we're only a few lines away from our script being completed. We had worked well together, compiling a list of characteristics for each actor, coming up with quotes, then combining the ideas together into a format. The scene was set in a pub. Kirsty had gone out for a commiseration drink after being dumped and finds that Mark has lied about there being nobody else when they split. She spies him as he sits with his other woman in the snug of the bar. Mark jots down the final line and crosses his arms over his body to shake hands with both Kirsty and I at the same time, Auld Lang Syne style.

'That's us, Teresa, ready when you are,' Mark announces proudly. The others glance around at us in curious anticipation.

'Would anyone like more time?' She enquires. Several head shakes and murmurs confirm they are happy to be done. My heart flutters as we make our way to the front of the group. I'm used to talking in front of groups, although there aren't many of my students that actually listen, but this feels like a dress rehearsal for the future. These could be our viewers one day. I cringe inwardly as I go over some of the raunchier and more foul-mouthed lines. I glance at Teresa's wrinkled face and at the woman at the front who reminds me of my parochial Aunt Gladys. God, I wish I had a wine to steady these nerves. Kirsty is up first, so I have no choice but to be thrown into the scene. She hurtles over from her place in the corner of the room, her face wild with rage as she looms up behind our backs.

'Who the *hell* is this?' Mark and I give genuine jumps in fright. I hadn't expected her to be quite as loud and aggressive.

'Kirsty, what are you doing here? It's not what it looks like, this is...this is my...'

'Mother?' She enquires sarcastically. I bristle indignantly and raise my nose in the air snootily, as rehearsed. 'At least this better be your mother since we only broke up...' Kirsty glances at an imaginary wrist watch, '...ten minutes ago.' The room gives a soft chuckle.

'Oh Mark, you didn't tell me your ex was so *earthy*. Where did you two meet, the local dump?' I throw a smug glance at Kirsty.

'You left me for an *older* woman?'

'I prefer the term mature,' I tut.

'Mature? You could have at least ironed your face before you came out tonight, love.'

Hang on, that wasn't in the script.

'How long has this being going on?' Kirsty demands.

'It doesn't matter,' Mark takes my hand. 'Grace and I love each other. I'm sorry, I feel I can relate better to someone who used to record the Top Twenty on an audio tape, like me. Someone who knows that *China Crisis* isn't that the local takeaway sent you sweet and sour instead of chow mein, and that *Dire Straits* wasn't the crap version of a hair iron before GHDs came along. This isn't just a one-night stand, babe, we're serious about each other.' Mark plays the dastardly, philanderer like he's done this sort of thing before.

'Oh please, the only serious relationship you ever had was with *this*.' Kirsty grabs Mark's right hand from me and thrusts it in the air. 'Your idea of commitment is spending more than one night a week in *Spearmint Rhino*.'

Most of the room laughs, Teresa shifts nervously in her seat, ready to pull the plug if we get too out of hand. Aunt Gladys looks on, rather confused at missing the humour.

'A diva with a daddy complex,' I retort. 'Somebody clearly missed their nap today. Are you even allowed to be in a pub?'

'Who shat in your cocoa, Grandma? Would you like me to help you cross the road to catch your bus? Come on, get your freedom pass ready for the driver.'

'I think you should stay away from buses, considering you look like you've just been hit by one,' I give Kirsty a sarcastic smile.

'Actually, I call this the just got out of bed look, because I did just get out of bed...with him!' Kirsty smirks to our enthralled audience.

I pick up my cup from the table and throw it over Mark, he stares at me in stunned silence. The mug should have been empty. Kirsty can't hide her delight that she got away with filling it up, unnoticed, when she popped out for a few props. Mark gathers himself and embraces his sudden soaking.

'Girls, we can work this out. Kirsty, it's not you, it's me...I'm just not ready to settle down yet,' he smarms. I stand, indignantly.

'It's not her, it's you. How dare you put this poor girl down.'

'You know what?' Kirsty spits venomously, 'it's not us, it's *him*. How dare he treat us so badly.'

Mark glances nervously at the cup that Kirsty is holding. She filled that too. The room laughs uproariously as Mark takes yet another soaking. 'Besides, if Mark likes older women so much then he can go back and stay with his mummy. You're not getting back in my place, you cheat.'

'Nor mine,' I add. 'In fact, well done, tonight you've gone from two girlfriends to none.'

Mark braces himself as Kirsty picks up the supposedly empty water jug from the table. But this time she's excelled herself. Leftover slops from our lunch rain down on Mark's head. She gives a smirking Ruth, watching through the window, a cheery wave.

'A dinner fit for the pig that you are.' Kirsty goes off-script again. 'Oh, and you know how I know nothing from the eighties? Well you know nothing from the noughties. Taylor Swift is not the name of a quick turnaround suit shop on Saville Row, and Arctic Monkeys is not a wildlife documentary by Sir David Attenborough!'

We take a bow and the room erupts with applause. We are so going to make a success of this, I just know it. Teresa looks like she may burst with pride as she wipes tears of mirth from her eyes. Why did it have to take a crisis for us to turn our lives around? I now know the full story of Kirsty after overhearing her in Dr Peter's office, listening in kept me awake last night with twinges of guilt. I know nothing of Mark, and they know very little of me. I want to change all that, when I can face it myself. I know when we get out of here the three of us will never be the same, but for the first time since I arrived, this feels like a good thing.

We head down to the canteen, full of high jinks and bonhomie. I plan to shake Ruth by the under-seasoning, over-cooking hand for her role in this. Who knew she has a sense of humour hidden behind that bird's nest hair and steely gaze? We are greeted at the door by Ariel and Dr Peter, Gabe scurries down the hall to be part of the welcoming committee.

'We hid at the back of the room and saw your play, it was fantastic,' Ariel gushes. 'Kirsty, we know you're leaving next week, but before you go, we would very much like the three of you to perform in our talent show. We decided that the whole facility should take part. It'll be a real spectacle. We decided everyone's talents need to be shared, if that's ok with you, of course.'

Kirsty gives a shrug and glances doubtfully at Mark and I. We all exchange a look as Ariel waits.

'Can we check our diaries and get back to you,' Kirsty sighs.

'Of course,' Ariel's anxious eyes dart between us.

'Ariel, for God's sake, we're messin' wi you,' Kirsty laughs.

'Oh, thank goodness! So it's a yes?'

'Yes,' we chorus. Where on earth did they get this chick from? She's like Snow White and Cinderella put in a blender, baked and sugar coated.

Gabe and Dr Peter shake us warmly by the hand.

'I think this calls for a celebration,' declares Gabe. 'Come on, Dr Peter. You know what I think we should do.'

Dr Peter gives Gabe an indulgent smile, while Kirsty, Mark and I practically drool in anticipation.

Wine? Vodka? Beer? Who cares! I'll take any or all.

'Ruth, open the lemonade!'

We all exchange looks of disbelief as our elation crashes.

'Look at their faces, they can't believe we've authorised it. This is a very rare occasion indeed,' sings Gabe.

Kirsty gives a tiny sob.

'No, we most certainly cannot,' I agree.

'Fucking lemonade? *Lemonade!*' Kirsty reiterates her disbelief.

'Oh, shush, we'll have all the booze and fags we can handle when we get out. Calm yer tits, hen.' I adopt one of Kirsty's favourite phrases.

'If you can't do a proper Scottish accent then don't even bother trying,' she haughtily announces.

'Well, I don't know about you but I'm quite enjoying this mini detox. I'm sleeping so much better, when dead dogs don't interrupt me, and I have the most amazing dreams. I mean, people would pay good money for the drugs that would give them my nocturnal adventures. Anyway, mardy-pants, are you joining Mark and I for movie night or are you going to sulk in the room for the duration?'

'Sulk. I'd rather be a party-pooper than a gooseberry. Anyways, I'm going to write to an old, dear friend tonight, so fill your boots.'

'Uncle Marion?'

'How do you know about her? I haven't even mentioned her to you,' Kirsty exclaims.

I start in panic, of course she hasn't mentioned Uncle Marion to me. A flash of inspiration hits me.

'Sure you have, you've talked about her in your sleep.'

Kirsty looks genuinely enthralled.

'I have? That's *crazy*. What else do I say?'

'Oh no, Ty. Not again! Leave me be, you rampant beast.'

Kirsty stares in horror at me before we both dissolve into fits of laughter. She grabs hold of me and we fall onto the bed. Silently shoulder shaking and clinging to each other in our mirth.

'Am I intruding on a moment here?' Mark appears in our doorway, looking ashen.

There he is again; my puppy. I instantly sober my mood and pull myself up on the bed, staring at the tiny dog sniffing around Mark's feet. What is going on in my head? I haven't even thought of Scamp today so I'm clearly not manifesting him.

'What is it, Mark. Why are you looking at us that way?' Kirsty has stopped laughing and is sat bolt upright on the bed.

'You know how Jim's sons were coming to collect him today?' We nod, mutely. 'Well, they were a no-show by lunchtime, so Ariel and Gabe took him over to the station so he could catch a train back to central London, then home to Somerset.'

'Mark, what is the point of this story?' Kirsty is exasperated now.

'He made it to Finsbury Park, then jumped in front of the train heading to King's Cross from Scotland. I guess he didn't think he was that important to anyone any more. He's dead, girls. Jim's dead.'

Chapter Ten

'Calm down, ladies. Come into the office but please keep your voices down. There are some very vulnerable people in here who need to be protected from this sad news.' Ariel frantically ushers us through to the room at the back of reception. We take a seat in stunned silence. Mark loiters awkwardly behind my chair, bristling with annoyance that we rushed down the corridor before he could tell us the conversation was overheard, and a private one between Dr Peter and Gabe.

'Why did you let him go alone, Ariel?' I finally find my voice.

'Grace, he was in great spirits, he really was. Have you ever tried to stop a six-foot, and goodness knows what, man from trying to get on a train? He was laughing and saying that the lads had probably forgotten, although we spoke with them last night and they assured us they would be here to pick him up.'

'Mania or smiling depression. There are just two examples of what that high spirited mood could have been,' Kirsty glares at Ariel.

'I know. Unfortunately, I've seen it a lot in my time here. He hasn't had an obvious, low episode for weeks and he always did so well in his therapy sessions. If someone says they have a second chance at life and don't intend to waste a second, you have to have faith in their resolve.'

'Has it happened before?' Mark asks solemnly.

'It has, but not frequently,' Ariel replies cautiously. 'People can relapse. We try our best but we can't interfere once people leave the recovery process. Life is indiscriminate at handing out blows and it can cause people to fall back into their harmful ways. It doesn't care who you are or what you may be going through. There will always be hardship to endure, no matter how desperate your circumstances may be.'

We all nod our agreement, it's hard to argue with her on that.

'We do offer outreach support too, nobody is sent back out to nothing,' Ariel continues, wringing her hands as she circles us anxiously.

'He wanted to be with his wife,' Kirsty shrugs. 'You can't stop the urge of that, no matter how horrific jumping in front of a train may be.'

'When you don't fear death, you don't fear anything,' Mark shudders. 'But he won't be seeing his wife in some grand, old reunion right now. There is no afterlife; when you're dead, you're dead. I suppose he is free of pain and suffering now, at least that's something.'

'Mark, our consciousness of existence is like an amoeba, on a flea, on the arse of a brontosaurus. Only an arrogant twat would assume that all we know is all that there is,' Kirsty flames.

'Bollocks! How come it has never been scientifically proven then?' Mark retorts.

'Your soul has a long journey yet if that's what you believe. Your body is nothing but a vehicle taking you to your destination, and when you get there, your soul no longer needs it.'

'Kirsty, that's beautiful,' Ariel gives a surprised smile at Kirsty's prose. 'It's all right for us to have differing or even no beliefs. We are all extraordinary and insignificant at the same time, but each of us makes up the rich tapestry of the universe.'

'Well, you can all debate until you're blue in the face, none of us will know who's right until we get there,' I try to close the subject. This lot are making my head hurt. I can barely get my thoughts around the awfulness of Jim's death. That poor train driver and those people on the platform who saw it happen. Those images will haunt them forever. They will go over and over it again, wondering if they could have stopped him or noticed his pain in that final, irreversible moment.

'Very true, Grace. We shouldn't criticise the opinions of others when we don't know for sure ourselves.' Ariel gives me a supportive smile.

'See, this is why I try to live in the moment. It's the scariest thing in the world to be deliriously happy with how things are at any given time, but knowing that in a split second, nothing may ever be the same again. Why waste that chance to be blissfully unaware?' I shiver at the truth of my own words. I've lived through that exact scenario more times than I care to admit. An eerie silence falls over us all as we ponder on this. As if the universe wished to reiterate my statement, the phone rings. We listen intently as Dr Peter's message booms out for Ariel to call him back immediately. William and Robert have turned up to pick up their father. There was an accident on the M4 and Robert had forgotten his mobile. William had dropped his in a puddle at a service station and now it wouldn't switch on. We look at each other in horror as Ariel makes her way out to reception and calls the doctor back in hushed tones.

'Fuck!' Kirsty voices the thoughts of all of us.

We decline the offer of an impromptu therapy session with Dr Peter, just the three of us. We go along to the movie as a distraction but I can tell that none of us are really paying attention. After it's over, we head morosely back to our rooms. I'm not sure how Kirsty can detach herself so easily, but she falls instantly into a deep slumber. She really should feel awful about all the horrible things she's said to Jim over the past few weeks. I look over at her doubtfully, it's unlikely that she will, but at least she made her peace with him. In his opinion anyway, I've heard no end of insults about him since then. My suspicions are growing that he was all but a playing a part in her fast-track plan to get out of here. I stare at her small body, shifting to a more comfortable position as she takes a deep breath. Maybe being deprived of love and care in those early years has numbed her feelings of empathy towards those who are suffering, she was largely neglected until her Uncle Marion came along. It could be that she distances herself from others because she assumes they will let her down. I have no idea; I doubt that she does either. A small whimper distracts me from thoughts of Kirsty's past. I peer through the half dark to see the silhouette of the puppy.

'Scampy?' I whisper cautiously. He gives another tiny whine followed by a large, noisy yawn. Is this my chance to make peace with this part of my life? My stomach churns. If he's not real then surely I won't feel him, and if he is just in my imagination, then where's the harm in playing along with it. I pat the bed nervously.

'Come here then, boy. That's it, come to your big sister.'

He disappears momentarily and I feel a pressure on the bottom of the bed. He bounds up towards me and burrows his head under my arm, his wet nose nuzzling my face. I laugh softly as he licks my cheek.

'Settle down, baby. There's a good boy.' I gently pull the cover from under him and wrap us both up. Throwing my arm around his tiny, quivering body, we drift off to sleep.

I awaken with empty arms and disappointment washes over me. Did I dream that my puppy had come back to see me? Will he ever be back or has my acknowledgment of his existence been enough to set him free? I pull aside the curtain and glorious, late autumn sunshine fills my eyes. A sudden breeze creates a whirlwind of orange, yellow and red leaves. Dappled, low sunlight streams through the barren branches of the oak trees. The window opens only a crack, yet it is enough for me to inhale the woody scent. I'm lost in awe at the beauty of the countryside and my heart swells. Snuggling in with Scamp, just like old times, had given me the deepest sleep I've allowed myself since arriving here. Even if it was all in my head, it felt good. I feel sadness wash over me when I think of Jim. He paid the ultimate sacrifice in his hope to be reunited with his wife, so firm was his belief that he would see her again. I feel that with his last breath, he breathed life back into me, that we all should learn from this tragedy. There is far too much beauty in the world to let go, without living every second to the fullest and appreciating each precious moment we have.

'Shut the window, you fuckin' eejit! I'm about to lose a nip here.' Kirsty breaks the blissful spell that nature cast over me. I close the window wordlessly and pull the cover back over my head. It smells of damp grass and puppy breath. I feel like he really was here.

'Reliving something you feel strongly about can happen to us all, Grace. When we last talked about Scamp, I really felt your emotion. It is important to be able to see that revisiting memories is one way for your brain to process what you feel.' I nod mutely at Dr Peter's words.

'When we feel strongly, especially negatively about something, we don't give our brains enough time to process what has happened. We can end up suppressing these memories if they are painful, then they can reach out to us in our most vulnerable times. Imagine stuffing a duvet into a cupboard and quickly shutting the door, every time I open the door, the duvet falls out. To stop this from happening I need to take the duvet out, lay it flat, fold it neatly and put it away. If I don't do this every once in a while, I will continually be stuffing the duvet back in the cupboard.'

'So, he wasn't really here?' I try to summarise his psycho-babble in one short sentence.

'I'm not sure, Grace. Would it trouble you if he was?'

I stare blankly at the doctor. He's very good at avoiding giving me the answers I ask for.

'If you believe Scamp was there and brought you the healing that you need, would that be so wrong?'

It appears I'm supposed to figure things out for myself. Well, I haven't done a very good job of that so far.

'Do you believe in ghosts, doc? Do you think that the spirits of our loved ones come back and help us when we are most in need? I'm a scientist like you, we're not supposed to believe in stuff like that, are we? It's just that...I'm seeing stuff that's conflicting with what I know to be true. How is it that only I can see this dog?'

'What is it you know to be true, Grace?'

'You know what I mean, I believe in proven facts. Not ghosts and fairies and unicorns. What do you believe?' I challenge him back. In typical therapist form, he asks me yet another open question.

'Isn't science discovering new and wonderful things every day? We don't know the cure of an illness yesterday, but today we do. It wasn't that the cure didn't exist yesterday, it was just our knowledge of it that didn't.'

I sit gazing at Dr Peter in wonder, he's so bright and unflustered. I wish I could be as untouched by life. Perhaps his has been charmed and nothing has happened to make him dour or depressed. When I get stressed I tend to drink. I drink until I can't feel. I'd had three large wines when I fell from the balcony, I'd had two before Josh even came round that night. It's funny how in here I haven't felt the need to numb myself as much. A crutch to suppress emotions, I imagine that's what this lot would describe it as. Actually, it appears that I'm beginning to see that now. In here I've been forced to feel and see things through sober eyes. It had stung worse than that jellyfish I stepped on, aged eight, while visiting Mum's parents in the Caribbean. I had a very skewed view of talking therapies when I came in here but they have, in most instances, seemed to work. OK, not for Jim, he was different, but for a lot of people. I see changes in them every day. Mark is new, he's a joker. I have no idea what he's all about and although I'm dying to know, I've learned not to push people and let them come to me in their own time. Like Brioche. I pull myself back to the session.

'Thank you. I genuinely feel I've come a long way today. Jim really shocked us all. The ripples from his suicide reached us immediately, and he was practically a stranger. I imagine how his sons must feel. The knock-on effect it will have on all those people at the train station. I suppose the driver has been enlisted in some kind of therapy programme right now and is sat at home wishing he could wash that image out of his eyes and mind forever. The passengers on the train and those on the platform will forever be terrified that they will see something like that again, or that one of their loved ones could ever consider such a drastic way out. It's just so horrific for all concerned.'

Doctor Peter nods calmly with a knowing smile.

'No more digging today, please. I want to keep a hold of this feeling. We're all in this together. There's no you, no me, only us as a whole. I get it. We are all one.'

The doctor sweeps his hand majestically towards the door and I stand before he can change his mind. He picks up his favourite, antique fountain pen and writes something at the bottom of my notes as I leave. He lays down his pen on the table again and studies what he has written. Only one line in the whole session.

Unity is clarity.

Chapter Eleven

I think I'm getting home next week. There was a shift in Dr Peter's demeanour in therapy and I've noticed a sudden air of expectancy around Gabe and Ariel. They appear to be treating me differently and giving me a little more trust. I was taking a look at the lake outside the front door earlier, just as Ariel was coming out of Dr Peter's office.

'Isn't it beautiful, Grace? Aren't we fortunate to have such a perfect view?' It was all she said. She turned on her heel and walked down the corridor, without so much as a backwards glance. That made me feel good, I hadn't planned to run off but to have her acknowledgment of that had mattered.

Kirsty has now had confirmation to leave next Thursday, that's six days away. Her sessions have gone from talking about and resolving her issues to creating a long term plan to deal with stress, depressive episodes, and exploring crisis strategies. She had spent a lot of time talking over her regrets where Jim and Brioche were concerned, with Dr Peter in her sessions. I like to think that they were genuine but the fact that she told me all this with a strange, little smile on her face made me wonder if this was all just part of her plan to be released. Kirsty concerns me a great deal, it's almost like she's missing the empathy chip. She has very little time for the problems of others. To be honest, she has little time for her own. I know the Celtic way often rejects self-indulgent behaviour and encourages a get on with it attitude, but this is something more, it's almost as though other people's feelings don't register on her radar. I have no doubt that she would fight tooth and nail to protect someone she cared for, perhaps not out of love or loyalty, but an almost animalistic approach. A survival instinct. She protects her pack to shield herself from harm. I don't fear her but I fear for her. I do have concerns about what she will be like without any boundaries or constraints. I suspect she may be a bit out of control.

The three of us work on perfecting and elongating our script in class that afternoon. Mark seems quiet and withdrawn today. There's an echo of sadness around his eyes and that once beaming smile looks forced. This really is the first shadow of depression that I've seen around him and I don't like it. I say nothing in front of Kirsty and wait until she heads off back to our room. I give a quick knock on Marks's door, his room-mate is off to therapy at the moment so we can have a chance to talk openly. We leave the door open, as instructed. There's a no closed door policy in Arcadia, when visiting someone else's room. I think it's to stop bullying but possibly shagging too. God forbid we find anything to get our kicks in here. Mark looks far away and detached.

'S'up, bro? You look like you're being haunted by the ghosts of tortoises past.' He gives me a wan smile. 'And budgies, hamsters and anything else you haven't told me about yet. I bet you were the type of kid to put bugs under a magnifying glass in bright sunshine too, weren't you?'

'Actually, I was quite bookish and into science. Bet you didn't get *that* from me, did you?'

I raise my eyebrows in surprise. There's another thing we have in common.

'Magnifying bugs could be described as science...but we don't do experiments that hurt living creatures any more. Anyways, you look down. Want to talk?' I adopt a gentler tone, the one I used to use with my students, back when I was blind to excuses and bullshit. I'd spent hours listening to tales of woe that meant homework couldn't be handed in. 'Your grandma died? You poor love. Don't even think about homework until after the funeral. I'm here, any time you need to talk.'

I was stunned to see said granny in Holloway Road Markies, buying a cheese and pickle sandwich to tide her over for her shift in the Cats Protection charity shop. She looked remarkably well for having been dead for over two weeks. After that first time I had been shocked, but not disillusioned. One kid out of a whole bunch had told me a lie, that was to be expected. Unfortunately, word had got around and I was inundated with dead "everythings" as an excuse for anything from absences to disruptive behaviour. I toughened up a lot in that first year. I bring myself back to the present and realise that Mark still hasn't spoken.

'OK, no worries, mate. You know where I am if you need me. I just hope you're all right.'

He pulls me back down as I stand to go.

'Grace, I absolutely adore you and I know I can trust you.' I give Mark a sympathetic tilt of my head which says I adore you too. 'I'm just, you know...struggling with opening up. I don't think it helps at all. Dr P has got a lot out of me but I don't want to be in here without you and Kirsty. It's just so exhausting having to think and let myself feel. My dad is very sick, I know I've let him down badly and I can't take back some of the things that I've said to him. He hasn't got long now and I don't want to be in here when he passes, I need to apologise and try to make amends. Actually, I don't know if he's even still alive. It could already be too late.'

'I'm so sorry,' I gasp. 'I never knew you were dealing with anything like this. What's wrong with him?' I can't imagine Mark saying cruel words to anyone, let alone his own family.

'He has liver cancer but it has spread to other parts of his body. He has third, let alone secondary growths. It got into his lymphatic system and now it's game on...or more like game over.'

'Have you told the doc about this?' I give Mark's hand a sympathetic squeeze.

'Yeah, he knows all about it, it won't change anything though. I'm not ready to leave and Dr Peter says that letting me go now could be more damaging than keeping me here. Reading between the lines, I know he's saying I've already tried to top myself once and the stress of this will make me try again. He apologised, but said he has a duty of care to me and can't take the risk.'

'OK, let's be proactive, not reactive. We need to get you out to see your dad as soon as possible. We need a plan to fast track your ass out of here, you need to examine the reasons that brought you in here and then stand up in group and tell everyone what it is.'

'Like you have?' He gives me a sarcastic smile.

'Point taken. My story is complicated and at the moment I'm working on just being able to share. That's my starting point. I've had a difficult past and I never worked through any of it. They've opened a can of worms in me, I'm having too much trouble just catching them all again to get them in any kind of order. I see imaginary dogs, for God's sake.'

'True, I'm just fucked up but you're an *actual* nut job,' Mark sniggers.

'Thanks,' I give a hollow laugh. 'Hmm, I have an idea that may just work. You could always ask if you can go see your dad with one or two of the staff members. If you're under constant surveillance, then I don't see how they could possibly refuse. Come on, why don't we go speak to Ariel right now. They surely can't deny you seeing your father for the last time. They are all about helping us in our emotional recovery and this can be your first step.'

'Grace, I love you, you know. I mean that.'

My insides switch to spin cycle. He *loves* me? I'm not at that stage yet, but I do care about him deeply. Instead of replying, I lean in and place a gentle kiss on his lips. He looks startled for a moment before a genuine smile spreads across his face.

'You're not the type to say I love you back, I can tell. You've made me feel a whole lot better, Grace. Thank you. Let's go see Ariel and see if I can get a few hours out of this shit-hole.'

Group therapy passes without event and without Mark. Ariel had thought my suggestion was a fantastic idea. She beamed at me with pride as she confirmed the details with Dr Peter on the phone. Mark had hugged me at the door of the office and took a seat in the back room to wait to leave. I haven't seen him since. In group therapy, we discover that we have a brand new Jim on board. Bob arrived two days ago and has shared at both sessions so far. Kirsty scowls over her crossed arms, slunk low in the chair, legs stretched out like a bored teen. There are those familiar heavy sighs and tuts kicking up again, but she's keeping them reasonably quiet in an attempt not to draw attention to herself. She's counting the days now, she doesn't really need these sessions any more, but Gabe thinks it will be a valuable lesson in empathy. That made me laugh; I've seen more empathy in a shark. All these sessions do is reinforce to her how whiny the world is when people have real problems, like homelessness and starvation. Gabe gives me a hopeful glance once Bob has finished, I avert my eyes from his gaze. I'm not ready to share any more just yet. I assume he's heard that I did finally open up a lot more to Dr Peter today. He had looked at me with delight and pride when I had finished. I think back to his words at the end of my session.
'Do you feel this is the breakthrough you've been waiting for?'
It seems that, after today's session, Dr Peter thinks I finally have some self-acceptance. I've been tormenting myself for years, constantly blaming myself for occurrences that really were out of my control. What I hadn't appreciated was that my unwarranted guilt had created a need to block out the pain, by abusing my anaesthetics of choice: alcohol, denial and humour. What I'm told I need to do now, is to allow myself to work through those emotions face on. I ponder on this, isn't that what I've been doing since I arrived? Also, if this has been a breakthrough, then where's my sense of relief? Those innocent lives were snuffed out and I still feel devastated by that. Scampy may have forgiven me, but I'm now waiting on this baby haunting me. Like in *Ally McBeal*, when her biological clock was ticking and the dancing baby kept appearing and scaring the crap out of the viewers. Creepy bugger gave me nightmares for weeks. I think I'd sign myself up in here indefinitely if that happened.
Dr Peter said that we should embrace our past and be empowered by our life story. Forgiving myself for the part I played will help let go of the suffering. He must have the patience of a saint to be able to do this day in, day out. A never-ending conveyor belt of sad and messed up people, I personally can't think of anything more depressing than constantly listening to the problems of others. He also thinks I need to allow people

to take responsibility for their own actions, rather than always be the fixer that I am. To let go of my need to try to always ensure a positive outcome, so that they don't make the same mistakes that I did. Before I arrived here, I had got to the point that I was starting to mistrust everyone. For instance, my pupils. I had zero tolerance for what I saw as their pathetic excuses for everything, from not completing their homework to not turning up for class. I recall one friend calling me, after a particularly bad day at work, to apologise for not getting round to forwarding me her decorator's phone number. Her aunt had been rushed into hospital that afternoon and it was touch and go that she would make it.

'Boo-frickin'-hoo,' was how I responded. 'I'm not interested in your excuses.'

She burst into floods of tears. I learned that day that I needed to separate my work life and real life, sharpish. I need to stop assuming that everyone is making stuff up. Josh hasn't done me any favours on that front, he has severely, possibly irreparably, damaged my faith in men. Karen rarely makes time for me and even when she does she quite happily drops me for every opportunity of a date. They think I'm worthless because I think I'm worthless. The place I currently call home isn't exactly des-res, but at least I feel valued in here. Ariel needs me to try and tap into Brioche's psyche and get her to open up, Kirsty would deny it, but she needs me to keep her on the straight and narrow. Mark needs me too but he just doesn't know it yet. I will be there for him, regardless of what happens between us. Although, I'm pretty sure something will after his earlier declaration. He's going through an extremely tough time and I know he will need massive amounts of support in the weeks and months to come. Like me, he also needs to forgive himself. I have no idea what he said to upset his dad but I'm quite sure his father doesn't hold a grudge against him.

Bob has finished his already familiar story and the slow, bored applause breaks me from my reverie. This man has the worst case of denial I've seen. The stockbroker in front of me had lost millions after investing in a company that went bust shortly after. It wasn't the first time there had been such an occurrence, it wasn't even the second. He was fired and subsequently his wife left, taking their three kids with her. His house was due to be repossessed and he was found by a neighbour, in his garage, passed out and surrounded by bottles of booze and pills. Of course, he was only drowning his sorrows and trying to get rid of a persistent, nagging headache from the stress of it all. Even the most hardened deniers amongst us had looked dubious at his tale. He was going to make his comeback, starting his own company, the second he was released from this dump. He was very well known and respected in the financial district and had no end of contacts who'd invest in his skills to take the London stock market by storm. All to help him make back the money he'd lost from the divorce. He wasn't bothered about the wife leaving; he'd been seeing his young assistant for over a year now. He missed the kids a bit but not the squabbles or school run. He was gutted about losing custody of the dog and he would miss the house. It was a bit on the small side but it had been home, none-the-less. He had to sell up to give his wife her half, but he'd move to a better area as soon as he made his first million or two. In the meantime, he had one of his many friends to turn to.

I roll my eyes at this familiar, peacock display and silently hope his wife screws him for every penny he has. Kirsty yawns noisily and stands to leave.

'I'm too knackered to watch the movie tonight. I may pop down to the library and see if they have a book on formatting scripts. We have the ideas but we never have checked the correct way to lay them out and pitch.'

'Great idea, I think I'll see what Mark's doing when he gets back. I'm desperate to know how it went with his dad.'

I sit for longer than usual in the canteen, willing Mark to walk through the door, so I can make sure he's all right. Brioche and I sit in amicable silence for the most part, as seems to be our new agreement. Rather than me try to get her to talk, I've gone more over to her camp and enjoy the calmness that surrounds her. I have absorbed more about her personality from her reactions and mannerisms, than I would have by talking with her anyway. I can now see that her silence appears to be a choice. Why not? People talk too much anyway. What's that quote? We are given two ears and one mouth for a reason. It's amazing how much you can pick up about a person from non-verbal communication. I probably know as much about Brioche as I do about my enigmatic room-mate, and she never shuts up. Kirsty will tell you what she wants you to hear and I often wonder if there's any more than a grain of truth in a lot of what she says. I do believe her about Uncle Marion and her mum being a prozzie, I don't know why, but that seems to stick as true. She wrote to her uncle, after all, Ariel took the letter from her to post. I must ask her if she ever got a reply. Any mail has to be inspected by the staff in case it contains threats or bullying towards us "vulnerables." I have no idea how I made it through almost forty years of my life without these glorified prison wardens breathing down my neck. The canteen door swings open and in walks an ashen Mark.

'Excuse me, please,' I smile apologetically at Brioche. 'He's just back from seeing his dad and I need to make sure that he's OK.'

Brioche nods her understanding, I pick up my tray and walk swiftly across the room. Mark is staring at the bland array of food, looking like the last thing in the world he wants to do is eat.

'Hey you, how did it go? Please tell me your dad is still with us. You've been away for ages so I assume so.'

'He was.' Mark looks like he's aged twenty years in the past few hours.

'What do you mean by was?' I gasp, preparing myself to hear the answer that I already know.

'Dad died not long after he spoke to me. He said he had been waiting and hoping that I'd be in to see him and now he could go in peace. I got the chance to apologise, but he said he's just a bigoted, old fool. I'm his son and he loves and accepts me the way I am.'

'The way you are? I don't understand. There's nothing wrong with you, apart from some prior episodes of pet homicides.'

'Well, we both know that. It's a generational thing, isn't it? The older ones are still a bit funny around gay people. They want to fix us or make us snap out of it, they tell you that you just need to meet the right woman and everything will fall into place.'

I stare at Mark in mute shock, unable to even contemplate formulating a sentence. Mark is gay? I finally meet a gorgeous, funny, creative, single guy, and totally misread the signals he was giving out. Actually, I should have known from this endless list of great characteristics that he wouldn't have wanted to be with me. Why is it that all perfect men are gay? He has no idea that I don't know, were the signs there and I missed them? He said that he loved me but he never actually said that he saw me as anything other than a friend. He did say in his creative writing that he had lots of female exes, maybe he tried to dabble in being straight. Come to think of it, when he got busted by that girl's father, he said he was helping her choose stuff for the prom. Duh! I slap my hand against my forehead, why didn't I see it? The laughter starts. Manic, side-splitting, pee-your-pants hysteria. Mark gives me a curious look before a hesitant smile spreads across his face.

'I don't have a bloody clue what you're laughing at, you mad bugger.'

'Never mind, Mark. You just couldn't make the shit up that happens to me. Come on, in the absence of fags and booze, let's go get messed up on a sugar high.'

Chapter Twelve

'Hi Grace. I'm so sorry, I've been meaning to call you for over a week. Carl's been away on a business trip and I've been trying to manage the three monsters...' I hear some muffled sounds down the phone before it clatters to the ground. 'Shit.'

'Shit!' echoes the voice of two-year-old Arabella.

There's a bit of a kerfuffle and she's back. Alice, the only work friend I choose to hang out with is currently on maternity leave with daughter number three.

'Sorry about that. I'm just changing the baby.'

'Oh, I thought you were quite happy with the one you got.'

'Ha-ha,' she monotones, drolly. 'Don't bloody tempt me, teething at two and a half months? What the actual fuck is that about?'

'Fuck,' mimics Arabella.

'I've barely had my bloody stiches out and Carl is already pestering me for a boy. Try explaining the X and Y chromosome thing, to a bloody idiot who's disappointed that you...*you*...have deigned to give him yet another daughter.' Alice gives a long sigh. I pause to check that she has indeed finished. It appears not. 'Once upon a time my life was rock 'n' roll, now it's just cock 'n' hole. I swear I would leave him if I had the energy. No, Arabella...do *not* crap in the fruit bowl.'

I hold the phone several inches away from my ear as Alice screeches at her toilet training child.

'Look, I can pop round and help you for an hour, if you want. We can't seem to get a lunch sorted. I think we've been trying to bring the mountain to Mohammed, how about I come to you.'

'Oh, Grace, would you? That would be amazing. I may actually be able to have a shower and get out of these vomit soaked clothes.'

I scrunch up my face in disgust, but it's too late to retract my offer now, she sounds so happy. The baby begins to squall and I hear the flustered sound of my friend trying to hold the phone, keep her grip on baby Maggie, and release a boob, all at the same time.

'I'll be there in twenty,' I shout, hoping she hears me.

I creep downstairs and pause at the corner, waiting to check that the coast is clear of Mrs Malik. I jump a little as I spot her out in the garden, I could be stuck for a good hour if I can't get past her. I press my back against the wall and slide slowly along towards the entry door. I see her, bent over and pulling a few weeds from the path and feel a pang of guilt. I promise without a doubt that I'll pop in and see her when I get back. I make it to the door and slip through unseen. Walking two streets back to the only place I could get parked, I curse myself for opening my big mouth. It won't be an hour, it'll likely be nothing short of five. Alice is so hungry for adult company that she spent forty minutes chatting to an energy salesman on her doorstep last week. He had realised in the first five minutes that she wasn't "authorised" to switch and had tried desperately to get away. Carl won't let her make decisions that involve anything more frivolous than what to have for dinner, even then he usually moans about her choice. Salad in October, tut. Casserole on the hottest day of the year, for goodness sake, Alice, have you taken leave of your senses? This once confident chemistry teacher, who was given a special mention for her impeccable manner with the students, by Ofsted, has become browbeaten by her barrister husband. She's criticised to the point of feeling the need to call him five times a day, to double-check her smallest of actions. Her eldest child, a petulant creature of eight years named Florence, is prone to throwing diva-like strops at having to get up in the morning. Perfectly normal pre-teen behaviour, but juggling this with getting the two youngest ready had proved tricky for Alice. It would be no mean feat for any parent, but Carl had taken to pandering to the child every morning, bribing her with treats to make getting her out of bed look easy, and therefore making Alice look incompetent. He would leave for work late to do the school drop-off, always with a disappointed shake of the head at Alice's so-called poor management skills. Oh, how I detest that insufferable man.

I pull up at their five-bedroomed, detached home, in its wide, tree-lined, Hampstead street. The magnolia is in full bloom and the scent of jasmine fills the air. Many times I have envied Alice's opulent home but there is no way I could put up with the man that goes with it. I push the brass doorbell and listen to the ring echoing, somewhere in the belly of the house. I glance back at my car, parked like an abandoned getaway vehicle, and glance up and down the street for any lurking wardens. I'll pinch a visitor's parking permit from Alice as all the pay and display spaces have been taken. One of those would have been ideal as it's paid for by the hour, meaning I'd have the perfect excuse for having to leave. Still, it passes a few hours of the endless half-term days and serves to reinforce the fact that I'm missing nothing by not being married with kids. Alice arrives at the door in a custom made by children, Boden t-shirt. I wince at the large, brown stain in the centre of it. I'm afraid to ask...

'A tsunappy. Bella just exploded on me,' she offers up as an explanation. 'I knew the bloody Noro Virus would get us eventually, nine of Flo's class are off sick with it.'

Today has just gotten a whole lot worse.

'It was pouring out of her like lava,' she continues, as we walk down the endless hall. 'I recognised the signs earlier, those familiar, grumbly tummy noises. It was lucky I did put a nappy on her, can you imagine the white Harrods rug with that mess on it? Poor Arabella, she must have been desperate. She ripped off that nappy. I'm actually quite proud that she's so well trained now that she tried not to fill it.'

I arrange a suitably impressed facial expression, despite not really wanting to know the details.

'I need to go rinse the Vera Wang before I forget, Carl would drop a bollock if he saw it full of shit. It was a wedding present from his sister. Bella may only be a toddler but even she knows what not to touch or Daddy will go ballistic. Unfortunately, that doesn't stop her. I think she thrives on the drama.'

'Jesus, you're in some nick. Give me the baby and go sort yourself out.' Not needing to be told twice, she drops the tiny, sleeping bundle in my arms. I glance down at Maggie's red cheeks and little rosebud mouth, her lashes flicker like tiny butterfly wings. What can this little scrap have experienced in her young life to dream of?

'Daddy say *no*, Bella!'

I hear a piercing shriek as my friend throws herself down the hallway at the toddler's words, almost in slow motion, towards Arabella and the MacBook dangling precariously from her arms. Alice just makes it and catches the computer as it tumbles towards the flagstone floor. She lifts her daughter down from the centre of the twelve-seater dining table.

'This house is so not child-friendly. She's not usually this bad, it must be because she isn't feeling well. Easy for that dickhead to say they have to learn not to touch, I could play for bloody Man-U in goal with all the training I get with this one around.'

I place baby Magdalena gently in the Victorian style crib and plonk Arabella on the sofa. Expertly flicking through the cable channels, I locate C-Beebies and the room fills with the sound of helium-infused cartoon characters. Alice looks at me in shock.

'No, Grace. Arabella never watches TV, Carl says...'

'Waybuloo,' shouts the tot. She picks up her stuffed puppy toy, Boggy, and settles down with her thumb in her mouth.

'Go!' I urge. Alice picks up the fruit bowl and scurries from the room.

An hour later she reappears, fragrant from her bath and the pained expression gone from her face. She glances in surprise at the table, where I've rustled up two pasta dishes with the meagre ingredients in the fridge, complete with homemade garlic herb toast and a side salad. Bella is down for a nap in her cot and Maggie gurgles happily in her bouncy chair.

'You're a bloody legend,' she smiles. She plucks three bottles of breast milk from the freezer, followed by a chilled Chablis from the fridge, announcing that Magdalena can have bottle instead of draught for the next few feeds. She plonks the chilled bottle down on the table and snatches up my car keys.

'I'll put mine on the street as I have a resident's permit, you can have the driveway and tube it home. This way I get to see you tomorrow too.'

She gives me a hopeful smile and I reluctantly nod my agreement. I hadn't planned on embroiling myself in another day of all this. She skips down the hall like an eight-year-old off to the funfair, her earlier, drained pallor replaced with a radiant glow.

'Oh, Grace, I've parked up but I'm sorry to tell you, some arsehole has knocked your wing mirror half off.' Alice pants as she races back through the house towards me.

'Yeah, I know the arsehole who did it, she was driving it at the time,' I reply, giving my friend a cynical smirk. Alice gives a soft chuckle and sloshes out a generous glass of wine each. Spatial awareness has never been my strong point.

'You're a tonic, Grace. I miss our pre-baby boozy lunches. Having kids has changed everything. I would love to go back to work and we *could* afford a nanny, but Carl says a mother's place is raising her kids. I just wish I'd known he would be like this before I had them,' she sighs. 'My wage would barely cover childcare.'

'You need to get your balls back, lady. Why should his say take precedence over yours? You're the one stuck at home all day, going stir-crazy and trying to entertain them without TV,' I give my friend a sly smile over my glass. Bella never watches telly, my arse. She knew what Waybuloo was and also recognised the two subsequent programmes I let her watch before she crashed out. Alice swirls her glass and gazes into her wine like it holds all the answers.

'I'm not strong like you, Grace. He says jump and I say how high. Look at the success you've made of your life. I envy you, I really do. What did my degree and teacher training give me? The ability to shake a rattle to the point that I'd happily beat myself to death with it? I'd love to work but I'm so out of the loop now that I can't imagine ever going back. My eldest daughter hates me, the other day I asked her where the sweet child I once knew had gone. She screamed back at me that she ate her.' Alice gives a hollow laugh and I smile at Florence's ballsy attitude. 'She's the only one who can keep Carl in check, he shouldn't have favourites but he does. I don't, they all piss me off equally. That's a joke, I promise.' she grins wickedly. 'Last week, Carl complained that I hadn't loaded the dishwasher and that dinner wasn't made. I had fallen asleep on the sofa when the little ones napped and had woken five minutes before school pick-up. Once they're all home and awake there's virtually nothing I can do in the house. These night feeds are slowly killing me, I'm lucky if I get two hours straight.'

'You have three bottles expressed, get Carl to take a shot tonight and see how he gets on.'

My friend smiles wistfully. I know she won't, but she should. Carl disappears at eight-thirty every morning and isn't back until after nine most nights. Preparing for cases in a place he can actually hear himself think, is his excuse. They split for a few months when Flo was Bella's age. Alice moved back to her parents cramped council house in Camden. He didn't even have the decency to give them the space they needed in this place. He has his empty starter flat that he's holding on to, he could have easily gone there, or at least let Alice use it while she got her head together. Even though she had post-natal depression, he didn't want to make it easy for his wife. He wanted her to suffer so that she'd come home and appreciate what he had provided for her. Predictably, she did. Now, another two kids later, she has further entangled herself in this unequal marriage. She claimed he knew all the legal loopholes to make sure she got very little in a divorce settlement. I knew the system didn't work that way but he had Alice brainwashed and scared.

I stayed until after Alice had walked to school to get Florence. The sparkle in my friend's eyes had returned and that wasn't just the two wines she'd consumed with lunch. It was good to see. She came back rosy cheeked and informed me that a little bit of Dutch courage had made her wave and shout a cheery hello to the posse of yummy-mummies that always stood in a huddle, whispering about the hot dads and the frumpster Mums, as they called them. The achingly hip group with their messy up-dos and chunky boots, skinny jeans and sloppy sweatshirts, would make anyone look frumpy. The carefully applied no-make-up looks, the Boden adorned babies and the trend of the moment buggy. I knew the sort she was talking about. I'd seen a few standing outside the junior school next door to Holly Berry High as I made my way in to work, always talking loudly into their iPhones.

'Yah-yah thanks, Nigel, sweet. My blog will be with you by nine at the latest. Of course it's not a problem, my kids are all sleeping by 7.30 on the dot. Yah, I don't know how I do it either. Pahahahaha.'

My friend is not frumpy in the slightest. In her opinion, she still needs to lose a few baby pounds. She wears Birkenstocks, which were more de rigueur ten years ago, but she is clever, kind and beautiful. That lot had knocked her confidence when she overheard them discussing one poor harassed mother's excuse for being a curvaceous fourteen to sixteen. 'You can't get away with calling it baby weight when your kids are four and nine, dear.' How they had cackled as this poor woman scurried by, head down, pulling her jacket in tighter around her stomach. I'd bet they were playground bullies back in the day too. That sort won't watch a movie that isn't subtitled, their kids' toys are expensive, Montessori wooden types and their dollies are racially inclusive and disability sensitive. Alice overheard one mother complain that the doll with missing limbs she ordered had cost an arm and a leg. She had smiled wryly at the unintentional pun that seemed to have escaped the group. This lot, combined with Carl's scathing view of her capabilities, had made my friend feel dreadful about herself. Today I see a spark of the former Alice. I pray that it won't be crushed by the first criticism to come out of her husband's mouth, as she greets him with a glass of Pinot Noir, this evening.

***

Dr Peter looks at me over his spectacles and jots something down on his pad. He places his fountain pen gently back on the table and waits for me to continue. I bring myself back from the memory of that day.

'I never want to give my power away. My friend had everything going for her and now she is a shadow of who she once was. She knew what Carl was like before she married him, he didn't like her going out with the girls and called her at nine every night, to make sure she was home. I don't mean to criticise her but part of me thinks she sold out for this imagined, perfect lifestyle. The big house, the wealthy and powerful husband, children, and a career too. I'm not convinced that anyone can have it all any more. Her kids are gorgeous and on paper she has it made, but still she isn't happy. I make her sound like a snob but that couldn't be further from the truth. Like me, she had very humble beginnings. You can't get too big for your boots when you know what it's like not to have any.'

'Do you think that this has affected your view on marriage, or say, a proposal from Josh?' the doctor prompts.

'I think I wanted to know I was worthy of a proposal. I don't even know what I would have said if he had asked me to marry him. I may have done the same as Alice, minus the kids, obviously. It's impossible to know how I would have responded. I guess some people chase what they think they should desire; what society tells them they should be doing. They may not listen to what their inner voice tells them they want.'

'I notice you're not sure how you would have felt about being married, why do you think that is?'

'I do feel pressure to have my shit together at nearly forty. I have the house and the job, but unless you have the full package you still feel like you've failed in some way.'

'Do you think Alice feels she has failed? You just inferred that, in your opinion, *she* has society's perfect package?'

'I *know* she does, but then she has a husband who reinforces her imaginary failings on a daily basis, just to keep her in her place. She's always telling me how well I'm doing.'

'You have done very well in your life, Grace. Do you think that maybe Alice, and possibly some of the other people surrounding you, may feel overwhelmed by your achievements?'

'Sometimes I wonder if what I have achieved pisses people off. Do they feel uncomfortable when they see someone like me exceed the boundaries they have created for me? It's not my problem if it makes them feel insecure, I'm not responsible for their successes and failings. Maybe Josh felt threatened by my promotion, by my independence. Maybe he found someone to fit the wife criteria that he desired. We were together such a long time and he would often dismiss my achievements as nothing special.'

'How did it feel to be dismissed by Josh?'

'If he thought my achievements weren't spectacular then maybe they weren't, I certainly didn't feel like anything special.'

'Let's imagine your situation is that of your best friend, what would you say to her?'

'I'd be pleased for her. I don't buy into that Schadenfreude way of thinking; I'm living proof that life can turn on a dime. Bad things can happen to anyone, we should be supportive of each other when the good stuff happens too.'

'Then why are you not deserving of such treatment, Grace?'

This hangs in the air for what seems like an eternity. While we sit in silence, my mind wanders back to my dog.

'Scamp slept with me the other night.'

'Why do you think that was?' Dr Peter gives me a cautious glance.

'I don't know. Maybe I never will be totally free of that memory.'

'There are lots of memories that never leave us, it is important to realise that that's ok. Scamp is a memory that sticks close to your heart, he was obviously very significant to you, and your first real experience of loss. Would you like to talk more about loss, Grace?'

I feel the panic rise in my chest, I can't talk about this.

'Not really,' I stammer. My mind is taken immediately back to getting out of the car. I start to panic, it's happening again. All at once I am there, I can hear the screaming row again, feel the cold night air…

'Remember what I said about the duvet, Grace, you must try not to block out your memories. Post-Traumatic Stress is a very overwhelming state of being…'

I can't hear him anymore. I see the traffic lights, hear a screech of brakes, a bus heading towards me. I'm there, I'm right there, fifteen years old again, watching it all from the ground. I feel blood rushing in my ears and press my hands against them to try to drown out the doctor. I take shallow gulps of air as the room starts to spin.

'It's ok, Grace, what colour is the shirt I'm wearing?'

'I don't feel so good.' Why is he asking me that? I don't give a fuck about the colour of his shirt, why am I even here? I cling to the side of the chair. I can't breathe, my limbs feel numb and tingly. Oh, my God, I'm having a heart attack. I hear Doctor Peter's voice in the distance.

'Breathe slowly, Grace. You're fine, I'm right here. Try and listen to my voice, remember we were talking about the colour of my shirt? We need to bring your focus back to the here and now.'

I try to head for the door, I need air. I don't make it, the head rush from standing has made me dizzy. This is it, I'm going to die. It's all I deserve after causing the deaths of so many others. I should have known all that I've seen wasn't normal, they really were coming to get me. Every fibre of my body is desperate to get out of this room. I gasp for breath and slump to the floor, the last thing I'm aware of is the doctor rushing from the room to get some help. The blackness takes over and I pass out.

Chapter Thirteen

'Gracie...Gracie...' The disembodied voice floats around me.
You're not there, Mum. None of you are real. Get out of my head and out
of my life. You're *dead*.
'We're here. We've always been here for you.'
'Gracie, it's OK, love. You're going to be fine, I promise you.'
Stop it, Dad. You're freaking me out.
I feel myself lifting, being pulled upwards. Am I going to join them? I'm
not done, I'm not ready to leave. Put me down!
'She's coming round. Grace, can you hear us?' Ariel's concerned face
swims into my vision. She peers into my eyes, fanning my face with a
sheaf of A4. She beams her relief.
'Dear girl, you gave us all a bit of a fright. Do you feel all right?'
'I feel fine.' I sit up and glance around me. I somehow appear to be lying in
a hospital bed, in a room that I don't recognise. Dr Peter and Ariel stand
on opposite sides of me with reassuring smiles.
'You had a panic attack, Grace. You hyperventilated until you passed out.'
'I'm never going to get out of here, am I?' I sigh.
'Of course you will, we just have a few more areas to explore that appear
to be causing you pain,' Dr Peter smiles reassuringly.
'I know they're all manifestations of my mind, but they're making me feel
like I'm crazy.'
'That's understandable, the mind is a very powerful instrument, it has
many ways of making us feel things that we may not be ready to feel.
Don't see it as a step backwards. Every session we have together I can see
you moving forward. It just takes time, you can only go at your own pace,'
Dr Peter pats my hand.
'I feel like I'm being haunted and it's scaring the living shit out of me. I
know I have to face it, but surely you can see how denial would be
preferable to this?'
'I understand, it can be very scary to face our demons. Sometimes we
need to see the past, as scary as it may be, to be able to move in our lives.
Stay here with Ariel for now, she can keep an eye on you for an hour or so
and then we'll take you back to your room.' I watch Dr Peter leave and
flop back onto the bed.
Ariel sits by my side and files some paperwork. I half-heartedly read the
book that she's brought me and try not to think about tomorrow's
therapy session. My extreme reaction means that Dr Peter will delve
further next time, I just know it. I won't be released until I've fully come to

terms with my past. In my darker moments, I do blame myself for the bus hitting my mum, dad and brother. For me to be the only survivor has caused years of anxiety and sleepless nights. I had lost four people, counting my unborn child, in that horrific moment.

I glance around warily. We're always here, Mum had said. Surely I'd feel the ever-present air of disdain that my brother had for me, he never quite got over losing Scamp. I was nothing but unpleasant to my younger sibling. Used to having years of attention, all to myself, I had resented the latecomer's arrival at the time. He was so young to be taken. Twelve years old; he had barely had a life. I carried a lot of guilt for not making those few short years more pleasurable for him, but I was a teenager, and a lot of teens are selfish brats. Are Mum and Dad here right now? I shake the thought from my head. Of course they're not. I'm a scientist, I know they've yet to find proof of life after death. It's just a reaction to dredging up the past. Post-Traumatic Stress Disorder, I've read a couple of articles on it. I suspected that I had it but I pushed it into the dark recesses of my mind. I guess it's one of the reasons why I hate the holidays so much; I can't escape from my thoughts. Even though I'm sick of teaching, it still gave me a reason to get up and go somewhere. I glance over at Ariel, engrossed in her endless sheets of paper. I'm bored here now, maybe I'll start a conversation to prove to her that I'm well enough to go back to my room.

'Do you like working here, Ariel?'

She looks up in surprise, as if she'd almost forgotten I was there.

'I do, Grace. Very much so.'

'Don't you ever feel depressed yourself, surrounded by suicide cases?'

'Quite the opposite, actually. I love to see our visitors recover and get back out into their lives like new people. Mental health was my calling.'

'How lucky that you discovered that, many people don't have a clue what they want to do with their lives.'

'I guess you're right, but better late than never. You and Kirsty have your script-writing career to look forward to.'

'I can't wait. I've always loved to make people laugh. Unfortunately, my students would laugh at me, rather than with me. I do feel I have another chance now. I know I blacked out back there but I'm ready to face things now. It's just that I've never really spoken about...you know. Friends knew what had happened but it never really was a subject anyone wanted to raise, least of all me. I went to see a guidance counsellor in school for a few weeks but they discharged me on the grounds that I seemed to be coping fine.'

'I know, love. It's a horrific experience you've had. I'm in awe of your strength.'

'If I was that strong I wouldn't be in here, would I? I wouldn't need therapy and see dead people and dogs if I was...all there.'

'Of course you're all there. You were just too strong for too long, something had to give. We all need help from time to time. You'll be out of here and back home in no time.'

'Do you know my release date?' I take the opportunity to fish for clues. Ariel gives an enigmatic smile.

'It is flexible, Grace, and dependent on your recovery. A major set-back can still change a leaving date.'

'So even Kirsty isn't home and dry?'

'Nobody is until it's time to leave, but don't tell her that. She's doing just fine and doesn't need the extra worry. I can't foresee any setback prolonging her stay.'

'My lips are sealed. I guess when some people get a release date they feel invincible and start being blasé about their therapy. They could give quite a lot away in those final days without even knowing it.'

'That's often how it goes, Grace.'

'Do you mind if I head back now? I feel much better and I'm starving.' Ariel gives that little rosebud pout, pops a thermometer in my mouth and takes my pulse.

'Off you go then, I'll come and check in on you later. Have a lie down after lunch today, you need a bit of recovery time before group.'

'Where have you been?' Kirsty shouts from our room as I make my way down towards the canteen.

'I passed out, I had to have a lie down for a bit until Ariel made sure I was feeling well again.'

She dismisses my comment with a roll of her eyes and waves a slip of paper triumphantly in the air, her face glowing with excitement.

'What you got there? Idris Elba's phone number?'

'I bloody wish! Actually, even better. It's Uncle Marion's.' Kirsty smiles at her piece of paper before folding it carefully and tucking it into her bra for safekeeping.

'Kirsty, that's fantastic news. She got your letter then. What did she say?'

'Well, I didn't get to speak to her but Ariel took the message. She says she'll come down to London to meet me when I get out. This is the best news ever, now I have back-up for going to Ty's to get my stuff. There is no way he will mess with her. She said she sends her love and that was pretty much it. I can't believe she's still at the same address after all these years. I was pretty sure it was a long-shot writing at all.'

I think back to Ariel's comments about nobody being home and dry over release dates. This will be just the incentive Kirsty need to stay on the straight and narrow. Of course, I'm delighted for her, but I can't help but have a tiny pang of envy at the thought that she will have a loved one turning up to meet her. I rally myself from my little pity party and we walk down the corridor to the canteen. There's a celebratory mood around Kirsty's posse. Jane also has her date to leave and my friend has her own good news to share about Uncle Marion. I take my usual seat opposite Brioche and she glances up with the hint of a smile.

'I wish we had something to celebrate,' I smile wistfully at the noisy group several tables away. 'Instead, I've spent most of my afternoon in a hospital bed after passing out on Dr Peter.' Brioche gives me a sympathetic glance. 'I'm fine, thanks. I hyperventilated until I passed out, I haven't done that in years. I'm not doing too well with some of the delving in therapy, but I really want to get home, so I'm going to have to suck it up. I have a feeling they won't give me a release date until I've achieved everything on their tick list. I guess that means opening up in therapy and group.' Brioche nods, sympathetically. 'My head is such a complete mess that I just don't know where to start. How do you even begin to process things that you've repressed for such a long time? I threw myself into my career and tried to make a difference, I really did. Once I discovered that I couldn't, I felt like a failure. I was back to having nothing, all over again. This is the new start I needed, the idea of writing for a living has given me the first thing to look forward to since I started my teacher training. Now I have to face the past before I can move on to my future. Any tips?' Brioche gives an apologetic shrug. 'Nope, me neither.' I notice her empty tray. 'Please, feel free to go. I have a lot on my mind that I'm trying to work through. I guess I can only do that on my own.'

She leans across the table and gives my hand a sympathetic pat. I watch as she leaves, wondering if she will ever open up and get her own discharge date. Maybe telling her my back story would be a good start, I know it won't go any further and I can tell she's an empathetic person. Maybe it would give her the confidence to talk to me.

My heart rate picks up at the thought of having to relive the awful day that I've tried so hard to forget. I think back to the panic attacks I suffered in the weeks after my entire family were wiped out. The several months I had spent in foster care had been awful. Not that the family I lived with weren't good to me, quite the opposite, they were wonderful, but they weren't *my* family. I had spent that time feeling like an outcast, as they cracked their private jokes and shared stories of their past. Of course, they had tried to include me. They spoke of holidays we could take, favourite places of theirs we should visit, and told me I most certainly didn't need to leave on my eighteenth birthday. But I wanted to, I needed out of their stifling care and bonhomie. I doubted that they would receive any funding for me after I reached adulthood, and besides, I just wanted to be alone. I received my small inheritance, eked it out well and spent the next year studying hard. The distraction was good for me. I needed to get the entry requirements for university after wasting the last year of school messing about and flunking many of my subjects. I stayed in a grotty, but cheap, bedsit until I got into my degree course. The landlord lived upstairs and creeped me out with his skulking around in the dark corners of the hallway, that stank of dirty mops and urine. Many a time I would come home and find things moved in my tiny box room. I knew he had a spare key and had caught him coming out of some of the other residents' rooms. He hastily offered up vague excuses such as checking out a damp spot or fixing a window that was jammed shut. That first year of having nobody and fending for myself was the longest and hardest of my life. It was then that I decided I could rely on no one but me, and to make money—serious money—to secure my future. It toughened me up, I studied like never before and aced my results. I got offered my first choice of university, moved into halls of residence, and found a job for my days off to tide me over financially. I learned a lot about myself back then. I realised that I was stronger than I ever thought possible. No free time meant I didn't dwell on my painful past and I found that worked well for me. Kirsty breaks me from my trance as she shouts across to see if I'll join them for class. I shake my head and she shrugs in response. I'm not in their mind-set and I promised Ariel I'd rest. Nobody in such high spirits wants a party-pooper dragging them down, so Kirsty will let it go. I've missed seeing Mark today, maybe I'll knock on his door and check in on him on my way back to the bedroom. He must be feeling dreadful over his father's death. I'm so glad I suggested he try and get out to see him. I poke my half eaten baked potato with my fork. I can't bring myself to eat any more than the bare minimum to survive. The food is awful and my clothes are hanging off me. It's not a good look. I went this way before, back then, the time I don't want to face. I wore layer upon layer in an attempt to hide my emaciated figure from school and my foster family. I dropped out of swimming class so nobody would see how thin I had become. No one bothered me about it, they didn't want to upset the poor girl who had already been through so much. I wish I had Kirsty's attitude. She couldn't give a shiny shit about the horrors of her past. Sure, she's totally messed up, but there must be some comfort in not caring what anyone thinks of you. I felt I had a lot to prove. I wanted to show that I could support myself and make a success of my life. My foster family had sent cards and letters every Christmas and birthday, but as soon as I finished uni and got my first job, they lost track of my whereabouts. A few grubby studios had tided me over until I got my job at Holly Berry High. I saved hard for a deposit and the day I got my flat was the best day of my life. I had a permanent home, at last, and spent months doing it up just the way I wanted it. I made new friends, people who knew nothing of what happened. I did say my parents had died but that was all. I became a master at avoiding difficult questions and the kids in school eventually cured me of the fleeting maternal instincts that I knew could never be fulfilled. I glance around the canteen, only Ruth remains, wiping down tables and watching me impatiently.

'Shall I help you clean up?' My voice echoes across the empty room. It's quite possibly the first time I've seen a genuine smile from her. I dump my tray into the deep sink full of scalding water and we work away in amicable silence. Ruth cleans the tables and I don some rubber gloves and scrub the food trays. Once we are done, she heads into a walk in cupboard and hands me a packet of cookies.

'You'll disappear down a drain if you don't start fattening up.'

I thank her and make my way down to Mark's room. It may not be wine or cigs but at least I have something that may raise a smile on his face.

I hear the shouting the second I leave the canteen. Familiar, raised voices float down the corridor as I pick up my pace. Brioche appears from her doorway and indicates for me to hurry. I run the last two corridors and see Mark, lying on the ground, held firmly by two of the security staff.

'Let go, you're *hurting* him!' I throw myself onto my knees and peer into Mark's face, contorted in fear and frustration. The man who shares a room with my friend stands terrified in the doorway, as Ariel and Dr Peter race towards us. That's when I feel the breeze, the first fresh air in the longest time. The curtains of the bedroom waft inwards as I notice the shattered glass on the floor.

'What happened, Steven?' I challenge Mark's room-mate.

'He tried to hurt himself, Grace. I walked in to find the window like this and he had a shard of glass in his hand.'

The security guards pull Mark to his feet, I watch in muted shock as they make their way down the corridor towards the office, with Dr Peter.

'Grace, ask Ruth for a dust pan and brush from the canteen,' Ariel shouts. 'We need to get this mess cleaned up immediately.'

I should have seen this coming. I spotted the darkness in his eyes yesterday. The shock hits me as I race back down towards Ruth, glancing curiously at me from the door of the canteen. I need to keep a closer eye on him from now on. I can't bear the thought that he would do anything to hurt himself. The last thing I need is the guilt of yet another death on my conscience.

Chapter Fourteen

'I need to see him. He'll talk to me; I know he will.' My eyes plead with Dr Peter as I sit opposite him in my session. It's been hours since Mark tried to hurt himself and I've no idea if he's OK.

'All in good time, Grace. You have your own recovery to think about too. Mark is fine, he has been through a lot today and needs rest.'

Why is he so infuriatingly calm? I know for a fact that Mark will open up to me. Who's going to be there for him on the outside? Not this lot, I'm betting, but I will. I glance at the doctor's determined stare and give in with a sigh.

'Fine, just let him know I asked to see him. Please. It's important that he knows he has people who care about him. I'll fight his corner when we get out of here, God knows, I know how it feels to not have support around you when you need it most.'

'As you say, support is invaluable to recovery. Who do you see being there for you when you return back to everyday life?'

'Well, Kirsty and Mark, I hope. Mrs Malik was there when I fell over my balcony, so perhaps I should be more tolerant of her need for company. She gets out and about a couple of times a week to some group she's mentioned, but I really should take more of an interest and spend some time with her. I do have Karen and a few other friends but they haven't been too involved with me of late. Busy with their own stuff, I guess.'

'What strategies do you have in place to help you if they are too busy, have you thought about it?'

'Not really, I'm used to it. When I got my promotion, I put it on social media. I had barely any likes and not one single text to congratulate me. Karen gave a tiny eyebrow raise, as if I thought I was something special. Even though when she was made partner at the law firm we celebrated all weekend, with a spa day and dinner and drinks out. I felt swept under the rug.'

'It must have been disappointing, it is important to celebrate your achievements and be proud of them. Do you agree?'

'Pride comes before a fall, that's what my mother used to say, and I did fall, literally and metaphorically speaking. My career fell nicely into place and then Josh left. Those closest to me have never celebrated any of my achievements; I've thought about this a lot lately. Before you say it, I know it says way more about them than me, but why wouldn't you want others to do well? I found myself emulating Josh's indifferent attitude when he set up his magazine and I hated myself for it. I wanted him to

feel what I had felt when he never acknowledged my promotion.'
'The friends you've made in here have the same aims as you, perhaps those friendships can fulfil you in the way that you need.'
'Maybe. Three nut-jobs, we kind of have to stick together.' I give a small laugh and the doctor scribbles something on his pad.'
'Right, that's time for today, Grace. Go get some lunch and work on your next masterpiece.'

I arrive early to class, itching to get started on my latest idea. Dr P got me thinking about my lack of real life support and those friends who seem to have it all. Can we really have it all? Are they really happier than I am? I would highly doubt it. They may appear smug in their big houses with their husbands, kids, and four by fours, but are they truly happy? Some of my friends who have hired a nanny, did so to go back to jobs they hated. They needed to feel like they actually contributed to society and the household income. One of my colleagues commented that she only made a hundred quid more than her child carer, yet missed out on all the wonderful things that the nanny got to share with the children. What has feminism done for us? Are we any better off? I pick up my pen and decide I will work this into a script by writing an argument for, and against, later.

For far too long women have been viewed as subservient to men. Phrases like, "wait until your father gets home," ensured that the female of the species remained tied to the kitchen sink in servile roles, seeking the approval of the males in our lives. We paid the price with our lives for the right to vote. We burned our bras and demanded equal rights to men. We smashed our heads against the glass ceiling. All the while, the menfolk stood above us on the roof terrace, entertaining themselves with patronising guffaws, clinking glasses and congratulating each other with hearty slaps on the back.
'Will you take a look at that lot,' they'd say. 'They want to be just like us. Silly girls.'
Yet, still we continue to create change. We fought for the right to have a proper education, a career, and to compete with men for all the top jobs. Good for us, I hear you cry, but hold on…what happens when we get home? Does equality exist in our home life? We can pay half the mortgage, bills and food shop. We even may have our own car if we're lucky enough. We can contribute to the world with our knowledge and expertise. But does the balance continue behind closed doors?

A typical day for one of my open and honest friends, starts whenever her children decide it will start. Often at 3am, with a screeching, teething baby. She paces the floor for an hour making soothing sounds, and administering Calpol and teething gel, as often as the packaging says she's allowed to. She falls back into bed around 4.30am, grabs an hour of restless sleep, only to be awakened by a potty training two and a half-year-old with a sodden pull-up around her ankles. Somehow, that tiny dribble you clap and cheer for in the potty, has turned into Niagara Falls overnight. Right through the mattress, duvet and if you're really unlucky, the pillows too. She then has her eldest to get ready for school, feed the entire family, and make up a packed lunch. With depressing regularity, a note will appear from her eldest child's bag with some last-minute, unknown-to-her, school related project. It's National Book day and requires a costume; there's a cake stall and all parents must make a contribution; there's a spelling bee and if she doesn't pass this time she'll drop down a group. You get the idea. She does all this, every weekday morning while her husband observes her disdainfully from over his Financial Times. This is just a snapshot of a few hours of one woman's life, but her day is far from over at that point.

My survey is small and based only on those around me, mainly from my own observations. Many won't admit their lives are nothing short of perfect but even the best actresses let their guard down at times.

Scenario one: Angela, the head of a high school department and beat three men to the much coveted title. She has two children aged five and seven. Her husband, Dick, runs an IT company and spends fifty per cent of his life on the golf course. I witnessed a call to her mobile in the staff room, her eldest child was being sent home from school feeling unwell. With Angela only working term time, Dick had decided that the au pair was no longer a necessary expense and dismissed her. Unable to leave, Angela calls Dick's mobile, it's switched off. She calls his office, only to be met with awkwardness. No, Dick isn't available...cue a long pause as the secretary searches for an excuse...he's in meetings all day. The child is dutifully picked up from school by one of our admin staff on a break, and deposited back to the high school office, where she promptly threw up on the fax machine. One hour before conducting interviews, a furious Angela had driven to the golfing range. She had a dramatic showdown with her errant husband, handed over one vomit covered child, and drove back to school, smiling and ready to meet her prospective new employee.
The result: Dick had the slightly mocking sympathy of the whole range. He

wasn't lying, his wife clearly was nuts. The only one who could see through him was the one he described as the pretty, young thing. The trainee bar manager, a graduate in hospitality management, who had worked no end of shitty jobs to make it into her current, low-paid position. He'd been telling her for weeks that his wife didn't understand him and he was sure that now she'd see sense.

Scenario two: Mary graduated from Oxford with first class honours and worked in senior management in a city accountancy firm. She fell pregnant and hid it from her boss until she could hide it no more. Two weeks after her happy announcement, she was informed that there were necessary redundancies due to recession cutbacks. Two were paid off, both women: a pregnant Mary, and a new mother returning from maternity leave, frantic with worry that she was behind the times in those short six months she had taken off before the guilt kicked in. Mary made no complaint, although she knew there were rules regarding what was effectively an unfair dismissal. Her husband told her that's just the way things are and at least he wouldn't have to wait until Mary rocked in at 7pm to make his dinner. Three months later, Mary discovered two new staff members were taken on, both male. Now she wants to go back to work before she falls behind the times, but her confidence is at an all-time low and the thought of a panel interview brings her out in hives.

With the right support, I can see how women could have it all, if responsibilities were split down the middle. Why shouldn't they be? Feminism is a fabulous thing, but what it has created in conjunction with our rights is that now, in many instances, we work full-time and do everything else. Childcare, housework, grocery shopping, making dinner; it often seems to fall on the same shoulders to carry the load.

I glance up from my page at the rapidly filling class. Kirsty waves enthusiastically from the door as she makes her way over. I turn my page over quickly. I'm unhappy with what I've written, I sound bitter and miserable. Where has my funny side gone? I slide the sheet under the table, fold it and put it into my pocket. So what if this is how some people live, they're not me. I should write about something relevant and positive. I have a healthy bank balance, I'm single and I'm successful. Single is a good start, actually. The women I have just written about all had men contributing to their issues, I can write about the many good sides of my life. Kirsty takes her seat and looks at me expectantly.

'You have that look again. What's on your mind?'

'The joys of being a singleton,' I smile.

'That will make an interesting read. It's you and me against the world now, hen. Who needs them?' A hush falls across the group and I close my eyes to visualise what my life was like with Josh.

'Singled out, by Grace Ellis.' I smile at my title. I like the "out" bit, it sounds like I'm opting out for now, maybe from now on, actually. I think back to the harmony in my life before Josh. Sure, I had dates but nothing serious. Back then I had a social life and endless hordes of singleton friends, all ready to drop everything to hit the wine bars or experience one of the latest trendy restaurants that seemed to pop up almost overnight. We were young and free, nobody was in a fluster, even by our late twenties. We had all the time in the world to find the right partner and settle down. Careers were what mattered; work hard, play hard. So often I'd had to catch the bus or tube to work in the morning, unable to consider myself fit to drive. I had a blast. Everyone had moved on, except Karen and I. They trickled away one by one until there were only two of us left. She has no interest in having kids, which is why she feels in no rush to settle down, like the others. I pick up my pen again.

Society would have you believe that unless you are coupled up with a significant other, you have failed in some way. It doesn't even matter to some that they aren't particularly happy. As long as they have someone to come home to and wake up with, they've maintained that level of success where the outside world is concerned. I'm in the fortunate position to have seen both sides of the coin. Here, I intend to outline two genuine Saturdays in my life, with and without my previous other half.

Scenario one: I awaken from my deep slumber and roll over. Reaching my arm out, my hand feels for another warm body. With a little shiver of happiness, I realise I'm alone. I stretch out like a starfish, enjoying the space on the empty side of the bed and the cold patch on an untouched pillow. The sweet scent of clean sheets fills my nostrils. The alarm clock tells me that it's just gone ten. I reach over to switch the radio on and the sounds of Classic FM fills the room. I enjoy the tranquillity of the moment and think of all the lovely food purchases I made yesterday. Do I opt for the eggs benedict or a toasted croissant with smoked salmon and cream cheese? Decisions, decisions. I shall ponder on this while I make a freshly ground coffee and enjoy a long, hot shower, with my brand new Molton Brown toiletries.

It's twelve forty-five and I've finally caught up with an exciting, new drama that I've been recording for weeks. I barely get time to watch TV these days, I'm either wrapped up in good books or out socialising with friends. Oh, there's a text from one right now.

'I've got rid of the man and kids for the day, fancy a boozy lunch out?'

I give my phone a warm smile and quickly type out my acceptance. The only other commitment I have is a date with Ant and Dec, on Saturday Night Takeaway, this evening. I click the record option, just in case I don't make it back by seven. I note with a frown that it coincides with Casualty and X Factor and roll my eyes at the first-world problem that is the recording clash. Oh well, we all have our crosses to bear. I will make the important choice on which programme I shall get on catch-up later.

I walk through to my immaculate bedroom and flick through my wardrobe. With a glance out at the unseasonably warm day, I choose a light blue cashmere pullover and my black skinny jeans. Wow, those evenings in the gym are certainly paying off, as are the early nights with nothing but a good book and a hot chocolate. I give my refection an approving once over, pick up my bag, and head out for the afternoon.

What fun my friend and I have, people watching and gossiping about a mutual friend's husband, who has been caught cheating for the third time. She says she will definitely leave him...this time. Another bottle of oak-aged Rioja? Oh, go on then. Cheers! Here's to a long overdue, girly day out. The festive music fills the air and a Christmas tree twinkles prettily in the corner. A cute guy walks by and gives me a shy smile. I smile back graciously and carry on chatting with my friend. Not today, sunshine, I'm busy. We are interrupted by her phone ringing. The kids are bored at the city farm and her husband has just had an urgent call to go into work. She gives a cynical eyebrow raise at this revelation, but he's an anaesthetist, she really has no option but to down the dregs of her drink and go, mumbling disappointed apologies. I sip on my wine and enjoy the fact that I'm in no rush. I watch as she makes a mad dash for the bus opposite, feeling fortunate to have such few responsibilities.

I arrive back at my flat and call out for my favourite takeaway. I slip into fleece pyjamas, switch on the tree lights, and pour a glass of my favourite red. I sprawl out on the sofa and watch a flurry of snow outside my living room window, as I agonise over the importance of which TV show to watch. Those cheeky, Newcastle chaps win and the theme music fills the room. The doorbell goes, my takeaway is here. Now this is what Saturdays are all about.

Scenario two: I awaken to the booming noise of the breakfast news and roll over to throw daggers in Josh's direction. He's awake so that means I am too, that's how he says it works. It's only gone 8.30 and I really fancied a lie-in after my long week at work. Josh shifts into a more comfortable position, taking up half of my side of the bed. Ugh! What on earth is that stench? It's coming from under the duvet, he does always say that Indian food gives him gut-rot. I may as well get up and have a shower, there's a new gastropub down by the Angel that I'm going to persuade Josh to try.

'Not so fast, missy.' An arm grabs me and I fall back onto the bed.

'You know fine well what we do on Saturday mornings.' I shudder as he pulls back the duvet to reveal his expectations. The newly freed smell hits me full on.

'Not today, sorry. I didn't sleep too well and my head is pounding.' I quickly pull on my dressing gown.

'Well, get us a cuppa then, love,' he calls after me in his best "Mockney" builder's voice. I head down the freezing hallway. Josh hates the heating on at night, he says it makes him cough. I always give in as it saves me lying awake listening to him, even though it's mid-December and I can see that ice has now formed on the inside of the kitchen window.

I dutifully deliver said brew and head off for a shower. As I rinse the shampoo from my hair, I reach blindly for my conditioner.

'Josh? Josh! Can you see if there is any more conditioner in the cupboard, please?' I wait patiently for a few minutes but he clearly can't be bothered getting up. I make my way precariously across the floor, banging my knee painfully on the toilet as I slip. I cling on to the sink and edge my way towards the cupboard. There is no spare one. I'm going to bloody kill him, fifteen quid a bottle and he wastes it on his perfectly straight, non-fuzzy locks. Thanks to my heritage, I'm now going to resemble a loo brush for the rest of the day. I sigh and head back to finish my shower. I reach for my towel on the rail to relieve my soap stinging eyes, it's not hanging in its usual spot. Ah, there it is, in a sodden heap on the floor in the corner.

I say nothing. Josh won't go out to this great, new place if I'm in a mood. He likes to intentionally go against anything I suggest if I have a pop at him. I pull out my blue cashmere pullover and black jeans from the wardrobe.

'You're not wearing that, are you? You look like someone's nan in that frumpy shade.'

I sigh and place my choice back on the hanger. He likes short skirts and heels, it makes the other guys jealous, he claims.

'Does that skirt still fit you? You've put on a few pounds since I saw you in

that last.'

Just to prove a point, I try it on. The zip jams three quarters of the way up and I turn away so he can't see. Josh was in before me three times this week, he couldn't be bothered to cook so had ordered pizza, Chinese and Indian, on three consecutive days. I'm usually careful with my diet, having lots of fresh fish, chicken and veggies. I like to save the naughty stuff for the weekends or evenings out. I pull out a skirt with an elasticated waist and turn to find Josh smiling smugly at me.

'Told ya,' he chuckles, snidely. I pick up his cup from the side table and wipe the surface of the wood with a tissue. I note with disappointment that he has ignored the coaster and a ring has appeared on the bedside cabinet. I'd admired and saved for that, as soon as I saw it in the antique shop, at Upper Street auctions.

'You fancy trying that new place down by the tube station today?' I keep an amiable tone to my voice, annoyed by the hopeful wheedle I hear in it.

'No!' Josh looks incredulous. 'We're going to my Mum and Dad's for lunch. You know the rule,' he gives me a smug smirk.

My heart sinks with overwhelming disappointment. This rule he mentions is that I have to drive and he gets to drink. I have no family, so there is no option for me ever to have a drink while he ferries me around. I'm not keen on his parents; his father is a guffawing bore. He and Josh drink port and slap each other on the back a lot. His dad worked in journalism too, for The Daily Mail. His mother generally gives me looks of disapproval when she thinks I can't see her. She had expressed surprise the first time she saw me.

'Oh! You didn't tell me your new girlfriend was black, Joshua.'

Those words have stuck with me since. Is she a racist? I have no idea. She's not likely to express those views to me, is she? Probably, because I have had to endure their opinions on refugees and immigration, and even though I'm as English as she is, she had asked what part of Africa I was from. She made some vaguely interested noises when I replied that my mother's parents were Jamaican.

'That's in the north part of Africa, isn't it, Joshua?'

It had greatly amused me to hear her say that.

Then I got the usual joke people make, from his father.

'Did she want to move here or did Jamaica?' It never ceases to crease me up. Not!

Can you see what I mean about remaining single? What is wrong with preferring a simple and pleasurable way of life? If it ain't broke, don't fix *it. Of course, I'm far from perfect and I'm sure I'm not a picnic to live with either.*

My friends will come out the other side of it. Their kids will go off to uni (or borstal perhaps, the way they pander to them) and they will be free...for a few glorious years, at least, until the grandchildren start and their own children piss off for childfree weekends to Paris.

Me? I think I'll favour the single life, unless someone remarkable comes along, and if they do, maybe I'll have a romance that involves a non-live-in relationship. That way I get the best of both worlds.

I put my pen down and start in surprise at the almost empty classroom. I'd been so engrossed in what I was doing that I never noticed people leaving. Kirsty stares at me with an amused grin. I slide my paper towards her and she reads through.

'Wow, you really sell single life. I may consider staying that way myself. Come on, let's go get some food, if you can call it that.'

We walk down the corridor in silence. Kirsty said she *may* stay that way herself? I hope she means in general and not that she's thinking of going back to Ty, we can't risk her slipping back into her old ways. I wouldn't take Josh back now if he turned up with the biggest diamond I've ever seen. But is Kirsty strong and confident enough to stay away? I need to try and be there when she leaves, I need to speak to Uncle Marion myself. I won't dob her in to the shrinks, but someone needs to know the importance of keeping her away from that man.

Chapter Fifteen

The rain batters against the car window, I press my hands protectively against my swollen belly. Where is Cal? I had visions of him riding his bike alongside the family car and forcing my dad to pull over. I had called him, in hushed tones, just before we left the house. I had heard him in the background refusing to come to the phone, but his mum had insisted he speak to me when she heard the panic in my voice. She knew about the baby; Dad had stormed round there to give Cal a piece of his mind after Mum found the test stick in my bedroom bin. It was stupid of me, I know. Normally I'm careful about covering my tracks but the bleeding I had experienced had thrown me. Given my age and the grief I would get, I was half hopeful that things were going to take care of themselves, so to speak. Another part of me was devastated. Mother nature had kicked in and brought out my inner tigress. After they hunted me down at a friend's house, I knew it was soon to be over. Cal mentioned on the phone that his mum had said it was maybe for the best. We we're both young and had the rest of our lives to worry about having children. In reality, I think she was more concerned about her place on the high school board of governors. Having a teenage son who had knocked up a fellow student didn't bode well.

I wipe the condensation from the car window. Mum glances round at me with a sympathetic smile and I scowl in return. My brother, Johnny, thumps me on the leg and shows me a model he's made from Lego pieces. I roll my eyes and look away again. I wish he'd stop pestering me, I don't have time for his childish nonsense. Dad is still prattling on about how necessary this clinic trip is. It'll ruin my future having a baby so young. What about my dreams of university? Of my career in science? I'll end up a single mum on that dodgy estate around the corner from us. My father thumps his fist on the steering wheel at the very notion. As the lights turn to red, I seize my chance. In the distance I can see a teenage boy on a bike. Is that Cal? It's hard to tell through the driving rain but it's the same jacket that he has and it looks like his trainers too. I open the door and Dad stares at me in the rear-view mirror. He revs the engine angrily to make me think he's about to move off. I glance quickly at the lights. They're still red, he's going nowhere.
'Don't even think about it, young lady.'
'Drop dead!' I scream, stepping out into the torrential rain.
The pain hits me instantly. I hear the horrific sound of crunching bone and

metal. The car is swept effortlessly to the side by the bus, I can just see it from my position on the ground. It lurches in slow motion towards the barriers of the bypass. I see the terrified faces of my family one more time, before the car flips on its side away from me and crushes against the archway of the bridge. I'm going to be sick. I feel so dizzy. A sea of faces looms above me, contorted in horror. I can see their lips moving but all I can hear is the rush of blood in my ears. I take deep, gasping breaths to control the world that's spinning around me, it makes things worse. A piercing sound pushes through to my consciousness. Is that an ambulance? I feel relief wash over me and then it all goes dark.

***

I sit up with a gasp, I haven't relived that scene in years. My pyjamas are soaked through and yet I'm freezing cold.
'What the fuck?' Kirsty sits up blearily and stares at me through mouse-like eyes. 'Was that you who screamed or did I dream it? Jesus, you look grey, are you all right?'
'Horrible dream,' I force out. Why have I gone through this again in my head? Is this some kind of preparation for talking about it? I know it's time to face my fears, speaking about it can't be as bad a seeing it first hand, or reliving it through nightmares. I would give anything not to have all of it flash back at me again. I swing my legs out of bed. There's no way I'll get back to sleep now, I'll head down to the washroom for an early shower and enjoy some hot water for once. Kirsty repositions herself on to her side and begins to doze again. I place my feet on the ground and wobble shakily to a standing position, adrenaline floods my limbs. I feel for my robe and slippers through the partial light and take a step forward. A searing pain shoots from my foot, right up my leg. I scream out in pain.
'Are you *actually* trying to make me have a fucking heart attack?' Kirsty screeches, sitting bolt upright once more. I reach down and pull out the lump of plastic that has embedded itself in my foot. I stare in shock at the little, red Lego cube.
'First Mum and Dad, then the dog, now *you've* decided to join the party?' I glare at the ceiling. Kirsty stares at me with a mixture of curiosity and amusement. Johnny always used to leave trails of Lego around my bed. Every morning he'd hide in the hallway and laugh at my agony. The little shit. I pull on my slippers and step gingerly towards the door. There's another, and another; I pick up a total of seven. I slip them in the pocket of my robe and limp down the corridor for my shower.

'This you cannot deny, doc. I am being haunted. It's exactly what he used to do when he was alive, torturing me by leaving bits of Lego around my bed. Then I'd go into his room to shout at him and Mum and Dad would tell *me* off. "He's only little. He didn't mean any harm." Well it's clear he still hates me, and worse than that, he *blames* me.'

'Extraordinary.' Dr Peter takes one of the Lego pieces from my outstretched hand and examines it closely. 'We certainly don't have anything like this in here. How interesting.' He turns the tiny cube over and over with his fingers, like it holds all the answers.

'It took me ten minutes to get to your room from mine, I'm still in bloody agony.'

'Ok, let's talk about last night's dream, before the Lego. Was it the same as always?' The doctor places the cube on the table, next to his notepad.

'Always the same. I see the exact scenario that I saw at the time of the accident. The last moments of their lives, shown to me over and over like a horrific, snuff movie.'

'Then let's talk about the dream. I want you to tell me all, as if you were writing a journal. Use the first person and be specific where you can. Try not to leave anything out and close your eyes if that helps. Take all the time you need.'

And for the first time ever, I give a full and honest account of the worst day of my life. I go through a variety of emotions, finally settling on laughter at the irony of my situation. I never wanted kids anyway. Was it really so bad that the option of ever having them was taken away from me? For years I had felt bitter that my choice had been removed. For what? My mind was already made up. My brother had already set the ball rolling in eradicating my maternal instincts. He was whiny, spoiled and demanding. He kicked off if he never got his own way and would suck up to my parents after we fought, giving me sly smirks at the attention he received. I know I shouldn't speak bad of him, he was denied a life, unlike me. But I'm not going to sugar-coat it, he was still a little shit. All those years I've wasted being resentful at the unfairness of it all, but it wasn't what I wanted anyway. I should be angrier at being denied my parents and sibling, I may have told them to drop dead but I didn't really want them to go. Even though Johnny pissed me off, I'm sure he would have eventually grown out of it.

'I hope today has given you a sense of freedom, it's hard to really relive something for the first time. It's important to be kind to yourself now, Grace, you have put yourself through a lot. Go and have some lunch and I'll see you later. I may just have the news you've been waiting for.'

I give a little skip as I leave the doctor's office and immediately regret it, as the pain shoots up my leg again. I head down the endless echoing hallways until I finally get to the canteen. I hug my good news to myself as I hum along to the song in my head, George Michael's *Freedom*. I glance around the canteen and see that Brioche is on her way out. She gives me a little wave before pointing to the corner. Hunched over, almost folded in half, sits Mark. I give Brioche a thumbs up and make my way down the line. Do I go for the chewy, bland macaroni cheese or the soup that looks like it was made from the leftovers floating in the sink after the trays have been washed? I give a little gag at that thought. Mac 'n' cheese it is. Ruth ladles an extra large amount onto my tray, the thought is kind but it tastes so bad that I'll barely manage a third of it. I thank her with a smile, help myself to a glass of over-diluted, warm blackcurrant juice, and head over to Mark's table.

'What's up?' I take a seat opposite him and try to look nonchalant. He glances up like the last thing he expected was to see someone choosing to sit opposite him. 'So, did the tortoise guilt get too much for you?'

Mark gives a soft chuckle. There's no smile there but it was exactly the response I had hoped for.

'Actually, it was the budgie. Qantas started flying down and pecking my eyes as I slept.'

'Nice dig at my dead dog,' I laugh. 'Qantas?'

'Budgies originate from Australia, Qantas also hold a fantastic flight safety record, which he did too until the ceiling fan got him. I told you I was weird.'

'Cool. What was the hamster's name?'

'Mr Nibbles; I lacked imagination around the teenage years. Sorry to disappoint.'

'I think I can forgive you. So, Kirsty gets home in a few days. Do we need to make any changes to the play for the show tomorrow night?'

'Shall we go over it in class later?' Mark looks hopeful, as if it hadn't occurred to him that I'd still want to associate with him after the incident the other night.

'Sure.' I give him a wide smile. It'll take more than another suicide attempt to put me off him. He's now a long-term friend in my opinion, even though I may have had slightly different hopes for us in the beginning. My stomach flips over at the thought of group therapy after lunch. I think I may just go for it and tell all, for the second time today. It's not a nice thought but I think it's important for Mark to hear that others are suffering too. It always seems to be the same people who stand up to tell their story, and quite frankly, it's gone way past boring now.

Gabe looks at me hopefully across the large hall. I know that Dr Peter will have made him aware of my breakthrough this morning, they will be looking for me to stand up and talk. I don't intend to let him down. I sit up straight, ready to brazen it out. Kirsty gives me a side-long glance, she knows what I'm about to do and is itching to hear the full account of what happened that awful night. She has a bit of an unhealthy fascination for gory details. I'm getting my date for leaving soon and this is my final hurdle. I'm flanked by my wonderful friends: Kirsty to my left, Brioche and Mark to my right. I can feel the moral support radiating from them, almost telepathically telling me it's all going to be all right.
Ariel takes her seat next to Gabe, which signals the start of the meeting. It's odd, but I feel a calmness descend on me. My mind turns to thoughts of my beautiful home. I'm not entirely sure what date it is but we must be getting close to Christmas. I want to be out by then. I visualise Kirsty, Mark and I, knee-deep in decorations making the flat look festive. A few glasses of wine, me making dinner for us all, and some cheesy Christmas movies to follow. We could even write a script for a Christmas special with a view to pitching it for the following year...
'Grace?'
'What?' I turn to Kirsty.
'What, yourself.'
'Did you say my name?'
'No, you bloody loony!' She tuts.
'Can you hear me, Grace?'
Who the hell is that? I can hear a woman's voice in my head but it doesn't sound like Mum. My throat feels scratchy and constricted, it makes me gag. I swallow hard. Focus! You need to get this done, it's only a stress reaction. Stop panicking. I raise my hand like Superman about to take off and Gabe gives me a beatific smile. Mark whispers for me to go for it, Brioche squeezes my hand.
'Don't fuck this up,' hisses Kirsty.
I stand and face the room, feeling a little light-headed.
'Hi, I'm Grace.'
'Hello, Grace,' the group choruses.
'It's taken me a long time to get to the stage where I can share my story. It's been hugely traumatic for me to even think about, let alone talk about it.'

All around the room I can see the warm faces of people who really do seem to care. Ariel looks hopeful, perched on the edge of her seat, urging me on.

'I lost my parents and brother in a horrific accident that I not only witnessed, but blamed myself for, for so many years.'

The room is deathly quiet. All I can hear is my own rasping breath. I cough to clear my throat. Great timing to be coming down with something, now that I've finally decided to share and we have the show tomorrow.

'I got pregnant at a very young age, my parents disapproved and wanted me to have an abortion. I was angry with them for pushing me into that decision and I ran away to my friend's house for a few days. My folks were understandably frantic, even my mate's Dad didn't know I was there. He was a single father and at work most of the time, my friend had a rule that he wasn't allowed in her room and he respected that. It was the perfect hide-out for a few days...until the police got involved. I was officially a missing person by that point. I was even on the news.'

Kirsty gives me an impressive raise of the eyebrows and I feel a bit bad, knowing that her mother didn't bother to look for her when she ran away.

'To cut a long story short, they found me. The kidnapping charges against my friend's father were dropped, as soon as Kate and I confessed that he had no idea I was there. My Mum and Dad were furious. They had told me when they found the pregnancy test in the bin that they would book an appointment for me at the abortion clinic. Me running away hadn't changed their minds one bit. I couldn't even be trusted to look after a dog, let alone a baby. I hated them for saying that, I was only ten when that happened and I never had come to terms with my puppy being run over while he was in my care. The afternoon that the accident happened, we had the worst rain I can remember. It was only four in the afternoon but the sky was black as night. The father of my baby, Cal, had given me no support whatsoever. The only time I had talked to him about it had been just before we left that day and he was forced to talk to me, by his mum. I thought I saw him at the traffic lights, I was planning on doing a runner at some point but when I saw Cal, something made me go. Had I waited just ten more seconds, I would have been crushed to death like my family were. The bus hit the car full force, knocking me over first. The last thing I remember of that moment was seeing was the faces of my family, as the car flipped over and smashed against the underside of the bridge. I passed out, and when I came around in the hospital, I was told that my family were dead and so was my baby. Not only that, but my internal injuries had been so horrific that they had to perform a hysterectomy.' I take a deep breath before continuing. My throat worsening by the second. 'I told them to drop dead. It was the last thing I said to my family and I never can take that back.'

I stare at the ceiling and try to compose myself. I'm not an emotional person, but out of everything, that is the one thing I cannot forgive myself for. The round of applause begins as a trickle, as people realise I've finished.

'Well done, Grace. I know that it isn't easy for you to talk about your past.' Gabe's voice fades away and a dizziness overcomes me. What is wrong with my throat? I feel like I have something stuck in it. I cough again and feel something push upwards. It better not be another bloody Lego cube, hidden in my pasta. No, I surely would have noticed even one of the tiny pieces. Ariel notices my discomfort and brings over a glass of water. I gulp it down gratefully as the group meet is called to a close. I sit for a moment, in amiable silence amongst my friends. Kirsty finally breaks the silence.

'Well, fuck me sideways.'

I come around from a deep slumber to see the backlit shape of a man in the doorway of my bedroom. I had headed back after group for a lie down, my throat was extremely painful and I felt feverish. It must be dinner time; even when you're sick they don't allow you to skip meals in here.

'Who's there?' I croak, offering up a variety of prayers that this isn't a fresh haunting. Who else have I inadvertently killed or pissed off? No one that I can think of.

'It's Dr Peter, Grace. Come on, it's time.'

'I'm not hungry. My throat hurts and I can barely lift my head off the pillow. I think I'm getting the flu.'

'You're not getting the flu, you're leaving us.'

'I'm going home?' I can't help but experience a buzz of hope through the misery of how I feel. My own bed would be the best cure for me right now. A hot bath, my electric blanket, my own private space. It sounds blissful.

'You will be, in time, but right now you need to leave us. You no longer need us here. Well done, Grace. I can't tell you how immensely proud I am of how far you've come.'

'Dr Peter, you're confusing me.' I sit up shakily and slide my legs out of bed.

'You'll know soon enough. It's time to go, Grace. I've enjoyed our time together.'

Chapter Sixteen

A blinding light fills my eyes. Am I dead? I've heard about the bright light but I'm not sure you're supposed to feel anything and every part of my body aches.

'Hello, Grace,' says a warm voice that I vaguely recognise. 'You're in hospital. You've been in an induced coma for five weeks after a fall from your balcony. My name is Dr Brown and this is Nurse Simpson.'

'Scott,' says the nurse.

I blink hard. I can just pick out their faces.

'Your latest scan came back with a massive reduction in intracranial pressure, you're going to be just fine,' the doctor assures.

'Brioche,' I rasp.

'We'll get you some food later. We need to check you over first.'

'The show,' I stammer.

'You will be feeling a bit disorientated but please don't worry. We will explain everything to you, but for now try to rest, your body has been through a lot and needs time to adjust.' They bustle around me, checking my vitals and coming out with a variety of scary sounding medical jargon.

'Where is Dr Peter?'

'I'm not sure we have a Dr Peter,' smiles the doctor.

'Isn't there one up in maternity?' The nurse enquires.

'Yes, actually.' The bespectacled doctor looks over her rims directly at me. 'Grace, I'm afraid Dr Peter is an obstetrician, it's not her field of expertise to look after you. But don't worry, I'm Dr Brown, and I am here to take care of you.'

The nurse and doctor have a conversation between themselves and I try to piece together what's going on. Who is Dr Peter and why did I just ask for him or her? I feel exhausted with confusion. I shouldn't be here. Where should I be? I'm not sure, but a memory flashes across my mind of another place. One with endless corridors and paintings on the wall. A purple room with a dog blanket on a bed? Was it my dog's blanket on the bed? How odd. I raise a hand to my brow, my head feels hot and heavy. For five weeks I've been in a coma, is that what they said? What hospital am I in? How did I even get here? I grasp on to fleeting memories of a place that's fading fast. A woman, black rimmed eyes and red lips. Another woman with a pretty face and smelled like summer. A circle of people talking.

'I was in another place. One with lots of people.'

'You were in A&E when you first arrived then moved to ICU, now you're

on Acacia Ward. You may have some memories of voices or of lights, this is very normal, don't worry. The brain will take a little longer to process all this new information, but give it time, it will all start to return to you.'
'But I sort of remember somewhere else.'
'You've been through a major trauma, as I said, it can be very disorientating. The brain can assimilate information while in a comatose state. Please try not to worry, I assure you things will get easier over time. As far as I am aware, you've only been here in this hospital, after your neighbour called the ambulance.'
'Lovely lady, Mrs Malik,' the nurse intones. 'She's been here every day to see you. She said prayers by your bedside and told you stories of what your cat has been up to.'
'I haven't got a cat.'
'Karen and Josh have been in to visit, your headmaster too. You're a very popular lady,' the nurse smiles.
'Josh...' I can vaguely recall that there's a reason that he shouldn't have been here.
'I think that's enough for now, have a rest and we will be back shortly. If you need anything, you have a buzzer right here by your side.'

I doze on and off for what feels like an hour or so, but given to the change in light, I know it must be days. I don't feel like I belong in here but it's a hospital, I guess that's normal. My progress is coming along well, they assure me. I'm now allowed to sit up and have small meals. My throat feels better, a little raw, but nothing compared to what it was. I guess it's to be expected having a tube rammed down it for several weeks. Mrs Malik will be in to see me tomorrow, I'm told. My curry lady; I hope she brings me something to eat. The food in here is awful. My choices so far have been chewy, bland mac 'n' cheese and runny soup, with ominous looking floating bits. Warm, watered down blackcurrant or orange juice to wash it down. Even the coffee is crap, I swear it's decaf. Now that I'm feeling a bit better, they've let up on their insistence of continual rest. I'm finally allowed a telly and I'm well enough to be feeling bored now. Mrs Malik had been put off from visiting while I recuperated but now I crave company and news of the outside world. I've just spent weeks sleeping but apparently I still need a lot of rest. I tried reading but my eyes lost focus after just a few minutes and it made my head pound. Dinner arrives, some kind of unidentifiable slop they said was curry. Strange colour for a curry, radioactive almost. I manage half, which is the most I've had all week. Scott comes in to ask if I'm up to seeing a visitor and I sit up eagerly. I saw from the bathroom mirror that I look like utter shit, but a guest does sound tempting.

'Sure, send them in.'

Josh bustles in past the nurse, a look of pained sympathy on his face. Didn't we break up? I'm sure we did. Unless I dreamt or hallucinated that too. What does he want?

'Somebody woke up again when my back was turned...' he sings, smarming over to my side. 'Oh, darling, I've been so worried about you.'

'You shouldn't be here. I don't think we're together anymore.' I eye him suspiciously.

'Oh, listen to you, silly. She's still confused, is that to be expected, nurse?' Josh gasps, dramatically.

'Of course. It'll take some time for Grace's memory to return and there may be some lapses.'

'You see? You're confused, my love. How are you feeling?'

'Brighton...you went to Brighton.' I pull my hand away from the clamminess of his.

'I'm often away on business, you know that,' Josh sounds uppity at the suggestion he may be gaslighting me. 'Hey, do you know what I was thinking? I could go to your place and get some of your own things. I think you'd feel better if you had them. Mrs Malik has a key, doesn't she?'

Does she? I have no idea. There's a spare somewhere but I can't think where.

'No, not necessary, thank you. I'll be out of here soon.' I can barely keep the chill from my voice. There's something in his tone that makes me nervous, but I can't think what it is.

'It's just...I also left something at yours, I think. I'm not entirely sure but the last time I was round, I had something in my pocket that I can't find now. I popped round twice but Mrs Malik was pretending to be out, I was going to ask if she'd let me in.'

'No, I'd rather you didn't.' Something in the dark and fuggy recesses of my mind is telling me to decline his request. 'I'm tired now and I'd like you to leave.' His eyes plead with mine but luckily Scott overhears and busies himself around Josh.

'Off you go, you heard her. Our patient needs to rest.'

'I'll be back to see you tomorrow, Grace.' Josh says as he leaves. It sounded suspiciously like a warning.

'I don't want him in here again.'

Scott looks up sharply from the chart he's marking off at the bottom of my bed and nods his acknowledgement.

'As you wish.' He gives a sly smile as if he personally would like to be the one to impart this information. Not today, though, that's far too easy. Let Josh go for now and drive all the way back here tomorrow, through the horrendous London traffic, only to be met by Scott and his dismissal. The nurse and I exchange a look. I think I have a prize bitch fighting my corner.

I sleep for most of the afternoon, drifting in and out of mindlessly dull, daytime soaps. What I wouldn't do for a good Netflix box-set right now. Around three in the afternoon, I hear a familiar accent floating down the corridor. I feel a rush of warmth for the neighbour who, quite probably, saved my life.

'Girl, there you are. Your looking better already, I seeing your beautiful face now there no tubes in the way.' Mrs Malik plonks herself down on the chair next to my bed. She's been cooking, I can smell the spices emanating from her clothes and it makes me hungry.

'They not letting me bring food. I try.' She shrugs, it's almost like she can read my mind. She opens the clip on her bag and pulls out a smartphone. 'Look, I get this thingy from my son. He said I not to be using my camera now, it is too old. On this, I can make phone call and take photograph, I can even check if my pension in bank. You seeing this before, girl?'

'I have, Mrs Malik. That's one of the fanciest ones you can get. Best not flash that about too much in public.'

'Look-it, cat is getting fat,' she giggles. I take the phone from her hand and flick through the gallery. What a spoiled kitty; he has a plush white bed with a hood, a three storey climber, and a box full of toys. Whoever the previous owner was doesn't stand a chance of him ever going back.

'Turmeric clearly loves living with you,' I smile. Mrs Malik's eyes widen in surprise.

'You hear me from coma? You know cat's name!'

'I must have, I'm not aware that I knew it before.'

'You not know it, I name cat after you fall and I take him in for you.' She leans in close to whisper. 'You know, I see you, girl. You come by my house and nearly frighten me to the death.'

'What on earth are you talking about?'

'I come to see you earlier in day, you lying asleep, as always. Then I putting out the bottles for the milkman and there you are. Right in front of me, like bloody Bobby Ewing in shower.'

'The soap actor from *Dallas*?' I laugh.

'Yes,' she whispers urgently. 'He come back from the dead and they saying it all a dream. I think you must be dead for sure, this was no dream

I have. You telling me you OK and they say you can go home. I hear you upstairs, clomp clomp clomping about. Then you go, with that girl and two big men. I see through peephole.'

'Who came to get me, Mrs Malik?' I lean in conspiratorially. 'I *know* I haven't only been here. I can't remember where but I just know, this lot don't believe me.'

'Was maybe four weeks ago. A girl with long blonde hair, too much perfume,' my neighbour wrinkles her nose in disgust. 'Big men: bald and black with beard, bald and white, no beard. They say they take you back to...Arca...denum? I no remember.'

'Arcadenum,' I repeat. 'Mrs Malik, do you have some paper and a pen?' She rifles through her enormous handbag and locates the items. I scribble down the details she has given me in a list. It's not a lot to go on but it's a start.

'I praying for you every day, girl, at my spirit group with other mediums. We put you on healing list.' Ah, so this is the group she goes to. Mrs Malik is a spiritual medium, I had no idea. 'That why when I see you, I sure you be dead; I never see no living ghost before.'

'Mrs Malik, do you have a key for my house?'

'No, I offer but you say not necessary as you hide spare. You keeping it under the plant pot.'

Is there anything this woman doesn't know about me?

'Can you go into my house and bring me in my bag and phone, please? I need to do some research. Oh, and some pyjamas, toiletries and clothes for going home in too. Not all at once if that's too much to carry, and just when you can.'

'I bringing my trolley,' she waves a dismissive hand in my direction.

'And please don't let Josh in if he asks, he's been at your door and will probably try again. He's not allowed in my flat anymore.'

'Oh, I see him but I not answering door, something not good about that boy. You see sense now you had a bump on head,' she gives a soft, girlish chuckle. 'I need to go now, girl. You go and sleep to get better, the body heal itself in sleep. This lot, they not know much as they think. Ayurvedic medicine is best, I heal you in half the time they do.'

My neighbour gets up to go. I'm not ready for her to leave but she's probably right, I want out of here as soon as possible and if sleep is the best healing, then sleep I will. Now I know how she feels when she wants company and it's a very interesting realisation.

'I come tomorrow with your things, girl.' She pats my hand gently, gold rings adorning every finger.

'Mrs Malik,' I call out as she reaches the door. 'Thank you. I probably wouldn't be here if you hadn't looked out for me. I appreciate all you have done and are doing for me.'

She tuts away my gratitude and heads off down the corridor.

'Everything OK?' Scott pops in to check on me.

'Yes, thanks. Isn't she hilarious?' I indicate towards the direction that my neighbour disappeared in. 'I just wish she'd remember my name. No matter how many times I tell her, she always forgets.'

'She knows your name fine well. I was on shift the first time she appeared and she asked where Grace Ellis was. I suspect she's just winding you up.'

The next day I awaken to a ruckus in the hallway. Josh's voice carries down the corridor towards me.

'She has things that belong to me and I want them back. The woman is a common thief! She has my fiancée's ring for a start, don't leave anything valuable around her. I swear, she'll knock it off.'

'Now, sir, I don't want to have to call security...' I smile as I hear the nurse intervene in the altercation between my ex-boyfriend and Dr Brown.

There's another scuffle and a thud against a wall.

'Hello, security? We have a disturbance in Acacia Ward. Yes, a patient is under threat.'

'Fuck you! Fuck the lot of you.' I hear Josh's voice becoming more distant, a cheerful ping announces the arrival of the lift. I sigh and lay back on my pillows as I hear the whoosh of the elevator door closing. Scott appears in my doorway, beaming proudly.

'Did you lamp him one?'

'No, that would be unprofessional,' he looks abashed. 'I merely helped him on his way.'

'You're a tonic, this place would be so dull without you.'

'Did you sell the ring? Please tell me you did, or you're going to. He so deserves it.'

'I have no clue what he's on about.'

A distant memory filters into my consciousness. I remember reaching out for something just before I fell. There was something sparkly on my neighbour's landing, the dodgy one, who I'm sure deals drugs.

'Hang on, I think I've remembered something.'

The nurse nods enthusiastically and takes a seat on the edge of the bed.

'I think I do recall a ring...an engagement ring. He didn't propose to me though.'

'No, he said you had his fiancée's ring.' Scott leans in in anticipation of some juicy gossip, but the memory is already fading.

'Argh! It's gone.' I smack my forehead with the palm of my hand.

'Best you don't do that, your poor brain has been through a lot.' Scott gently pulls my hand away from my face.

'God! Do you know how frustrating it is not to be able to remember anything?' I rage.

'I've had a few nights out where I've kind of lost track of what happened, but no, I guess not in the way you mean.'

'Scott, do you know of a hospital called Arcadenum?'

'Not that I know of, I've lived in London all my life and it doesn't ring any bells,' he shrugs. 'Do you really believe you weren't here the whole time?' I nod solemnly. 'It probably was the drugs or hallucinations, like the doctor says,' Scott shrugs.

'No, it was real. I can't remember it but I can feel it. There were lots of people there, Mrs Malik saw some of them too.'

'What do mean? When she was here visiting?'

'No, she said I came home four weeks ago and scared the shit out of her. She said I spoke to her, went up to my flat and then left, with a blonde woman and two men.'

'What the fuck? That's not possible. You've been in a coma.' The nurse presses his hand across his mouth. 'I'm sorry, sometimes I forget you're a patient and not a friend.'

'That's nice,' I smile. 'Don't worry about it, I'm not exactly the most professional person when I'm at work either. Maybe I could get hypnotherapy, can I get that on the NHS? I can pay so it's not a problem if I can't. I think I have money.'

'Let's get you well again first, shall we?' The nurse's demeanour changes back to business, as the doctor enters the room.

'Yeah, let's get me well again and I'm sure I'll remember everything, all by myself.'

The better I feel, the longer the days take to pass. If I thought the school holidays were bad, then this is teaching me just how awful things can be. Today, I had a visit from the headmaster of Holly Berry High. I'd spoken to Scott about handing in my notice, the thought of going back into that place depresses me so much. I need a career rethink. Scott buzzed expectantly past the door to my room a few times, desperate to overhear me quit my job. I felt awful seeing the look of relief on John's face at seeing me on the mend, knowing the bombshell I was about to drop. I can't think of one person that will take on the stressful and time-consuming job of department head. He's going to have to recruit externally. Still, I've had a wake-up call and intend to live a little. I had been stunned when Mrs Malik had brought in my things and I could check my bank account balance on my phone. I remembered I'd always been a keen saver but couldn't remember a precise figure. Numbers seem to be muddling me and my short term memory is fractured at times, I'm told that's normal while my brain recovers from the trauma. All the signs are very encouraging and with every day being exactly the same, it's not unheard of to forget what day it is. I do that all the time in the school holidays, so I don't think it's an indication of there being anything wrong.

John had taken a seat, awkwardly by my side. It was a rather overly intimate scenario. Who wants their boss seeing them in their pyjamas with not a scrap of make-up on? I could tell he felt just as uncomfortable as I did. He began by saying that there was no rush to come back, after New Year would be fine, but I could take longer if I needed to. I felt some mild pressure in his statement, not through nastiness, more of desperation. Smarmy Mr Wilson had been asking after me and had hoped he could pop by. I made it very clear that it would not be necessary for him to pay me a visit. Bloody creep. A few times I had tried to steer the conversation towards leaving my job, but on sensing my hesitance to commit to a return date, John kept changing the subject. I had glanced at the doorway a couple of times to see Scott waving his hands frantically to hurry me along. Finally, I had taken a deep breath and gone for it. John appeared shocked, then confused, when I said I wanted a career change. What would I do? I told him I had thought of travelling for a while or maybe doing something creative. Like what? He was flummoxed, as academics often are with arty-farty stuff like creative arts.
'I don't know...maybe writing?' I had blurted out.
Scott's face had appeared at the corner of the doorway mouthing, 'what the fuck?'
I don't know where the idea had come from but I reckon it could be quite a fun job, now I think of it. I've never tried writing, other than a thesis. It sounds soothing. I could turn my spare room into a writing retreat. I visualise soft lighting and the relaxing sound of Classic FM floating out from the radio as I work. John had looked at me hopefully but the more I thought of it, the more I was convinced that it was the right decision.
'I'm sorry, John, my mind is made up,' I told him apologetically.
'Take your time and think about it, Grace,' he'd said. 'I'm not going to accept a final decision while you're recovering from a serious head injury.

I'll take on a temp for the moment, I'm sure you'll see sense soon.' He gave me a warm smile and placed some magazines on the bed in front of me. 'My wife thought you'd like these. She sends her regards.'

I feel guilty after he leaves. Is he right? Maybe I am being hasty in ditching the entire career I've worked so hard for. I have no idea if I even have a flair for writing. On the other hand, haven't I just been handed yet another chance in life? Twice over now I should have been killed but I wasn't. At this rate I'm going to rival Turmeric on lives. I've seen him dodge buses on the high road, he's pretty street smart but I panicked every time I saw him.

'What do you want for dinner, our budding little JK Rowling?' Scott appears in the doorway with today's menu list.

'What are my choices?' I sigh.

'We have a posh one today, fillet of salmon with a side salad and toasted brioche, or beef casserole and dumplings. Bizarrely, you asked for brioche when you first came round. Not the most profound word I've ever heard from someone coming round from a coma.'

'Did I? How absurd. I'm not aware that I have a lot of brioche usually. Ok, let's go with that.'

Scott turns to go, his crocs squeaking all the way down the corridor. What a strange thing to ask for when I came round.

Brioche...the face of a woman pops into my head. Brown shoulder length hair and the saddest blue eyes I've ever seen. Someone from work? Someone from this strange place that I'm told doesn't exist?

'Who are you?' I think aloud. The image fades, I sigh and pick up one of John's magazines. I've learned over the past couple of weeks that if I don't push these images, they tend to resurface and give me the answers I need.

Chapter Seventeen

It's now been three weeks since I came round from the coma and I'm itching to get home. Mrs Malik still comes in daily and it really helps to break the monotony of my time here. She brought in my laptop and I now spend several hours a day coming up with funny sketches and scenarios. Who knew I had it in me. I seem to have a flair for writing scripts. The nurses and doctors print them off and pass them around the other staff and patients. It gives me such a buzz to know that everyone finds my words funny. It's everyday things that I write about: going out with friends who have kids, what people say and what they really mean, and what I love about single life. It's not Dickens but it keeps us all entertained. I have another scan tomorrow, then they will assess my progress and decide when I can get home. I'm now allowed up and about more and just having clothes on has made a huge difference to how I feel. The list that I started on the missing chunk of my life now has a few more items added. Words that mean something and nothing, which is frustrating. The name Shelley, my fixation with brioche, although I never eat the stuff at home. Most oddly, an elderly nun. Scott says I was probably unhinged before my fall and not to worry myself about it too much. He would get a total bollocking from Dr Brown if she heard him say that. Already, Scott is talking about bars we will go to when I get out. I know that's not how nurses are supposed to behave, but he's fantastic, he makes my stay in here so much easier and I really miss him on his days off. The other nurses are lovely, of course, but Scott is more like a friend to me now. We keep it under wraps, he would be in trouble for fraternising with a patient. Not in that way, he's not into women. Best of all, he's single too and has no intention of breeding, as he calls it. At least I know I'll always have two mates childfree like me. Saying that, the other one has been strangely absent from my life. I've messaged Karen twice since I woke up from my long sleep and she said she'd come in. She's working on some big case just now that's taking up a lot of her time. She's also settled on one particular man and has come off of the multitude of dating websites she was on. He's a workmate and newly single after a bitter divorce. He has four kids that she has no intention of ever meeting.

Scott has asked around the staff to see if anyone knows of a place called Arcadenum. No one has, and my Google searches have turned up no results. There's a similarly named respite place, in Milwaukee, but even I know that's a bit of a long shot. I'm beginning to realise now that I probably was either hallucinating or dreaming. If you *can* dream under such heavy sedation. Anyway, I've decided to let it go and focus on my future. Scott has a mate who works for Charpollo Productions, responsible for the smash hit drama series of the year and up-and-coming in the world of comedy. He's putting out a few feelers for who I can send my scripts to.

It's just gone ten when Mrs Malik arrives, with a fresh gallery of pictures of Turmeric. She has smuggled in some well disguised bhajis, wrapped in foil and hidden in an ancient Somerfield carrier bag, along with some boiled sweets and multipack cartons of Ribena. The bhajis are quite possibly the most heavenly thing I've ever tasted. She has already cooked up a storm and filled my freezer, cleaned my flat, and set the heating to come on for an hour a day so my pipes don't freeze. The woman is a wonder. I feel a pang in my heart when one of the nurses comes in to check on me and Mrs Malik refers to me as her girl. It's almost like we're playing the absent roles in our respective lives. She being the mother I don't have, me being the daughter she rarely sees. She updates me on who she thinks committed the latest murder in Emmerdale and I share my ideas on what to write about next. I was allowed downstairs to help her pick out some flowers from the hospital shop. It's her late husband Adi's birthday and she wants to put some on his grave. She has a few bhajis for him too, which she crumbles over the ground ceremoniously. He loved them and said they were even better than his mother's, she smugly informs me. Her son has invited her up north for Christmas but she couldn't leave Turmeric. Go, I urge her, I will have the cat. She tells me my landlord wouldn't allow it and I roll my eyes, much to her amusement. Anyway, she was planning to ask me for Christmas dinner. From a religious point of view, it's not a festival she would normally celebrate, but when her children were growing up she wanted to embrace all cultures to encourage them to be rounded individuals. She now puts her tree up every year and can't wait to see Turmeric's face when he sees it. She says she will wait for me to get out so we can do it together. I accept the invite gratefully and she adds that I can invite my new friend, Scott. She had already asked him what he was doing for Christmas and he replied that he was just going to hang out at home. He could go to Spain, where his ex-pat parents have a karaoke bar, but last year's celebrations had ended in a huge fight. His parents got hammered and argued about his mother's affair, which had ended before Scott and his brother were even born. No, he didn't need the drama. I had laughed when Mrs Malik had told me that, the man lives and breathes drama.

The next morning I'm awakened at nine, as my hospital room turns into a hub of activity. Dr Brown stands by my bedside.

'Scan day, Grace. We're going to see how your brain function is doing. I see no reason to have any concerns and I'm hoping we can get a discharge date for you.'

Scott does a happy dance behind Doc Brown but stops quickly when she turns to look at him and stares nonchalantly at his fingernails. I try not to laugh as the doctor tells me what to expect, all I can think of is Scott telling me that they call her Doc Brown, after the crazy scientist in *Back to the Future.* It was one of my favourite films growing up. Her white, frizzy hair is the reason for the nickname. Now it's all I can think about, Scott barely conceals his glee at my discomfort and my stomach aches from trying not to laugh. She gives a small sigh at my obvious disinterest and tells Scott to call a porter.

'Right, missus, let's get you into the wheelchair and ready to go. No metal on? What about the gansta' grill? Open your mouth. Good girl, you took it out. You need to poop? You'll be a good half hour in the scanner...'

I shake my head and give a soft chuckle at his fussing over me.

'Hey, if you're out by next week there's a fab comedy show that my ex is hosting. You'll piss your pants, Grace, I promise.'

'You think I'll be out by then?' I ask hopefully.

'Between you and me, totally. There's eff all wrong with you now. Not my call though and I don't want you flaking out on me at the gig, so let's see what Doc Brown says. Maybe she'll arrange for you to go home in her DeLorean. Let's hope she's fixes the flux capacitor in time. Hey, maybe she could take you back in time so you can knock on your neighbour's door instead of balcony skydiving, I can just see her climbing the hospital clock to fix a line to the car's aerial.'

'It didn't go to the aerial, you nutter,' I laugh. I stop abruptly as something comes back to me. 'Ariel! There was someone named Ariel in the place I was at.'

'Can I take back my promise that you'll be out next week? What on earth are you on about now, Grace.'

'Pass me my notepad, please.' Perfume...jasmine? Long blonde hair.

'Scott, I remember something proper at last. I can even see her face.'

'We have got to get you that hypnosis once you're all clear; you could be a medical wonder. We could do all the talk shows and be rich, with me being your agent, of course. Oh, my God, I'll meet Her Royal Highness Queen Oprah,' he breathes.

My scan came back clear and I'm finally allowed home. You cannot believe how happy this makes me. It's now the seventeenth of December and Mrs Malik still doesn't have her tree up. She's beyond excited when I call her with the news.

The next afternoon, I unpack my little cupboard and drawer and neatly fold my clothes into my hold-all. Scott has just come off the day-shift and offers to drive me home. We turn up the radio and roll down the windows. It's bloody freezing and Scott moans, but I've been starved of fresh air for so long that I'd run naked down Upper Street, just to feel it on my skin. Scott carries my bag upstairs and I knock at my own front door. The key wasn't under any of the plant pots so I can only assume Mrs Malik is inside. She opens the door and I feel a rush of heat and curry. It smells and feels exactly like her house. Turmeric curls up on my chocolate brown throw and opens one sleepy eye, to give me a smug glance.

'He want to welcome you too, girl. Come, come. Dinner is ready.'

My table has been cleared of the papers I had been marking and has been set with a pristine, white table cloth. A bottle of red is breathing in the centre and candles flicker prettily in the half-light. My house feels like a proper home.

'Grace, Scott. Sit!' She orders. 'I already change bed and do washing, I fill fridge with food...'

I smile, that's the first time I've ever heard her call me by my name. Tomorrow we will put our trees up, so I'm told. Tonight, I am allowed only to eat and drink, moderately, and then rest. She acts like a real mother to me, the only one I've known since my mid-teens. Rather than feeling stifled, it makes me feel good.

I have the first proper meal in what feels like forever. For the first time in weeks, I clean my plate. Mrs Malik washes up, although I try to show her the dishwasher. She tells me a machine cannot be expected to get dishes clean. By the time they are ready to leave I feel overwhelmingly tired and my bed beckons. I see that Mrs Malik has unintentionally chosen my favourite duvet set, she's turned on the bedside light and electric blanket. She blows out the candles and bundles Scott and Turmeric out of the door. I undress, crawl into bed, and allow the familiar sounds of my neighbourhood to gently lull me off to sleep.

'Two hours she kept me, Grace. Two. Fucking. Hours. I know for a fact that should baby Sanjeev ever commit a crime, I could confidently pick him out of a line-up. From behind! Sleep well, hun. See you tomorrow for tree decorating xx'

I curl up with laughter at Scott's text message, from the comfort of my own bed. This feels so good. I stretch my arms and legs out and roll over, face down in my soft pillow. I inhale the lavender scent from the washing powder and give a contented sigh. The alarm clock goes off and the radio kicks in.

I should be getting up for work. Did you hear what I said? I *should* be getting up for work. I give a small squeal at the prospect of no more Holly Berry High. Instead, I brew myself a freshly ground coffee, make some toast with butter and jam, and run a bath. Filled to the brim with gorgeously scented bubbles, I soak in the hot suds. I think how long it has been since I had toast and jam. It was my favourite supper as a child. I haven't had it since the night I came back here and...

Came back here and what? I visualise standing in my hallway, half drunk, realising someone was in my kitchen.

'Grace, you're not well, dear,' the lady with the long blonde hair says. Ariel?

I slip under the water and listen to my heart pounding. So many things are left unanswered. The ring; what ever happened to it? I wonder if I can spot it on the neighbour's balcony. I pull the plug from the bath and wrap a towel around myself. Peering out of my bedroom window, I glance to the left. There he sits, smoking a joint, staring blearily at my face.

'Hey, you're home. I thought you were dead when I saw you on the ground, man. Got myself a new sixty-inch telly. Wanna come through for a smoke and see it?' He drawls. I guess that answers my question, he found the ring. I shake my head and disappear back into my room.

'Gift from the Gods, it was. Rained pennies from heaven, Grace, man.' Pennies from Josh's overstuffed wallet more like. I would've posted the ring back to him, had I found it. It highly amuses me that smoky Joe over there has found it and furnished himself with a brand new flat screen, it's all Josh deserves.

Today we put the Christmas trees up and I'm starting to feel really festive all of a sudden. I spend a few hours online shopping, to turn the spare room into an office. A desk, chair and a lamp is all I really need. Though now I have the time, maybe I could decorate it too. I lose myself in Farrow and Ball colour charts and why shouldn't I? I nearly died. We should enjoy what we can, while we can. I settle on a lavender, which I think will be calming and conducive to creativity. I order an antique style bureau and a black leather chair; a vintage style desk lamp finishes my purchases.

I head downstairs to Mrs Malik's house. By the time we've finished, an hour and a half later, my neighbour's home largely resembles Santa's grotto. I have to say, she has impeccable taste. No tacky mismatched colours, just classic red, green and gold, it's somehow reminiscent of India in its colouring. I'm on the cooking tonight. I've been craving a good old, British Sunday roast for ages. I bid Mrs Malik goodbye and head off down the length of Upper Street, to the big Sainsbury's, by Chapel Market. All around me the buzz of Christmas fills the air. People hailing cabs with armfuls of presents, the throng of revellers outside the Steam Passage pub, and a half pissed busker with a Santa hat on, singing about how he wished it could be Christmas every day. I smile contentedly as I wander past the brightly lit shops, going through the shopping list in my head. It's good brain training for me.

One large chicken, parsnips, carrots, potatoes, green beans...

I stop in my tracks as I hear an angry, Scottish accent float out from the pub.

'Ty! You absolute bastard, give me my fucking keys back. I am not going without my stuff.' Through the haze of cigarette smoke, I see a scuffle ensue between a petite, blonde woman and a designer-clad, black man.

'Do let me deal with this. Excuse me, hen.' An extremely tall, and impossibly glamourous woman, gently moves me to one side.

'Hello, Tyler. How are you, son? My name is Marion and I believe my niece would like her house keys back.'

I move swiftly along as this elegant woman raises a fist and punches the guy to the ground, it's a right hook that any bloke I know would be proud of. Rifling through his pockets, she triumphantly holds them aloft before poking the man on the floor with a stiletto heeled shoe, just to check she hasn't killed him. He groans and rolls over, clutching his stomach. I hurry away. This can be the downside to the area I live in; yummy mummies by day and scummy dummies by night. It's certainly an entertaining place to live. I continue along the street and begin my shopping list over again.

One large chicken, parsnips, carrots, potatoes...

'Grace? Oh my goodness, is it really you?' I turn back towards a voice that I vaguely recognise. Oh fan-fucking-tastic. Steve's wife stands in front of me, baby in a sling across her chest.

'I am so sorry, I heard about your accident. You really have been through the mill,' she adopts a sympathetic tone. 'Hey, I was devastated to hear about you and Josh splitting up. You know, he said if I saw you, could I ask you if he can come round? He thinks he's left something valuable in your flat, and with the magazine not doing so well, he really needs it.' She clamps a hand over her mouth as she realises she's just given away too much. I glance at the baby snuggled into her chest. Poor kid, stuck with snooty, mercenary people to teach him his way in life. I glance back at the woman's expectant face.

'Josh...' I repeat.

'Yes. Your...ex, Josh?'

'I'm sorry, I've had a bump to the head, I'm not really firing on all cylinders.'

'I know, poor love. It's all together just been a rotten time for you.'

She reaches out and touches my arm. I channel my inner mad woman, it's the perfect way to get out of this.

'Who are you?' I hiss. 'Did *they* send you?' I stare up at the sky. 'I can see you, you know!'

Steve's wife stares at me in shock, before glancing fearfully up at the sky. She edges a few feet away from me and mutters something about the baby needing a feed. I give a genuine belly laugh as she hurries off, picking up speed now that I'm laughing manically. I don't think I'll be bothered by any of them again. How fantastic to know that the magazine is doing badly, he poured all his savings into that. Twat.

Chapter Eighteen

Christmas eve arrives, I have a meeting today with Scott's contact at Charpollo productions. I have spent days perfecting a script encompassing all the previous writing I've done. It's a sketch show about a forty-year-old, successful, single woman. Predictably, her friends have moved on to marriage, babies, and having conservatories fitted. The only thing missing from my heroine's cliché is that there are no cats involved. To get into the festive mood, its set at Christmas, part of the sketch is based at the office party. It follows my heroine, Bryony, through dating, working, and meeting up with friends. I'm using her voice, both inside her head and out, for the whole script. The only thing I lack is a name, I don't even have a working title. Me, Mrs Malik and Scott had brainstormed over it for hours and had come up with nothing. I hope this doesn't go against me, I'm a complete novice and I fear that it'll show. I sit nervously in the studio's carpark, drumming my fingers on the steering wheel and hoping for a last minute flash of inspiration. Regardless of a lack of a name, what if it's not funny enough? What if they stonewall me, before politely declining? I think I'd die on the spot. Mrs Malik and Scott both loved it, but Karen critiqued it.

'I've seen something like this before,' she'd shrugged. 'It's a bit Bridget Jones, not really my thing. Good luck with it though.'

She'd wrinkled her nose and slid my script back across the table, via a small puddle of condensation from her wine glass. My good news dismissed, she had immediately launched into where Graham was taking her on holiday next week. A five-star hotel in Skiathos was all I heard before zoning her out. She's really knocked my confidence with her comments. A real friend shouldn't do that. Maybe point out a typo or say, 'hey, how about for the follow-up she does this?' But not give comments loaded with indifference the night before I'm pitching. I made a decision that night that I no longer wanted Karen in my life. It sounds harsh but it's very much a one-way friendship. I text, I call, I drop everything when she's free. She never showed up once after I came round from the coma. She had only visited for twenty minutes while I was sleeping and Scott said it was almost in a voyeuristic, gawking way, the kind of thing old ladies do when they see a car crash. Well, I don't need it. I'm getting rid of anything in my life that makes me feel bad about myself. I simply put my soggy script back in my bag, finished my drink, and made my excuses to leave.

'But it's only half seven,' she'd wheedled. 'Graham doesn't finish for another hour and I don't want to have to get the tube.'

The old me would have ordered another round and calmly accepted that when Graham arrived, she'd be off, regardless of whether or not I had some wine left in my glass. She'd ruined my script, I only did four copies and then ran out of ink. I didn't know how many would be meeting with me to discuss my ideas. I had to traipse to the other end of the High Road to get refill cartridges after I left her. I had rallied myself assertively. 'Sorry, no can do. I have a deadline and don't want to be hungover for tomorrow. Bye, Karen.'
I left her indignantly gaping after me and not one single fuck was given. I did have another wine, but at home, in a bath full of bubbles.

I'm really going to have to go in now. Ugh, I hate things like this. I wish Scott was here to support me but he's on shift today. Right, stop the procrastinating. Look, it's starting to rain, do you want to sit opposite people you're trying to impress with a giant afro? I glance at the clock. It's ten to one. I need to get my arse in there. It's a big building. One of those that had you known how far you'd have to walk, you'd have considered taking sponsors. I push open the car door and open my brolly out. I dash to the studio, fastening the suit jacket that I hope makes me look quirky, and walk into reception.

Travis glances at me critically over his thickly framed spectacles and hipster beard. Sebastian gives a gentle sigh, like he's seen it all before. Finally, Travis places my script down and stares at me intently.
'What makes you think our viewers would like to watch this?'
'Well, it's real life and relatable. I think there's something in there for everyone,' I blurt out nervously.
'Like what?' he looks bored. He gives a large yawn without covering his mouth and looks unashamedly at the clock on the wall.
'Like...there are loads of women my age who have coupled up friends and kids. They bore the pants off you, discussing how they'd love to move out west but the Chiswick rate for the tooth fairy is double that of Hackney. They edit their profile pictures on Facebook to this dewy, youthful yummy mummy, to the point you don't even recognise them on the street. I saw my friend Emma's mum, last week, out with her grandchild. I shouted across the road, "Hi, Joan, is that you on babysitting duty today?" It wasn't until she glared at me and stormed off that I realised it wasn't actually Joan, it was Emma herself. She didn't look half as good as she did in her latest uploaded picture, complete with soft focus filter.'
Is that a shadow of a smile I see on the faces opposite me?

'What challenges do women face as a singleton, thinking of putting themselves back on the market?' Travis now has a bit more warmth to his tone.

'I think it's all the ridiculous avenues you have to go down to find dates, especially those dating websites. You know the story; cute guy, nice profile picture. You try to muster up a witty message to send, including some joke to make you look funny, but not too funny. Anyway, you send what you believe to be *the* perfect message, only to be met with a dick pic response. Well thanks for that Gary, 42, from Barnes, but I've seen better.'

This time there is a soft chuckle and my confidence builds a little. Time to pull out my favourite Karen story, in memory of our friendship. By the time I finish telling them about her ex tying holly sprigs to her tampons, they are openly laughing.

'I want to take Bryony down a journey that everyone can recognise. I have loads of ideas for her, I can get a second script to you in a few days, if need be.'

'I guess we could take a look at another one?' Sebastian and Travis exchange a non-committal glance.

'Fantastic, I have to do one for Poppy anyway, so I'll send it on to you guys too.'

Their eyes almost bulge from their heads. I stand to leave and they almost trip over themselves, manoeuvring around the intimidatingly large desk to shake my hand. We say our goodbyes and I skip off down the endless corridors. I know they think I mean Poppy Andrews, from their rival production company, Elmbank. I actually mean Scott's Shih Tzu, Poppy Simpson. I've been looking after her for a few days, after doggy day-care asked that she no longer return. There were several dogs, including a Staffordshire Bull Terrier, that were terrified of her. I genuinely had promised Poppy that I'd have a second script ready in a week. She's whimpered and lifted a tiny paw up towards me. I shook it ceremoniously and we sealed the deal, there and then.

My stomach fizzes with anticipation as I turn into yet another, seemingly endless corridor. Beautiful landscape pictures frame the length of this wall, I glance at them on my way by. Suddenly, out of one of the rooms peers the curious face of a Jack Russell puppy. I freeze on the spot. I'm having another flashback.

I close my eyes and go with it. Behind me and to the right is my bedroom, two corridors back and a left turn is the canteen, and Ruth. Who is Ruth? I press my arm against the wall to steady my balance. I hear a voice.

'Oi, Fantoosh. You gonna go see the movie tonight? *Girl Interrupted* they're putting on. Kind of ironic for this joint, don't you think?'
 I glance behind me. I know that voice. Is she a friend of mine? I don't think I have any Scottish friends and the corridor is empty.
'Come here, Russ. I'm so sorry, did he scare you? He's only a puppy, see?'
A funky looking redhead, in striped tights and an impossibly short black skirt, steps out from a room in front of me.
'Oh, not at all. He just reminded me of a dog that I lost.' I pat the pup and he reaches out to sniff and lick my hand. 'What a gorgeous boy.'
'Aw, I'm sorry you lost your dog. Are you going to get another? He has a brother who's looking for a home, you should give the breeders a call.'
I leave with the phone number on a slip of paper, that I promptly put in the outside bin as I go. I can't be trusted with the responsibility of a dog again. I'm just about to pull out of the carpark when I pause. Should I retrieve the note from the bin? I think back to the day I lost my Scamp and the heartache I felt. No, I'll leave it be. One step at a time. I indicate left, back towards Islington. There's a sudden, loud bang from the main road. I watch in shock as a lorry veers towards a hedgerow by the studios, heading toward the cars on the opposite side of the road. I reverse back into the carpark and take off at a sprint towards the scene of the accident. Utter carnage surrounds me. I look quickly around to see what I can do to help. To the left of me is an old Volvo with a trickle of smoke coming from under the bonnet, past that is the lorry, jack-knifed, with a stunned looking driver stepping down from the vast height of the vehicle. To my right, a car has run into a tree. It's just a fender bender and the occupants of this vehicle seem fine. They wander blearily by the roadside, trying to make sense of the situation. I head towards the car to the left, dreading what I'll find. A woman is slumped over the steering wheel and another is sat up in her seat, moaning painfully. In the back, I see a child of around three, seemingly unscathed. She holds a stuffed toy towards me.
'Take teddy. He not like this,' her little eyes brim. I pull on the back door to reach the girl but it's jammed shut. I rush round to the other side and see that the boot of the car is buckled, jamming both rear doors shut. The driver's side door will open and I quickly check the woman over. Even to my untrained eye there are no signs of life, I think it's too late for this one. I yank several times at the seatbelt and it finally pulls free, throwing me back onto the grass. I drag the woman from the seat and put her into the recovery position on the grass, a few metres away.
'For goodness sake, will somebody help me here?' I scream to the onlookers.

'Grace, I'm here. What can I do?'

'Sebastian! Can you get the other woman out, please? I think this car could go up any second.' He runs around to the opposite side of the car, I pull the driver's seat forward and free the child from her car seat.

'Has anyone thought to call an ambulance?' I yell. A man caught up in the tailback pulls out his phone and dials. I hand the little girl to the man from the car on the opposite side of the road and run back to the driver. Always go to the quietest at an accident scene, my first aid instructor's voice filters into my head. I roll her onto her back and check for a pulse. Finding nothing, I begin chest compressions. After a few minutes, I check again and put my ear to her mouth and nose. There's still no response. I begin CPR again and repeat the cycle for a good fifteen minutes, before I hear the distant sirens. I flop back exhausted onto the grass. I really don't think I should have been exerting myself so soon after my own injuries. All that activity has made my head pound.

The passengers are taken away in three separate ambulances and the police arrive. I stand at the side of the road, covered in mud, with an equally grubby Sebastian next to me. We exchange a look.

'Don't go to Poppy, Grace. In fact, tell her nothing, she's a Rottweiler in disguise. Trust me, her bark isn't half as bad as her bite.'

That's when the laughter starts. Uncontrollable, convulsing laughter.

'Are you in shock?' Sebastian looks aghast.

'No, it's not that, don't worry, I'm absolutely fine,' I sober myself. 'I'm just relieved that the kid is OK. I think the passenger will be too, but I reckon we've lost the driver. God, if I hadn't hesitated at the junction I would have been caught up in all that. That poor kid, I wonder if that was her mother.'

'You're a good sort, Grace. You just risked your life without a second thought.'

'So did you. Anyway, I'm like a cat, I seem to have a lot of lives.'

'Well, long may it continue. Listen, I wanted to catch you up to explain about what happened in the meeting. Travis is a bit of a twat and likes to make new, prospective writers feel awkward. I don't know why, it is a bit of an elitist industry, I guess. I need you to know we both loved it and he's already talking about who could star in the pilot.'

I give Sebastian a grateful smile. It's good to know they think I'm on to something. Mind you, this could be awkward. How will I break the news to Scott's dog that I may not be using her services? The police stop measuring marks on the road and approach to take our statements. An hour later and I'm finally on my way home. If this wasn't Christmas Eve and I didn't have plans, I would happily crawl straight into bed.

'She was asking for you, Grace. Her mum is dead and her aunt is some jet-setting businesswoman, over here on holiday from America. You need to go and see her. Poor little scrap, stuck in hospital for Christmas.' I give Scott a withering look and turn back to the cooker.

'She has no father to speak of, her aunt told the hospital that he hasn't even seen her since she was born. Grace!' Scott takes my hand and pulls me round to face him. 'You asked me to check in on the kid and I did. I could have got into a whole lot of trouble looking up records in A&E. it's not my department. I went to see her and she asked for the lady who took her out of the car. That *was* you, wasn't it?'

'Yes! Look, if you really want to help me then fetch me a wine. I'm glad the kid is OK, it's all I wanted to know. Leave me be for five more minutes and then I swear, I'm all yours.'

Scott sighs and leaves the room. It's not that I don't care about the child, it's just not my place to get involved. She has family and she's not mine to worry about. I check the curry on the hob and wander back through to Scott. He has his back turned to me, huffily pouring out two wines at the dining table.

'What do you want me to do? Adopt her?'

'It's not a bad idea. Poppy is getting a bit bratty being an only child,' he smiles. I can't help give a small chuckle and it cheers up Scott's mardy face a bit.

'Why don't you adopt her?' I narrow my eyes at him over my glass.

'I don't want kids.'

'Neither do I.'

'She'd be more at home with you, *culturally*,' Scott smirks, thinking he has one-upped me.

'Oh, you mean *English?* Well, last time I checked you were English too.'

'Yes, but she is Afro-Caribbean English and so are you. They like putting children with adoptive parents of the same ethnic background,' Scott smiles smugly.

'I'm mixed race, I think you'll find. Anyway, there's nothing we can do right now, so can we please enjoy the evening. Merry Christmas.' I reach across the table and clink glasses with my friend. We did invite Mrs Malik but there is some kind of explosion happening in Emmerdale tonight and she can't miss it. We'll see her tomorrow for Christmas Day. Scott's staying over in the spare room and we have enough wine to see us through to New Year. At the rate that he's refilling my glass, I'm going to have to try hard not to ruin Christmas Day by being hungover. The timer goes off in the kitchen, setting Poppy the dog off.

'Shush, Poppy,' Scott chides her gently. I dish up a plate for Mrs Malik and turn off the hob.

'I'm just going to take this downstairs, I'll be back in a second.'

'Poppy, what on earth has gotten into you, girl,' Scott scolds. The dog is now on the window ledge barking furiously at the road outside.

'Does she need the loo?'

'No, I only took her fifteen minutes ago and she did both loos. She's just a mad bugger; I think she gets it from you.'

'Your bedside manner is flawless,' I roll my eyes at a chuckling Scott.

I carefully make my way through the dark corridor and down the stairs to Mrs Malik. That idiot across the hall from her wasn't content in just taking the bulb for their landing, he's also nicked my one too. She opens her door and mutters a frantic apology. The bomb has just gone off and her favourite character has run into the barn to save his son. I hand her the plate and urge her to go, she slams the door in my face. I tut indignantly and turn to leave. A feeling of being watched prickles at the back of my neck. I pause, holding my breath, too scared to turn around and look.

'Is someone there?'

'Yes.' A voice echoes in the darkness.

'Who are you? Are you here to see me?' I feel my heart pound in my chest. The hall is pitch black and there's no way Mrs Malik will hear me scream over that din in her living room.

'I'm not sure. Is your name Grace Ellis?'

Chapter Nineteen

'For the past three weeks I've been having these crazy flashbacks. I couldn't get your name out of my head, so I checked the electoral register and found you. For some reason I knew you lived around this way.'

I stare at the young woman opposite. She looks vaguely familiar but she's not the usual kind of person I'd be friends with. I know that sounds terribly snobbish but she's far too young, for a start, and has an edginess about her that verges almost on the aggressive side. I'd probably run a mile if she spoke to me on the street. She helps herself to another ladle-full of Caribbean chicken, from the crock pot in the centre of the table.

'This is lush, Grace. Did you make it yourself?'

I nod mutely, Scott looks as stunned as I am.

'So, Kirsty, remind me, how do you think you could know Grace? She's been in hospital for weeks, following an accident,' Scott asks haughtily. I can tell that he's concerned that this woman may be a scam artist and about to steal my identity.

'That's the problem, I have no idea. I've been in hospital too. I tried to kill myself; I took and overdose and slashed my wrists in the bath,' the woman shrugs nonchalantly. 'My soon to be ex-husband found me. I've left him now though. He's a dealer and probably baying for my blood to get the money back that he was laundering in my account.'

Scott's eyes widen at Kirsty's words.

'Get her the fuck out of here,' he mouths when she's not looking. But I can't, I'm fascinated by why we feel we know each other. We've both had experiences recently where we have been unconscious, and despite Scott knowing that I physically hadn't been anywhere, I have also been having these strange flashbacks. I'm intrigued to know more but finding it difficult to find my words. I focus on the woman: peroxide blonde hair, a thick black slug of eyeliner almost covers her upper lids, a shocking red lipstick that gives her mouth a mean appearance. I'd say she's a fair bit younger than me, could she have been a student?

'Kirsty, did you go to Holly Berry High School?' I enquire.

'Nah, I went to school in Glasgow, or rather, I didn't go to school in Glasgow. I *was* supposed to though.' She pours herself another glass of white wine and makes a face.

'Would you rather have something else to drink?' I smile politely.

'I'm more of a vodka and shots kind of girl,' she shrugs.

I head off to the kitchen, I'm sure I have some vodka at the back of the drinks cupboard, left over from a barbecue I had in the summer. I pour one up for her and now Kirsty looks more at home, vodka and coke in hand.

'Tell me more about these flashbacks,' Scott breaks the silence hanging over us.

'Apparently, when I came around I was shouting for my Uncle Marion.' Scott and I exchange a look. 'I haven't thought about her much in years. Since I ran away from home, really. I find it easier to forget about people from my past rather than cling on to them. Anyways, the nurse asked who she was and then got in touch with her. It was a nice surprise when Uncle Marion came to fetch me from hospital. We went back to my flat, my soon to be ex hadn't picked up the message that I'd be coming home, and we walked in to find him in a compromising position with the neighbour. Both stark-bollock naked and high as kites. He hadn't even bothered to visit me while I was in hospital. Me and Uncle Marion have been staying in a B&B since then.'

Neither Scott nor I want to be rude enough to ask why Marion is an uncle but is referred to as a she.

'Dessert, anyone?' I breeze enthusiastically.

As the drink flows, so does the conversation. Scott is now referring to both Kirsty and I as the bat-shit bairns, which he says in Kirsty's accent. We both find this hilarious. We discover that Uncle Marion is sat over in my local, waiting for Kirsty. Intrigued to meet this character, we order her to text her and get her over. I immediately recognise the woman from the Steam Passage the other day, she's the one who decked that guy. He must have been Kirsty's ex. How funny that just days ago they were strangers that I wanted to avoid and now they're sat at my table, drinking like we're all old friends. We talk some more about our flashbacks. We both think the name, Arcadenum, sounds familiar. Kirsty keeps thinking about a large, older man, with a West Country accent. His name was Tom, maybe? We both recognise the name Ariel, but Kirsty doesn't have this fixation that I have with brioche.

'I bloody hate brioche,' she announces with disgust.

Midnight comes and we wish each other a merry Christmas. Kirsty and Marion head back to their B&B. We now know that Marion is transgender, something that is slightly more noticeable up close, but otherwise she looks just like any other glamorous, older lady. We arrange to meet up for New Year, to see if we can come up with anything else about this mystery place that exists in our heads. I tell Scott to leave the washing up and crawl into my bed. I pray that tomorrow won't bring the killer hangover that I rather suspect it will.

Surprisingly, it doesn't. Perhaps I'm still drunk or it could be due to the jug of water that my favourite nurse put by my bed. I awaken to a pristine flat and Scott at the cooker, making a fry-up.
'If you were straight, I'd marry you,' I announce, taking the flute of fresh orange that Scott offers me.
'Bucks Fizz,' he smiles. I wince as the bubbles go up my nose. 'There are only a few days a year where alcohol is acceptable before eleven in the morning: Christmas, New Year and any time you find yourself in an airport. Enjoy.'
I join in his toast and head off for a quick shower, before Mrs Malik arrives for breakfast. It's far too early for me to drink so I leave my glass on the dining table for now. What a difference from last Christmas. Josh and I were barely talking. We'd had had a massive fall out, days before, at his work's night out. Things never fully recovered after I apparently, "made a fool of myself," in front of his boss and work colleagues. I had bought and wrapped loads of presents for Josh throughout December, but he only had two for me. A new kettle, because he hated my whistling one, and pyjamas. Hardly the stuff of romance novels. We had spent the day watching telly, stuff that he liked and not the festive nonsense that I wanted to see. It was worse than the Christmases I'd spent alone in my grotty bedsit. At least I could watch what I wanted through the snowstorm of interference on my old black and white TV, with the metal coat hanger stuck in the back as an aerial. I had suspected then that we wouldn't see out another year together and I was right. I took his kettle back to Argos and got myself a spiralizer instead. He never even noticed.

Mrs Malik shows up. We have breakfast and exchange presents. She laughs heartily at the onesie I got her, it's white with bunny ears, and she loves it so much that she wears it for Christmas dinner. I also bought her a star and named it Adi, she hugged me for a good minute upon receiving that particular gift. I'm taking her to the Royal Observatory next weekend to see it. We will make a night of it, with dinner at a place of her choice. For Scott, I spent a bloody fortune on two tickets for the sold-out Beyoncé show at Wembley, from one of those shameless sites that buy in bulk and triple the cost. He screamed so loudly that I expected the police to come round and check there hadn't been a murder. Mrs Malik gave me a beautiful earrings and bracelet set, that I'd admired in the antique shop along the road. I put them on straight away and she told me they made my eyes sparkle. Scott bought me three courses of hypnotherapy to get to the bottom of my flashback fixation, once and for all. Never before have I had such great presents. Well, not since my space invaders game and puppy.

We pass the afternoon watching *The Wizard of Oz* and playing charades, with Mrs Malik winning because many of hers were Bollywood ones that we'd never heard of. She got my choice of *Emmerdale* in under thirty seconds. We drink wine and play carols in the evening. Turmeric lies on the sofa between Scott and I, in a turkey induced sleep. It's the best Christmas I can remember.

As soon as it gets dark, we head outside into the chilly, drizzly night, to see if we can see Adi's star, from the chart they sent with the certificate. Mrs Malik decides that it must be the one that's twinkling at us, right at that moment.

'He waving at us,' she laughs.

Scott and I stay up until around eleven, then decide it's time to turn in. I lie in bed listening to carols on my radio and reflecting on our wonderful day. Tomorrow, Scott is back to work and I'm back to writing my second script for Travis and Sebastian. With ideas filling my head, I curl up under the duvet and drift off into a sleep of sheer contentment.

'Honestly, Grace, they are such little bastards at Holly Berry. I am so jealous that you'll never set foot in that place again. Two hours I was locked in a fucking cupboard for. I swear to you I would trade places with you in a heartbeat.' Mandy jiggles the baby on her hip and takes an iPhone from her bag, to keep the toddler distracted from jumping on the dental surgery's plush sofas.

'You ever tried to have a filling with two under three in the same room? During Christmas dinner it chose to fall out. I was in agony and in bed before the kids.'

I notice the deep furrows on Mandy's brow, she looks knackered. Not only is she a fulltime teacher at Holly Berry High, she has four children, and an even bigger one in the form of a husband who claims he can only cope with two of them at a time. Preferably the older ones. She's currently acting deputy head and has to deal with a nanny who calls in sick almost every Monday morning. I really do feel for her, just doing my own job was hard enough without all the other stuff. Her husband had decided that in the run-up to Christmas he would get a conservatory fitted. The builders would have little else on so it was great timing. Mandy went ballistic and told him there's a reason why people don't chose a stressful and freezing time of the year to have major work done to their homes. Then the builders, having already started, declared that they always take two weeks off for Christmas and New Year. They left a howling gale blowing through a hole in the kitchen wall, badly covered by a tarpaulin. Delightful.

'Oscar? Who are you talking to?' She swings around in horror as her toddler chats animatedly to someone on the phone. She prizes it off him. 'Oh, I'm so sorry! No, we don't need an ambulance. My child must have swiped and hit the emergency call button by mistake.' She hangs up quickly and peels the toddler off of an elderly lady, looking rather taken aback at being clambered on.

'Grace, I have to go. Let's do a lunch. I have no bloody idea when but I'll call you.' She takes off out the door after her tiny escapee.

I take a seat and glance around at the others in the room. There are seven people waiting, I really hope we're all seeing different dentists and mine isn't running *that* late. I absent-mindedly pick up a copy of the Islington Gazette, dated the second of December. The photograph on the front shows the police dealing with a jumper, at Finsbury Park. God, how awful. Some people can get used to news like this, even seeing jumpers as an inconvenience, but I can't. A man named James Dibble had thrown himself in front of a non-stop train, after a stay in hospital. Poor guy, perhaps had he been told he was terminally ill. What a way to go. How awful for the driver and bystanders, I don't imagine I'd ever get that image out of my head. I flick to page three, where the story continues. There's a picture of his two sons laying flowers on his grave, it had only been a year since they lost their mother. Down the bottom is a picture of James in a brown woollen jumper, the rosy complexion of a farmer. I stare at the man for the longest time. Neddy...the word echoes through my mind. I scan the article for the names of his sons. William and Robert, so who is Neddy, and why do I feel like I know this man? I take my phone out and take a photograph of the article. I will ask Kirsty if she recognises him when I see her in a few days.

I head over to Scott's house after my appointment. I've been roped into going to see the little girl I pulled out of the car on Christmas Eve. He has popped in to see her on his breaks, she is being held in hospital until they can find appropriate foster care for her. All the emergency placements were full. At least I know I won't be taking her home, I may have been a teacher and thoroughly vetted, but I haven't jumped through all the necessary hoops required for fostering. Scott has banged on and on about this kid for days and it's wearing rather thin. I feel terrible for not wanting to take her on, but isn't it more unfair to have a child when you don't really want one? They're not status symbols to tick off on a list of what you're expected to achieve in life. I genuinely do seem to be missing the maternal chip that most women have. I used to feel like there was something wrong with me but I refuse to beat myself up about it now. There are enough people in the world without me adding any more into the mix, even if I physically could. My phone buzzes in my bag.

'What you up to?' it's a message from Kirsty.

'Going to visit a kid in hospital. Long story,' I reply.

'Mind if I come too? I need to see you. I remembered something else.'

Grateful for having another person to help me find the kind of conversation that would interest a three year old, I agree. It also gives me a chance to show Kirsty this picture of James Dibble.

'Hey, Clarissa. How are you, sweetie?' I take a seat on one of the tiny plastic chairs in the children's ward. Because she's not actually unwell, Clarissa is allowed up and about to monopolise every toy possible. At the moment she's carefully wrapping a baby doll in a shawl and placing it in a pram.

'Who's that?' She points to Kirsty.

'This is my friend. I told her what a lovely girl you are and she wanted to come and see you too.'

The child pushes the pram over to Kirsty's chair.

'I need you to do me a favour. Can you babysit the kid, please?'

'Sure,' Kirsty laughs and shrugs in my direction. Clarissa heads over to the play kitchen and pours an imaginary drink into two cups. She wanders back over to me and hands me one.

'I got shot of the kid. Wanna get wasted?'

I stare at her in shock as she clinks her plastic cup against mine. Kirsty's chin almost hits the floor, before anger flames her face. I watch as she walks the baby back over to Clarissa, role-playing along.

'I'm sorry, she wants her mummy. She just won't settle with me.'

We watch on carefully.

'Fine,' she sighs, and unwraps the dolly. She bends the legs into a sitting position and places the doll in front of one of those wind up, musical TV sets.

'You can watch cartoons 'til bedtime. Mummy has things to do today. Ok?'

She picks up a play handbag and glances back at the dolly before heading over to the drawing table.

'What the fuck was that all about?' Kirsty hisses. 'How can she think that is normal? This child needs a loving home and someone to guide her.'

'Oh, don't you start...'

'Do you want to see her grow up in the care system? She's so little and has her whole life ahead of her. Somebody needs to do something.'

'They are doing something; they're finding her a temporary placement for now. Foster carers are in short supply. Look at her, you really think she won't be snapped up by some loving family?' I look guiltily away from the child, drawing a house with a garden, in crayon.

'Anyway, what did you remember that you wanted to tell me?' I ask.

'Oh, yes, I forgot about that. Does the name Gabe mean anything to you?'

'Gabe,' I repeat. I close my eyes and a vision of a large room pops into my head. There are lots of people and Kirsty is there. I can see a gentleman in a tweed jacket and spectacles, talking to us. I tell Kirsty what I see, she scrunches up her face and shrugs.

'I'm not getting that but it may come to me.'

'Here, take a look at this picture and tell me what you think.' I load up the photograph of James onto my phone and hand it to Kirsty.

'That's Tom,' she gasps.

'Could it have been Jim instead? His name is James Dibble.'

She spreads her fingers on the screen to zoom the image and stares at the article for a long time.

'What a pity he's dead, I want to ask him what he knows. Why do you think he jumped? Was he was depressed? Was he in hospital because he was suicidal too?'

'We're not likely to find out now, are we?' I shrug. Kirsty pulls out her phone and Googles his name. She finds the article in the online version of the Gazette and locates the picture of his sons. She starts to hunt them down on Facebook. I watch over her shoulder, shocked by her lack of tact.

'You can't contact them, Kirsty, they're *grieving*.'

'We can just say that we knew their father and wanted to send our condolences. Then we can do a bit of fishing for answers.'

The child interrupts us by wandering back over with the picture she's drawn.

'For you,' she smiles shyly and hands it to Kirsty. 'There's me and there's you. We been making cakes 'cause Grace is coming for tea. See?'

She points to me, wandering in from the far side of the picture. I take a look at her interpretation of us. Jesus, are my teeth really like that? I could give Red Rum a run for his money. I press my lips together, self-consciously.

'Is that your cat and dog there too?' Kirsty points to the two animals in the picture.'

'You bought them for my birthday. I'm gonna be four soon.'

Kirsty's face softens.

'That was kind of me, what are their names?'

'How would I know their bloody names,' the girl shrugs. 'We have to choose them together.'

Kirsty texts me the following evening to say she got a reply from Robert, one of James Dibble's sons. She forwards the message on to me. She says she doesn't know why but his story makes her feel angry.

Hello, Kirsty. Thank you for getting in touch. I know I haven't met you but it's lovely to hear from a friend of Dad's, who knew him from hospital. We were devastated when he took his own life, but sadly, we weren't surprised. He attempted suicide a few months ago and had been in hospital since then. He never really got over losing Mum, right at the beginning of their retirement and just when they were about to head off on holiday. He lost his favourite horse around the same time as Mum, which I know many would say doesn't sound as bad, but they don't know the bond that he had with Neddy.

Anyway, thank you for getting in touch. I trust that you're recovering well from your own stay in hospital.

Best wishes,

Bob Dibble.

I read through the message several times, each time feeling that I recognise this story more. This place from our heads, was James there too? It would make sense that we all shared this experience. Kirsty texts again.

'You don't have to answer this, but me and James were both suicidal. Were you?'

'No, I fell off my balcony trying to reach a ring that I threw away.'

'Ah, OK. I thought I was on to something there. Never mind.' she replies.

'Scott and I are going out for dinner. You and Uncle Marion want to come along?' I message back.

There's a long pause before she finally replies.

'I'm going to see Clarissa. I'll call when I'm back and see where you are.'

Wow, this kid has really tugged on Kirsty's heart strings. I've been feeling bad about not going to see her but I don't want her to get attached to me. Scott says she's been talking about Kirsty non-stop anyway. I've dropped out of favour and I'm quite relieved. I settle down to read through the latest escapades of my character, Bryony. This time she's at a New Year's party and has discovered that her ex is there, with his new girlfriend. She's going out of her way to flirt with as many men as possible and has just got into a row with a girlfriend of one of her targets. I chuckle along to the script. I reckon this one may be better than the Christmas episode and I think Sebastian and Travis are going to love it. Satisfied that It's grammatically correct and punctuated perfectly, I email it off to Charpollo. Now I can fully relax and enjoy the build up to the New Year.

Scott and I sit in a gastro-pub by the Angel tube and go over the latest revelations in mine and Kirsty's flashbacks. He's increasingly convinced that we were "somewhere," but the science side of both of our brains is telling us it's impossible. Mrs Malik takes the opposing view. She sees the spiritual side, and as she pointed out, how could she possibly have seen me in the entryway while I was unconscious in hospital? I originally thought she may have been imagining it, but she gave me names that made sense and I have a vague recollection of it happening. My first hypnotherapy session is booked for the Monday after New Year and we're all eagerly anticipating what will transpire. Kirsty agrees with Mrs Malik, our memories have too many similarities for it to be a coincidence. Scott is intrigued by the whole thing, he's not quite sure what we've experienced, but I can tell he's hoping it's true. Uncle Marion declared us all bat-shit.
Much to Kirsty's delight, Marion has now decided to stay on in London and retire from her various business ventures. She had voiced some rather unladylike language at the price of houses in the city, to be able to buy somewhere, she had decided to sell up her properties in Scotland. Uncle Marion offered her niece the opportunity to move in with her. Kirsty has decided she wants to stand on her own two feet and get a job. She's offered some great input into my script ideas and I've asked her if she would consider working on a joint project. She has quite a bit of savings, thanks to Ty's money laundering tactics. He had demanded it back but Kirsty said she'd go to the police if he threatened her again.

I tell Scott all about the girly dinner date with Mrs Malik yesterday, and how her eyes shone as she looked up at Adi's star in the Royal

Observatory. We had the most amazing night for star-gazing. Mrs Malik claimed that Adi had blown all the clouds out of the way so she could see him. She chose an Indian restaurant for our dinner out, then critiqued the whole meal, informing me on how she could do it much better. Indian dishes have been westernised for our delicate palates. Tikka Masala isn't even a proper Indian dish, it's pretty much just a tin of tomato soup thrown over some chicken, in her opinion. I was concerned that she wasn't enjoying the evening but she had declared it the best night out she'd had in years.

Kirsty and Marion walk into the pub, Scott gives them a cheery wave and they make their way over to us.

'I have to tell you something,' Kirsty looks coyly at us over the top of the specials list. Marion shifts excitedly in her seat, ready to observe our reactions.

'Wee Clarissa has got me to thinking, I'm nearly twenty-seven now and it's probably about time I settled down. My Ma was an alcoholic prostitute and I didn't have a very secure upbringing, until you came along,' she squeezes her aunt's hand lovingly. 'I can't be arsed with any more dick-heads in my life but I reckon I'd make a bloody good mum.'

'If you cut out the bad language,' Scott admonishes.

'Aye, well obviously I wouldn't be swearing at the bloody bairn,' Kirsty tuts.

'I had a meeting with the adoption people and it turns it you don't even have to be perfect to give a kid a home. In fact, they actually like you to have some life experiences because you know what challenges the kids might have been up against.'

'Go on,' I urge.

'Well, it's a long process, but I said I know a kid that needs a home. They said first of all it would be a good idea to have a home myself,' she rolls her eyes. 'Clarissa will be going into foster care for now, so me and Uncle Marion are going to start flat hunting for me. I want that wean, and I'm not going to give up until I get her. They have said they will look into it and see if she can get a long term foster carer until I pass all my inspections. They were chuffed I've been in to see her every day.'

'That's amazing news.' Scott beams at Kirsty and throws a look my way that says that I rank somewhere between pond life and a dog turd.

'Clarissa will be lucky to have you,' I smile warmly at Kirsty.

'We just have to get you a home and a job now, hen,' Marion chimes in.

'Grace and I are going to work on a script together.' Kirsty smiles contentedly and I catch Marion's eye. I know we're both thinking the same, that after all that Kirsty has been through, this is exactly what she needs.

Chapter Twenty

The next couple of days move at a glacial pace, as I anxiously wait on news about my script. Five times I've checked their website. It says they are definitely open between Christmas and New Year. That's it, they hate my script. I just know they do. Now that I think of it, the Christmas one was much funnier. I'm a one-trick pony and they've seen me as the fraud that I am. I can't write, what was I thinking?

I distract myself by viewing properties with Kirsty. Uncle Marion can afford to pay for a flat outright and effectively mortgage one to Kirsty. My eyes boggle when she tells me that she had five guest houses, aka brothels, in and around Glasgow. They spoke of business ventures but never for a second had I taken her for a Madam. She had sold two of her places and made just over a million. She was happy renting for now, to see that she really did want to be in London, but also to prioritise Kirsty's adoption process and quest for her own home. I walk enviously around the three-bedroomed luxury flats, overlooking Highbury Fields. I love my draughty, old pad but these are serious property porn. All integrated décor and large, open-plan spaces. On the third day of looking, Kirsty settles on the very first one she saw. The estate agent nearly wets himself when Marion says they'll be paying by bank transfer. Happy New Year to you, mate, what a deal to fall into your lap. Just imagine the commission he will get. I head for home to get ready for Mrs Malik's New Year's Eve bash. She's doing a massive pot of goat curry and a chicken one for the wimps, who can't stand the thought of eating goat. I grew up on it so I don't fall into that category. I sit down in front of my laptop and click on to my email. There are five new ones in my inbox, one from Charpollo Studios. My stomach flips over as I click to open it.

Hi Grace,
We would be delighted to accept both scripts to pitch on your behalf.
Would it be possible for you to come in next Wednesday at 2pm to go over the necessary paperwork and legal stuff?
Wishing you a very happy new year, I have a feeling it will be a good one for you.
All the very best,
Seb Clark.

I whoop with joy as I click reply, I'd be delighted to have their representation. I send the email to the printer so that I can show the others. I have a feeling that Seb is right, this is my year.

Mrs Malik gives me a hug and tells me she's so proud of her girl, now all I need is a husband and I will be a complete success. I tut at her, as she good-humouredly launches into a lecture about how I can never be fully complete without someone to love, and to be loved in return. I'm relieved when I hear the door go and Kirsty and Marion arrive. Now I can escape her rantings. Scott arrives half an hour later, we charge our glasses and Mrs Malik heats up the curry. Kirsty has brought along a Scottish country dancing CD and makes us all try out some of the complicated reels. My head spins as I collapse exhausted on the sofa. It's good for all of us to have a night off from all the day-to-day stuff like scripts, adoption, nursing, and for Mrs Malik, to keep from fretting about Emmerdale and whether or not Turmeric is getting too fat.

At midnight, we all hug and go outside to watch the fireworks over on the fields. There's something about tonight that feels like a fresh page. Not just because it's a new year, it feels like we've all turned a corner. In a couple of days, I'll be having my hypnotherapy. I really feel it will give me the answers that I need. Mrs Malik picks up Turmeric and carries him back inside. She doesn't want him out amongst drunk people, she tells us, as she pours herself another wine. I had no idea this lady could be so much fun. All this time I've lived here and been too busy to spend time with her. Actually, that's a lie, I wasn't too busy. I just assumed she would be a pain had I given her any encouragement.

The evening ended in hilarity, as we put Mrs Malik to bed. Marion and Kirsty cleaned up the kitchen and fed the cat, Scott blew out the candles and tidied up the front room. I helped Mrs Malik into her onesie and ran horrified to Scott with her false teeth, which she handed to me in a napkin. He put them in some kind of fizzy liquid. We locked up and posted her keys back through the letterbox. We carried on partying at mine, playing music from the eighties and nineties. I knew for a fact that I was going to feel like utter shit in the morning, my hangover was already in the post. I don't even remember Kirsty and Marion leaving. I woke up at 10am, on the sofa with Scott and Turmeric. I could've sworn we left the cat downstairs last night. I take the boy back home, Mrs Malik opens the door fresh-faced and in great form. She physically recoils when she sees me. I hand the cat over wordlessly and climb back up the mountain of stairs to my bed.

'Never again. Never a-fucking-gain,' Scott announces when we finally surface, sometime around two. 'That's it, I'm having a dry year.'

I can't even speak. I stagger out of the kitchen with two paracetamol tablets in one hand and a pint of water in the other, trying to gear myself up to take them without throwing up. In my mind, I'm agreeing with Scott. I have got to calm down this year. I remember so little of last night and yet I cringe at the memories I do have.

'Did I really flash my bra at an elderly taxi driver, after Mrs Malik told me I had to find a man?' I finally find some words.

'Yes, you did,' Scott confirms solemnly, with a judgemental raise of the eyebrow. 'I know I said never again, but maybe we need a hair of the dog,' he ventures.

I gag at the thought of another drink and head to the bedroom. I crawl back into my foul smelling bed. It's like someone poured an entire bottle of gin in there and I don't even like the stuff. I have a flashback of raiding the drinks cupboard, somewhere around daybreak and holding the bottle proudly aloft.

'We still have booze!'

Urgh, I *smoked*. Why did I do that? That's right, Kirsty and Marion had gone out to the garden for a final cigarette before giving up. I thought I'd prove how over smoking I was, by having a fag. My stomach flips over and I force myself to take a few sips of water. Scott wakens me an hour later, to tell me he's off to the tube station. I reply with a weak wave from under the duvet. By early evening I'm feeling well enough to have a shower. I call out for pizza, Coke and doughnuts, and spend the entire evening on the sofa watching trashy movies that I don't have to think too hard about.

By the following morning, I have finally slept and eaten away my hangover. I spring out of bed with that new year resolve that I always get. Tomorrow I have my hypnotherapy and Wednesday I have the meeting with Seb and Travis, at Charpollo. Today, I'm hitting the gym and stocking up on healthy food to embrace the new me. The air is crisp and frosty as I make my way round to my car, there is a promise in the atmosphere of better things to come. I turn up the music and the heating, feeling invincible for the first time in months. I've gone from feeling lonely and dissatisfied, to having four lovely, new friends and an exciting career change. Who knew that a knock to the head could do me so much good. I work out in the gym for two hours then hit the pool, swimming fifty lengths. By the time I leave my limbs are like jelly, I feel both exhausted and revitalised. I love the fresh, chlorinated smell that reminds me of feeling pumped up. I jog back through the car park, vowing to come here at least five times a week from now on. I was prone to slob out in front of the telly with a wine in the past, mentally exhausted from a ten-hour day attempting to teach those reluctant, eye-rolling teens. Now I have all the time in the world to fill my day with positivity, health, and ambition. It feels good. In fact, I don't remember ever feeling so happy.

My Sainsbury's trolley overflows with veg, salad and lean protein. Hummus and carrot sticks replace bags of crisps and a rainbow of fruit will be blended into smoothies. I don't even go near the wine aisle and throw a disgusted look in the direction of the cigarette counter as I leave. I'm enjoying this feeling of being in control and feel rather smug as I see the harassed mother next to me, loading carrier bags into her boot, laden with chocolate bars, cheap cider and crisps.

'Hi, Miss Ellis,' a voice floats out from the back of the car.

'Oh, hello, Britney. How are you?'

'Pregnant! Look.' She pulls up her tracksuit top to reveal her bulging stomach.

'Wow, you certainly are,' I stare in shock at the year nine girl, sat next to a toddler in the back of her mother's beaten up Ford Focus.

'I said don't touch my stuff,' she shouts at the child, yanking her headphones back from his hands. I give a small eyebrow raise at this example of her potential child-rearing abilities.

'She's a fucking idiot,' the mother growls. 'Why she'd go and get herself knocked up at fourteen years old, I do not know. I'm far too young to be a nan,' she points aggressively towards the tot, 'this one will be an uncle before he's even three.'

'Hey, Miss Ellis, is it true you went nuts and threw yourself off a balcony? I didn't think we were *that* bad,' the girl laughs. Her mum retreats a little away from me.

'Now, Britney, you know better than to gossip. Remember when there was a rumour going around that your dad was in prison? That wasn't true either, was it?' She stares at me in mute shock, her mother glowers at me. 'No, dear. I just decided to have a career change. I did have an accident and luckily it knocked some sense into me to stop wasting my life. Good luck with the baby. I'm sure you and your future husband will be very happy together.'

I start up my car and pull out of the parking space with a cheery wave.

That was bitchy but it felt good. I know the boy she's been seeing and he won't be sticking around. That girl was one of a group of four who aimed to disrupt every class I taught them. I separated them, but it only served to dilute what little attention the others paid. I feel relief flood my body that I don't need to be part of that any more. I head for home to put away my shopping and spend an hour having a cuppa and a chat with Mrs Malik. By seven, a warm bubble bath and a chamomile tea sends me off into a wonderful dreamlike state. Grateful that I'd changed my bedding this morning, I slip into the fresh sheets that I sprinkled with lavender and fall asleep immediately.

If yesterday I felt invincible, then today I feel rocket fuelled. I buzz with excitement as I drive towards Camden, and the private practice of this esteemed hypnotherapist. Scott had chosen him on the recommendation of two friends. One had given up smoking and the other had been cured of panic attacks. Almost a year on, the positive effects were still evident in both cases. I pull up into a wide, tree-lined street and take a deep breath. I really hope that I'm about to have all my questions answered. Paul answers the door with a welcoming smile, he has an air of calmness around him and this is reflected in his home. Spiritual artefacts adorn the room he works from. I admire the feathered dream catcher hanging in the window, its jewelled stones catching the light and throwing rainbows onto a nearby wall. The sun filters softly in to where I sit, bathing me in light. I already feel rather trance-like, with the atmosphere and the scent of a jasmine incense stick.

'I hear that you've had some experiences that you'd like to revisit, Grace.' Paul's voice is soft and monotone.

'I'm hoping to,' I say quietly, careful not to disrupt the air of tranquillity. 'I can't be one hundred per cent sure that they are even real and not just hallucinations. I was in a medically induced coma and to be honest, I don't even believe in some of the stuff I seem to be able to recall.'

'The mind is a powerful tool, if there is some memory of that time then we will do our best to retrieve and make sense of it.'

We talk for a while about what I have recollected so far, and I set the voice memo on my phone to record the session, so that I can play it back to Kirsty later. I barely even notice when I slip into the warm, comforting blanket that is hypnosis. I feel fully in control, but in that lovely mid-way point between sleeping and awake. Paul asks me to tell him what I see, as I stand inside this place in my head.

'There's a long corridor, with paintings on each side. The visitors have made them. They're quite good.'

'Is there anyone with you, Grace? Tell me what you can see.'

'To the left of me I can see a curved, wooden reception desk, but it's empty. Behind and to the side of it are what look like offices. I'm walking down the corridor now and there are rooms where activities take place: baking, writing, painting. On my right there's a room with a large screen TV and chairs set out in rows. The corridor reaches a kind of junction. To the left and right there appear to be bedrooms.'

'Very good, Grace. You're doing so well. Do you know what this place is? Do you have a name for it?'

'No.'

Around halfway down I see the tiny, furry face of a Jack Russell puppy. 'There's a dog here, he looks like my old dog. He's peeking round from the corner of the corridor.' I turn to the left and continue down the hallway.

'I'm outside a place that feels familiar. It's a bedroom with purple walls. There are two single beds; one with a crumpled, tartan blanket and another with a patchwork quilt. Out of the window I can see leaves swirling like a mini tornado in the breeze. The location is beautiful and rural, like Hertfordshire or Surrey.'

'Is anyone else there with you? Any names of people coming to your mind?'

'No, but it feels like there should be lots of people here. That there have been many through these doors. I'm back in the corridor now. I feel safe in this place, but watched. Watched very closely.' There is an air of melancholy over this place, a sadness to it in that it holds many secrets. The end of the hall is guarded by wide double doors. 'I can see something that looks like a canteen.'

A sudden noise from one of the rooms catches my attention.

'There's someone here!'

'Who's there, Grace? Remember that you are safe, nobody can harm you.'

Curled up on a bed lies a man, tormented by sadness. He rocks as he mumbles anxious words. I draw closer to him and he stops in fright. His eyes widen as he stares at me.

'Mark...Mark is here. He was my friend. He's done something terrible to himself and he's cut. He can see me.'

Mark hastily pulls himself up and presses his back against the wall.

'I'm sorry, I didn't mean to frighten you.'

I back away and he stares at me until I'm in the corridor. Further down and to the right of me seems to be a shower block. I hear the sound of running water from the other side of the door. I push it open gently and a sad sigh fills my ears, as if it has been magnified a hundred times. A lady reaches out from the cubicle for her towel. Burn scars mark her body from her wrist to her shoulder and all down her torso. Something is telling me not to get too close. I keep back a safe distance, so as not to startle her.

'There's a lady in the shower. She has burn scars. She's very sad.'

'What is her name, Grace. Try to remember.'

'She never speaks to me but sometimes she will smile and she always listens.'

I back away further as she wraps the towel around herself and steps out.

'Brioche,' I murmur. 'I think her name is Brioche.'

Paul walks me back down the corridor, asking me to notice anything new that may give me a clue to the place I'm in. I hear heels click-clacking on the floor behind me and turn to look.

'Grace? What are you doing here?'

'It's Ariel. She is asking me why I'm here. She's telling me that I'm all better and I can go home. The doors are opening and there's a bright light shining in.'

OK, Grace. Stay with me. I'm going to count back from ten and when I reach one, you will be awake, alert and remember everything we have spoken about.'

Paul counts down softly and I feel as though I'm being unfurled from a warm duvet. I try to hold on to the place I've just visited, grasping for a name.

'One. Open your eyes, Grace.'

I blink and readjust to the light in the room.

'How are you feeling?'

'Blissed out. It was strange, unnerving and comforting, all at the same time.'

'You did really well, Grace. Do you feel you have many of the answers that you needed?'

'Kind of, I'm disappointed that I didn't get the name of the place.'

'Perhaps next time, you do have three sessions and it's best not to push what doesn't come naturally.'

I feel calm and tranquil all afternoon. I relax on the sofa and watch back to back episodes of *Come Dine with Me*, just because I can, now that there's no Josh on the scene to moan about it. Kirsty will be round in an hour or so and we are going to listen to my recording. She's all up for getting a takeaway and making a night of it. I'm supposed to be on my health kick but already I'm swithering. It's been so long since I had fun friends to do things with that my attitude is all a bit "why not?" I have a feeling she will easily talk me into it. I doze on and off on the sofa for an hour, trying to revisit the place in my head that I went to today. I'm still trying to figure out why I said the shower lady was named after a French pastry. Surely I must have got that muddled, although Scott says I came round asking for Brioche too. And where is Mark? He was a friend of mine; I know that now for sure. I felt a strong bond there. Is he out there looking for us or has he forgotten everything? He was the third person I now know from there who had suicidal tendencies and I'm the only one who was in there due to an accident. Did they perhaps think it was intentional? It's the only explanation that I can come up with.

Kirsty arrives, and judging by the clattering coming from her carrier bag, so do bottles of wine and vodka. Bang goes my detox, only two days in. 'I'm not being really bad,' I chide her. I have a meeting at two tomorrow, over at Charpollo.'

'Yeah, yeah,' she waves a dismissive hand towards me. We listen back to the audio and Kirsty nods at parts that she recognises. Once it's done, she tells me that the name Brioche makes sense to her, but not the burns. We need to find both Mark and Brioche, we decide. Where do we start when that clearly isn't the woman's name and we don't have a surname for Mark? We order in a Chinese takeaway and sit at the dining table, surrounded by sheets of paper, brainstorming what we already know. At the top we write Arcadenum. It doesn't appear to exist but it's the only name we have to go on. Under that we write down that it seems to be either a hospital or an institution, maybe for people with suicidal tendencies. Then we write our names, James Dibble, Mark and Brioche. Kirsty taps the pen against her teeth agitatedly. We're missing so much still. Kirsty is worried about the bright light I saw but I'm less bothered. 'Why did Paul tell you to stay with him?' She says ominously. 'What would have happened if you had walked into the light?'

I shrug. we seem to be chasing our tails here.

'What we need to do is find Mark,' Kirsty tries to motivate me. 'Can you call Scott and get him round?'

He answers the phone on the tenth ring, like he couldn't decide if he should or not.

'I'm on an early tomorrow so don't try to ply me with booze.'

I can't help laughing as he lays down his conditions before I can even say hello.

'We have Chinese,' I cajole.

'Fine. Save me a spring roll and I'm all yours for an hour.' He hangs up and comes straight over.

'Where would someone go if they tried to kill themselves?' I question him as soon as he arrives.

'Depends how successful the attempt was. A&E to begin with, then either ICU or Psych,' Scott takes a seat and dips a chip into Kirsty's curry sauce.

'We need you to find someone for us. His name is Mark and he has brown, longish hair. Do you think you could do that?' Kirsty asks.

'Mark who?'

'We don't know,' I sigh.

'Are you kidding me? There are probably over a hundred Marks in my hospital alone. You want me to go and look at each one to find ones with brown hair? Even if I did have access to every file of every hospital, what's to say he's even in one? You're not and neither is Kirsty.'

'It is pretty stupid,' Kirsty admits. 'Can you not think of his surname? See if that comes back to you.'

'I don't know if I ever knew it,' I shrug. 'Oh, forget it, Scott. It was a dumb idea. The only one we both remember for sure is James Dibble, and he's dead. Maybe Mark is too.'

'I do have some news but I'm not sure how much it's worth,' Scott says doubtfully. 'I was on the phone to my Mum earlier and I asked her if she knew of a hospital called Arcadenum.' Kirsty and I glance up hopefully. 'She didn't.' Kirsty's shoulders slump. 'She did say that years ago there was a psychiatric facility called Arcadia but she doesn't think it's there anymore.'

I rush through to the spare room and switch on the laptop. Kirsty and Scott stand behind me as we wait impatiently for it to load. I type Arcadia into the browser and immediately an old picture of a large, white building appears on the screen. I read aloud.

Arcadia was a mental health facility situated in the outskirts of Hertfordshire. It opened in 1947 and its practices are now considered to be forward thinking for its time. Many of these types of establishments deemed a patient be institutionalised for life. Arcadia was unique in that it offered short-term treatment and used talking therapies in place of Electroconvulsive Therapy, more commonly known as ECT.

The institute was heavily criticised at the time, as people feared that not only would the treatment not be effective, but that it re-introduced psychiatrically distressed people back into society. In the case of many of those in their care, health practitioners thought patients should remain institutionalised, for the safety of themselves and the wider community. Their apprehensions were confirmed when a returning patient set fire to the building, in 1968. Due to the high security nature of the hospital, the windows were barred and doors were locked. Seventy-three lives were lost, including those of staff and patients. Arcadia remained a ruin for several years until it was demolished, due to lack of available funds for rebuilding. Many modern therapists have adopted the practices first used in Arcadia, and the popularity of talking therapies continues to rise.

'Well, you weren't in there, were you? Unless you want to also add time travel to your myriad of unlikely events,' Scott scrolls back up to take a look at the photograph again. Kirsty and I exchange looks of despair. 'Maybe my next hypnotherapy session will come up with something. You could try it too, Kirsty. It would double our chances of finding out what went on,' I urge, trying to grasp on to a thread of positivity.
'Yeah, I suppose so, but I better not start clucking like a hen and running around with my knickers on my head. Give me his number and I'll try and get a session.' Kirsty takes my phone and leaves a message for Paul. We all decide it's time to call it quits for the evening. I'm a little disappointed that I didn't get more information from my hypnosis. Maybe Kirsty will have more luck than me, but if she does end up doing the knickerless chicken then that will be just as entertaining.

Chapter Twenty-One

I arrive for my meeting at Charpollo. Travis has had a sea change in attitude towards me, he shakes me warmly by the hand and even makes me a coffee. I had watched as today's young hopeful appeared from the meeting room, red-faced and flustered. Travis was dismissive in his farewell, telling her they'll be in touch, with an air of boredom and disdain. By the look on his face, I doubted she'd be holding her breath for a positive outcome, just like I hadn't.

I sign all the necessary paperwork for Charpollo to promote my scripts, it's all rather jovial and I can't help but notice that Sebastian keeps holding my gaze for slightly longer than necessary. I give thanks for my dark skin, that doesn't defy me with a blush too readily. I'm on my way out when Sebastian chases after me down the corridor.

'I forgot to ask you, Grace. How is the little girl from the accident?'

'Her mum died, which I think you probably guessed. They tried for almost an hour to save her in Accident and Emergency, but her injuries were too bad. I'm amazed the child was pretty much unscathed, just a few cuts and bruises but nothing life-threatening. Her aunt doesn't want her. She's going into the care system but my friend is hurrying through the background checks for adoption and is hoping to take her on.'

'That's fantastic news about your friend, I really hope she's successful. So...what are you up to this afternoon? Working on your next masterpiece?'

'I actually don't have any plans for today, other than coming here. Maybe I'll go to the gym, I really kicked the arse out of Christmas and New Year and I need to get back on track.'

'Oh, that's a pity, I was hoping to hear some more of your ideas. Could I tempt you into meeting for a drink later? Just a coke, since you're being good.'

'Sebastian, are you asking me on a date?' I give a nervous laugh.

'God, no! Well, unless *you* want to call it a date. I was just hoping to get one over on Travis and get some inside info,' he winks.

'Well, judging by the look of things, he put that poor woman through the wringer, so why not. I think it's the least he deserves for being a meanie to the newbies. Where were you thinking?'

'I'm in Barnsbury, so how about the High Road?'

'Oh, you're not far from me at all and I love your local. Shall we meet for dinner and then head there after?'

We exchange mobile numbers and I walk back to my car feeling lighter.

He may call it an interest in my work but I know a hot date when I see one. I'm starting to love this year already and we're only a third of the way through January.

Kirsty comes round in the afternoon and we listen to the audio from her hypnosis. Paul had a last minute cancellation and managed to squeeze her in this morning. She wanted to surprise me, so just showed up at the front door instead of texting. She too saw the long corridors and rooms, but being more open and spiritual than me seemed to work in her favour. She appeared to have people around her in the hospital, and the place was definitely called Arcadia, it came back to her the second she saw it. She seemed to experience part of a typical day there and recalled writing humorous scripts and sharing a bedroom with me. She saw Mark and Brioche, Ariel and Jim. She could feel herself in a therapy session with a man named Dr Peter. According to Scott, I also mentioned a Dr Peter when I first came round. Kirsty looks thoughtful.

'What is it? You want to see if we can find a new Arcadia that was built in another location?' I enquire.

'Leave it with me, you go and enjoy your date. I have a theory that I need to research but I don't want to confuse everything by mixing it in with your thoughts. I don't mean to be rude, but you scientific types like to piss on the parade of others with your stats and facts. It'll only muddle me more.'

With that, she goes off, leaving me even more confused than I already was.

I arrange to meet Sebastian in the Greek restaurant that I've been wanting to visit for months, Josh hadn't taken me up on it and this feels a little bit like sticking two fingers up at him. I arrive first and order a half carafe of red to calm the nerves. I'm on my first date in almost ten years, I've arrived early on purpose as I hate being the one to walk in last. I scan the menu. The wonderful cooking smells coming from the kitchen are making my stomach rumble. I order some pitta, hummus and olives, to silence it, and people watch to while away the time. Ten minutes later and my heart gives a little leap, as I see Sebastian passing by the window. The bell above the door gives a cheerful jingle and I give a shy wave to attract his attention.

'Sebastian, you're looking rather dressed up for a non-date,' I laugh.

'Is that aftershave I can smell?'

He gives an embarrassed chuckle.

'Hey, you can call me Seb. Only my mum uses Sebastian now. Anyway, you're the one who called it a date, I didn't want to turn up in tracksuit bottoms and let the side down. Nice joint this, Grace. Good call, I love Greek food, my favourite place in the world is Santorini. You ever been?' Seb babbles away and it helps to calm me.

I needn't have worried, the conversation flows as well as the wine. He tells me a channel of note loves my script. They have some reality TV personality in mind for the role of Bryony, who wants to try her hand at acting. This makes my heart sink a bit. I hadn't envisaged my lead as a bottle blonde, with fake nails and boobs, but I guess a sale is a sale. He won't tell me who she is so I pour him another wine to loosen his tongue. We talk about where he would love me to take my heroine and I make mental notes of some of his great ideas. I still haven't been able to come up with a name for it but he and Travis are working on it too.

We move on to my stay in hospital and his break-up with a long-term girlfriend. I try to hide my delight that the main reason for the break up was that she wanted kids and he didn't. He's pretty much the full package: intelligent, ambitious, doesn't want children. Easy on the eye to top it off. Now I don't even have to go into not being able to have kids, he's put his cards on the table so it's a non-issue. We chat about my teaching and how he's considering starting up his own production company. He owns a three-bedroomed cottage just down the road, near The Drapers Arms. It's one of my favourite watering holes and has a real country pub feel to it. The last thing I thought I wanted was to get into another relationship, but I have to admit it, this feels right.

We finish up our food and head off for a drink. I could now write the next few scripts based on what we've discussed alone. We make another date for the weekend, I will cook and then we brainstorm. His ideas are great but they make me feel very amateur. I guess I am, in comparison to Seb. There's an amicable lull in the conversation, I'm just thinking how my good intentions of cleaning up my act for the new year have ended in disaster. That is just *so me*. It's then that it hits me.

'I have a great idea for my character...and a name. I actually have a name!' I announce to Seb and half the pub.

'What is it? Tell me!'

'I was just thinking how bad I've been already this year. I said I wouldn't drink until at least February, and even then, only at weekends.'

'Out with it,' Seb laughs.

'Well, Bryony has all the mishaps that so many of us face, but imagine she's having to do all that sober. We start the series with her coming out of rehab and having to do her first booze free Christmas.'

'I like it!' Seb gives me a warm smile.

'Really?' I'm slightly taken aback with someone constantly loving the things I come up with and not putting me down, like Josh did.

'And this is the best bit...we call the show So-Bryony, like sobriety, but everything she does is so Bryony. That could be our hook at the end of every episode. Maybe it's the wine going to my head but I love that name and it feels like a fresh idea. I haven't seen anything like that before on telly and it puts some humour into what can feel like a dark situation for many people.'

'I totally agree, there is humour in almost any situation if you look for it. Travis is going to love it. He already adores your ideas but this adds a new spin. I think this could be the break he's been looking for in the comedy market.'

We chat excitedly and scrawl notes on napkins, until the loud sighs and tuts from the barmaid sends us scurrying apologetically to the door. Seb offers to walk me home but I decline, I'm literally only a few streets away. There follows the first awkward silence of the evening. I keep a bit of distance so that he doesn't try to kiss me goodnight. Then we do that strange hug-dance that people do. Finally, we settle for a peck on the cheek and handshake combo, then head our separate ways. I check my phone and see a missed call and a voicemail from Kirsty.

'Hey, Grace, I need to come by tomorrow. There's something I need to speak to you about. I'm off to bed, so call me now and I'll wring your bloody neck.'

I barely slept. The first few hours were wine-addled unconsciousness but from 3am I tossed and turned, intrigued by what Kirsty had pieced together in her head. By seven, I'm sat in front of the computer, googling Arcadia staff members. None of them are familiar to me and due to patient confidentiality, I can't find photographs of any of the residents. I do find an ancient article linked to a local paper, it's an interview with the father of one of the women who died in the fire. He spoke of his guilt on sectioning his daughter for her own safety and how it had led to her untimely death. He had chosen Arcadia for the fact they tried to help people in her situation. They didn't treat mental health issues like some dirty, shameful secret, as many other institutes would. His daughter had suffered severe depression after her only child was stillborn, her father didn't want her locked away indefinitely. He wanted her to go on and lead a full and happy life again and be free of the darkness that plagued her. My phone buzzes with a text from Kirsty.

'I hope this doesn't waken you, message me when you're up. I can't sleep.'

I text back that I'm already up and for her to come over when she likes. I leave the article on the screen for her to see and head off for a shower.

Kirsty arrives an hour later and I make us both a coffee. She dumps down a bag of breakfast pastries and sits down at the computer. 'Wow, that poor man,' she sighs, as she reads through the article. 'Do you think he's still alive?'

'I would doubt it. It's almost fifty years since it happened and he says the daughter was almost forty at the time of her death.'

'Yeah, so he'd be well over a hundred now. That's a pity.' Kirsty scrolls through the article. 'Dorothy Elizabeth Lewis. Why don't we look for an obituary pic and see if we recognise her?'

'Why would we recognise her? You surely don't think we were there, it's not even possible. I only googled it out of curiosity.'

'See, this is why I told you nothing last night. Be quiet and help me look.' We search the local newspapers from 1968, me sighing at the pointlessness of it all and Kirsty digging me in the ribs to shut me up. After an hour of searching, we finally find an obituary for Dorothy, in a Harrow publication. Kirsty clicks on the link.

'Bingo! We have her, Grace.'

A grainy image of a woman, smiling in happier times, appears on the screen.

'Brioche,' Kirsty says quietly. I feel myself go cold all over.

'But...it's not possible. How can we remember her when she's been dead for nearly fifty years?'

'Because for that period of time when we were unconscious, we weren't here.'

'Of course we were here, Scott checked my stats every day,' I give an irate tut.

'Physically we were here, but the real essence of us wasn't. Come on, you're a scientist. *Think* about it.' Kirsty is becoming exasperated.

'I assume you're talking about our souls,' I roll my eyes. 'Existentially speaking, we cease to be without our human bodies. Anything we experienced while unconscious was simply drug related hallucinations.'

'*Bullshit,* we have proof. How can we hallucinate people that existed but we never knew?'

'No, at the very least we were in a suspended state...like Schrödinger's cat was to the outside world. What state was the physicist's cat in? Was he alive? Was he dead? That's what I think of when I think of us in there.'

'Exactly! Now we're getting somewhere. What's to say we weren't in a place in which we had a lesson to learn? I had to learn to let go of the past and that suicide wasn't the answer. The other road I could go down was to take my shitty childhood and make something better of it. That is why I'm going through all this gruelling crap that the adoption agency is throwing at me. I can't change my past, but I can make another child's life the best it can be. I want to raise Clarissa as my child and I won't stop until she's home with me.'

'I'm not convinced; what's my lesson?'

'You had to accept your own misfortunes and forgive yourself for the part you felt you played in it all. Oh yes,' she smiles slyly, 'I revisited that in my hypnosis session. I know all about your parents, brother, baby...*and your little dog too.*' Kirsty laughs as she mimics the witch's voice from *The Wizard of Oz*. 'None of it was your fault, Grace. You also needed to learn to be less materialistic and to do what makes you happy. You were spared a life when others weren't so lucky, so fucking well live it.' She looks triumphant in her conclusions.

'You think we went into this kind of limbo type place to come back as better people?'

'Yes, I do. Well, to come back as whole, more stable people. Brioche—I mean Dorothy—didn't make it. She died before she could get well. My theory is that she was there to help us and to teach us something. Compassion? Determination? I'm not sure, but I sense that she was part of it. She had been in there forever, I remembered that in my session with Paul. She never emotionally got out because she never physically got out.'

'She never got out because of the fire...' I'm struggling to get my head around Kirsty's theory. 'What about Jim? What about Mark?'

'Well, we both know what happened to Jim. Not everyone can be fixed, I guess. Mark? Who knows. We may have to let that one go. There were loads of people in Arcadia, I can't see us having some grand reunion in a Schrödinger's cat type support group.'

'So, you think that everyone who has a near death experience goes through this?' I'm questioning her, but it makes a bit more sense than I'd care to let on.

'I haven't got a clue. You hear of people seeing a long tunnel and a bright light, with loved ones who have died meeting them at the end of it, don't you? Maybe this is the coma version and a lot of people genuinely don't remember it, or explain it away with your drug-induced hallucinations reason.'

'You do hear of people floating above their bodies at the scenes of accident or during surgery, I guess. You knew my name and came looking for me,' I shrug. Kirsty's theory is a bit far-fetched but I'm struggling to explain it away.

'Let's go see Mrs Malik.' I grab the bag of pastries and we head downstairs.

'Yes, it is possible. You are having a life lesson to learn and you come back, so enjoy your second chances.' Mrs Malik had been completely unsurprised by our revelation.

'That's it?' Kirsty had clearly hoped for a bit more drama and excitement.

'How can we find Mark?' I enquire. 'Do you think your group could somehow...communicate with him?'

'We can try,' she smiles enigmatically.

I can't believe these words are coming out of my mouth. I'm a scientist for goodness sake. I pause as I recall something being said to me before. "Yesterday we may not have had a cure for a disease but it didn't mean that the cure didn't exist, just our knowledge of it didn't."

I see myself sitting opposite a man with glasses. A fountain pen and a notepad by his side on a small round table. He has his legs crossed at the knees and eyes me as if I was a specimen. Dr Peter, is that who he was? I tell the others my thoughts and Mrs Malik smiles.

'He a wise man, your Dr Peter. There is so much we are not knowing about. We just need to open our eyes, and our minds, and we see it.'

Kirsty and I leave with a homemade takeaway, placed in an ancient Fine Fare bag. We eat in silence at mine, both of us trying to figure out the next move.

'We need to let Mark go,' I say finally.

'Not necessarily, let's have faith in Mrs Malik and her crew.' Kirsty shrugs. She places her plate in the dishwasher and puts on her coat. 'Right, sorry to eat and run but I'm off to see my daughter-to-be. Her foster carers are being great about me hanging around so much. I have another meeting next week with the adoption people and then it's just all the red tape to get through.'

'Kirsty, that's great news. You'll be a fantastic mum.'

'I've had to be honest about my own childhood, my mum isn't suitable to be around Clarissa, but they know I have no intention of allowing that woman back into my life. I am a bit worried it'll put them off though.'

'You'll be fine; the kid dotes on you as much as you do her. They'd be mad to turn you down because of someone from your past.'

I walk Kirsty out and knock on Mrs Malik's door, to return her Tupperware. She gives me a wide smile.

'Good news; Mark alive! We have emergency group circle and we all feel a living soul. Where he is, I don't know. Sorry.'

That's good enough for me, we may not have had a happy ending for James Dibble or the lady we called Brioche, but Kirsty and I are going from strength to strength in our new lives. Mark is alive, that's all I really need to know.

'Thank you, Mrs Malik. I appreciate all you've done for us. Right, I better get back to work. I need a new script as a follow-up for Seb. I promised I'd have something to show him at the weekend.'

'You no show him anything,' she scolds. 'You wait until marriage for that.' She gives me a cheeky wink and I head back upstairs, laughing at the woman I used to avoid, who has now become one of my greatest friends. One of many, actually; Seb, Scott, Kirsty and Marion, every one of us thrown together from nowhere in this haphazard way. How strange that our lives crossed through such dark circumstances. It's hard to believe the place I was in emotionally, just a few months ago. It was filled with sadness and loneliness. My trip to Arcadia was indeed a light at the end of the tunnel. I made it back, unlike some. Now I won't, I daren't, waste another second of this precious thing we call life.

Epilogue
December 2016

I sit anxiously in the audience, with Seb and Travis on either side of me. The first live recording of So-Bryony is due to start in ten minutes. To say I'm bricking it would be putting it mildly.

'Don't worry, darling, it will be fine.' Seb takes my hand and gives it a squeeze.

'Get a bloody room,' Scott awkwardly manoeuvres himself along the row. 'Sorry, oops, was that your foot? It's lucky that I'm a nurse, isn't it?' He finally sits down heavily next to Travis. 'My new man sends his apologies for not making the show, guys. He has his book launch tonight but will come along to the after party.'

'Grace...Grace? Where you at, girl.'

'We're here, Mrs Malik. I saved you a seat next to me,' Seb waves.

'You no butter me up, boy. Until you make an honest woman of my second daughter, I give you no more curry. Living in sin! I not know why you people cannot wait.' My old neighbour takes her seat and rustles around in her bag, producing a large packet of sweets. She passes them along the line and we each take one.

'Come on, my angel. Look, there's Auntie Gracie over there.' I look up to see my friend arriving with her daughter and Marion. The child plants a kiss on my cheek and I give Seb a soppy look.

'Not a chance!' He stares at me aghast.

'Oh, come on. You know I'm broody.'

'OK, maybe...get more than five laughs and I'll consider it,' Seb chuckles. Clarissa settles down on her mother's knee.

'You've got your shoes on the wrong feet, silly,' Kirsty chides affectionately.

'They're the only feet I have. How can they be the wrong ones?' Clarissa pouts.

Mrs Malik pats the child's head and hands her the whole sweet bag. Kirsty tuts good-naturedly and tells Clarissa to go ahead, but not too many.

The lights go down and a buzz of anticipation fills the air. Having seen the rehearsals, I was pleasantly surprised by Sophia's portrayal of Bryony. Known only by her first name, I had been a bit sceptical of this girl. Who did she think she was, a Madonna or an Adele in the making? But she was funny, I had to give her the benefit of the doubt. Hadn't I been a science teacher with a dream? Everyone needs a chance to be someone new. Look at Uncle Marion, happily living as the woman she always identified with. Kirsty, she's gone from homeless gob-shite to doting mummy, and not in the annoying way that some of my old friends were. Seb too, he doesn't know it but I'll make a daddy of him yet. Even Scott, the eternal singleton, has been venturing out there. He's met some guy on Grndr and we all get to meet him for the first time later.

My hapless heroine wanders onstage to a round of applause. The script has Sophia saying Bryony's polite responses, whilst a voiceover speaks the part of what she really means. She's seeing some friends for a Christmas night out, for the first time since she came out of rehab. She's just spotted her ex-boyfriend and his new woman on the other side of the bar. Jane, a friend of Bryony's arrives and hits the bar for a wine.

'Bryony, it's good to see you. How was rehab? I bet you feel much better for it,' Jane says patronisingly.
'Is that a double to go with your shot?' My lead's voice-over booms out from a speaker. 'I'm thinking perhaps you should have joined me.'
'Yes, I feel fantastic, thank you. Looking forward to no hangover tomorrow,' beams stage Bryony.
'I do love a tonic water on its own, it tastes so refreshing,' Jane gushes.
'Not as refreshing as seeing you ten pounds heavier with the face of a Bull Mastiff. You're clearly in the throes of some brutal, festive overindulgence,' the voiceover chimes in.
'Gosh, I know. I could almost convince myself there's a gin in there,' states the chirpy, stage version of my character.
'But how have you really been?' The mock sympathy oozes from Jane as she reaches over to clutch Bryony's hand.
'I've dropped two stone, bought a designer handbag, and not woken up at the end of the tube line in twelve weeks,' deadpans the voiceover.
'Life is good. I've even been on two dates with a guy I met at AA, he's new to recovery too.'
'My goodness, an alcoholic who works for the breakdown service. That doesn't sound safe,' Jane clutches her chest dramatically.
'And yet they deem you safe to breed,' tuts the voiceover.
'So, how do you get your kicks now? I remember that you liked to smoke a bit of marijuana in college...'
'I do online shopping, spending all the money I saved from getting wasted all the time.'
'Still, I do remember when a hashtag was hanging around someone you knew had a joint,' chimes in the voiceover.

Kirsty clutches her hands to her daughter's ears.

'You said this was appropriate,' she hisses. I give a nonchalant shrug. Yes, I wrote the script but Seb edits bits in and out to give a better flow. Voiceover Bryony is getting all the laughs. I look at my friends in the row and all seem to be finding it hugely entertaining. The pilot finishes with a showdown between Bryony and the drunken girlfriend of her ex. Clarissa has gone from bored and restless, to laughing raucously at the drinks being thrown around the stage. The show ends with a standing ovation for the cast. The cheering seems to go on relentlessly and I feel rather embarrassed by my part in all this. I've never enjoyed having attention drawn to anything I do and it'll take a bit of getting used to. Worse still, they turn the spotlight on to me and announce my name as the playwright of the show. I give an awkward wave to those around me and turn my attention back to the stage. Sophia has acted out my script better than anyone else I could have imagined. I scold myself for snootily looking down on her abilities.

We head back home for an after show party. Seb puts on some music and Mrs Malik heats up the curry. My show is receiving a lot of praise. For the first time, I realise I could successfully make a career of script-writing. I just have one final surprise for this evening and it's on its way into the front room, right at this moment.

'Uncle Sebastian, we have a present for you,' beams Clarissa, carefully carrying a box towards Seb.

'For me, Lissy? But it's Auntie Gracie's big day.' Seb crouches down to the little girl and eyes her suspiciously.

'Shush,' Clarissa tells the box, with a slight hint of Scottish accent. 'Well, you see, Mummy said I needed a cousin, so...'

Seb pulls the ribbon on the box and the lid bounces open. A Jack Russell puppy stares up from the inside, tilting his head adorably.

'Grace? Why is there a dog, in a box, in my living room?'

'Like the girl says, she needs a cousin. I did warn you I was broody.'

'What's his name, Lissy?' Seb picks up the pup, who wriggles in his arms and tries to lick his face. The child thinks for a moment, Kirsty urges her to pick one from her range of choices they discussed earlier.

'Rainbow,' she states. We all make the appropriate noises and Clarissa goes off to set out the puppy's bed and toys, shouting back to us that he's had all his jabs and can go outside now. Kirsty had kept the dog all week, to keep the surprise for tonight's celebration. She assures me that he's now fully toilet trained. She is seeking compensation for a well-chewed bedroom chair and a Barbie doll, however.

'Please tell me we are not calling the dog Rainbow.'

'Shh, Seb. Only when Lissy is around. Don't worry, you can choose something manly and butch for him.' I pat his hand reassuringly.

Mrs Malik shouts us through to the kitchen to take our curries. I watch the stampede and smile contentedly at my friends. So much has changed for me since Arcadia. Yes, I have finally accepted that something strange went on while we were asleep. Kirsty and I needed a rocket up our arses to get us out of our self-destructive ways, as she herself so eloquently puts it. Marion has moved into my place and finally has her rightful title of auntie. She and Mrs Malik have become firm friends, although they bicker as much as they get on. We often get those calls saying, "guess what's she's gone and done now," from either party. Marion has gone from brothel to bingo these days and can comfortably retire on the money she's made from her business ventures.

Seb and I? Well, we got engaged a few weeks ago on holiday in Santorini. It was completely unexpected on my part, but it felt right, so I said yes. The doorbell interrupts my thoughts.

'I'll get it, shall I?' I shout to the oblivious noisy bunch in the kitchen. I make my way down the fairy-lit and garland filled hallway. Seb had thought it rather over the top but I love the festive feel. The hall is scented with apple cinnamon and gingerbread candles. They flicker warmly in the breeze as I open the door.

'Hello, you must be Grace. I'm Scott's boyfriend. Oh God! Please don't tell him I said that,' he laughs. 'I'm not even sure if we're at that stage yet.' I give a soft chuckle.

'Your secret is safe with me, come on in. Oh, look, it's starting to snow.' The man steps over the threshold and together we watch the snowflakes swirl around the street lamps.

'Gosh, isn't it beautiful. I'm sorry, I didn't catch your name.' We walk down the hallway and into the brightly lit front room, filled with noise and activity. I turn to get a proper look and see if Scott's boyfriend is as hot as he claims.

'Mark Green,' he smiles.

'Mark! Oh, my goodness...let me get you a drink,' I babble. Mark gives me a strange look as I turn back and pull him into an impromptu, tight hug.

'It really is just so amazing to see you.'

Scott makes his way over to us.

'Bitch, please! Put my man down at once, we don't want him to go off and bat for the opposition.'

I make my escape and head to the kitchen to fetch a drink for Mark, grabbing Kirsty on the way by.

'Look,' I demand. 'Recognise that face?' I point towards our new guest and wait for her reaction.

'No fricking way...'

'Yeah, way. He seems totally oblivious though. There was nothing, not a single bit of recognition on his face when he saw me.'

'Do we mess with his head and tell him? In his opinion he's only just met us and probably doesn't want to admit he was once suicidal,' Kirsty whispers.

'No, leave it be, I reckon. What are the bloody odds of that though? Just a chance, online meeting with one of our friends and now Mark is standing *here*, in my front room?'

'You know, I've been doing some more thinking about what happened to us, Grace.'

I roll my eyes at the next chapter of Kirsty's over-active imagination heading my way.

'Don't be so dismissive, just *listen* to me. You know how Dr Peter was the therapist at Arcadia? Well, my theory is that because we were all in that Schrödinger state, we got a little glimpse of the afterlife too.'

'Yes, I know, you've told me all of this.'

'No, this is different. Hear me out,' Kirsty insists.

'You're obviously not going to shut up until you've got it out of your system. Go on, I'm listening.'

'OK, what if Dr Peter was Saint Peter? The gatekeeper of Heaven? He decides if we get in, or sent back to learn from our mistakes.'

'Kirsty, you know I'm not religious. Next you'll be telling me that the group therapy leader was the Archangel Gabriel.'

She throws me a sarcastic look.

'That was actually where I was going next. Do you know that the name Ariel is Hebrew for lion of God? She may have seemed like a pussycat but she wasn't, was she?'

'Kirsty, you've completely lost the plot now. I'm not drunk enough for this conversation.' I push my way past her, heading to the fridge for a top-up of wine.

'Is that so? Well hear this. Pastoral paradise; that's the definition of Arcadia, according to poetic fantasy. What does pastoral mean, Grace? It means concerning or appropriate to the giving of spiritual guidance.'

I lean my head against the coolness of the fridge door.

'You see? I telling you Mark is alive. God only know how that boy made it, after all he put himself through.' Mrs Malik breaks the terse atmosphere and takes Clarissa out a juice box from the fridge.

'Why you girls fight when neither of you have the answer? You not got a clue what is out there for us after life. I should be knocking your bloody heads together.'

'Does absolutely nothing faze you, Mrs Malik?' Kirsty stares at her in awe.

'No, what will be will be. You meant to meet again and so it is happening. Don't argue about shit you know nothing about.'

Kirsty and I exchange reluctant smiles of armistice and make our way back over to Mark. Kirsty stares at him unashamedly until I give her a nudge.

'So, Mark, we hear you're a writer,' I can't help but quiz him. I need to know why he got into it, did I do that?

'Well, this is my first attempt but I got lucky and signed a book deal a few weeks ago.'

'Wow, that's fantastic. What do you write about?'

'It's a humorous, fantasy fiction, I had a bit of a life-changing year and I've had an urge to write since. I think Scott has his copy with him. He said he saw someone reading it on the tube and told him he'd been on a date with me. Shameless, that's what he is.'

Scott holds the book triumphantly aloft.

'Give us a look then, Scott,' Kirsty makes a grab for it.

'Don't mess it up with your curry hands. Go and wash them. This is the first signed copy.'

She heads off to the kitchen with a sigh and I catch a glimpse of the front cover, it features a white building that looks exactly like Arcadia. Bedlam; that's what he's named his book.

'I need to read this, you got any more with you?' I thumb through Scott's copy until he grabs it from me.

'No, I'm sorry, but I'll get you one tomorrow,' Mark smiles benevolently. 'Call it an early Christmas present.'

'I have spares,' Scott unclips his backpack. 'I was going to wait until you were all drunk and make you buy them, but I can see there's no need.'

Mark hosts an impromptu signing at our dining table. Kirsty puts a sleepy Clarissa in her buggy, to go home with Marion and Mrs Malik. Her aunt is taking the little one for a sleepover, so that Kirsty can have a rare night off.

I move the puppy into the bedroom with his training pads, bowls, and bed. I did say I wouldn't let him sleep in with us, and here I am breaking the rules, an indulgent mother already. Kirsty puts on some music and we spend the next two hours squabbling over the mountain of CDs dumped in the middle of the table. It has taken a huge effort not to mention anything to Mark about what Kirsty and I know, but surprisingly, we do manage to keep schtum.

By the time 2am arrives, I'm exhausted. Seb sends me off to snuggle in with the dog, which in his drunken state he has decided he will name either Jack, or Russell. It ain't happening, I'll call him Rainbow over either of those unimaginative names. I see my friends off and crawl into bed, noticing briefly that one of my slippers has been reduced to a pile of foam. I pick up the puppy and tuck him under the duvet beside me. He pushes my arm up with his nose and falls asleep instantly. I inhale his warm doggy smell and listen to him breathing deeply in my arms. It may have taken nearly twenty years, but I'm finally ready to trust myself to care for another living being in a way that I couldn't before.

I waken early, to a wet nose and enthusiastic licks to my cheek. 'Bugger off, Seb. It's not even light outside yet.' I mumble sleepily. A grunt from other side of the bed makes me realise that an amorous fiancé isn't the culprit. I open my eyes to my new baby's enquiring face and my heart gives a little leap of joy. 'Come on then, let's go pee-pee.'

I shiver out in the snow in my night clothes and Ugg boots, as the little dog has a good sniff around. He's probably already been, judging by the mess I saw in Seb's good work shoes by the side of the bed. I feel a rectangular shape in my dressing gown pocket. Ah, yes. I remember now. I put Mark's book in there last night, after I picked it up from the dining table on my way to bed. I never even got round to opening the first page. He's signed it for me and written a dedication too.

My Dear Grace,
I want to thank you for being there for me. You thought I didn't remember you, but I do. Thank you for coming back to me one last time, to help me find the incentive to leave. Shelley sends her warmest regards.
Love Mark.
xxx

As I stand outside on this Christmas eve, looking up at the barely lit sky for Adi's star, the snow falls gently around me and my dog. I hear carols float on the breeze from a nearby church, as the parishioners have their early morning practice for tonight's concert. *O Holy Night!* I adore that song. It makes this old sceptic smile, every time.

See, I don't know who's right, I don't know who's wrong, but looking up into this vast space makes it difficult to believe there isn't something more out there. We'll find out for sure when we get to where we are going. What I do know for sure is that we are all linked together. We live on forever in the hearts and memories of our loved ones, making our own individual marks on the world that can never be undone. I have a vague memory of discussing this before. Who was it with? It was like I'd awakened, from a time that now feels like a hundred years ago. Every person we meet has an effect on each and every one of us. Good or bad, right or wrong, they all have something to give us so we can learn and grow.

'Come on, baby. Let's go inside and warm up.' I pick up the puppy and take one last glance at the sky. There it is, Adi's star. It twinkles down on me and I give it a wide smile in return. I get it now, I wasn't asleep all that time in Arcadia. I was waking up. To life and to love, and to the only truth that we have in our lives.

We are all one

Louise Burness is a fiction humour author from the north-east of Scotland. Her career began after friends jokingly suggested that she write a book about her unsuccessful love life.

Her first book, *Crappily Ever After,* became a Kindle best seller.

Louise released her second novel. *Ivy Eff,* in 2014. She has also written two children's books, illustrates many of her book covers, and enjoys making song parodies for her YouTube channel.

She is currently working on fiction humour book number four and the audiobook narrations for two of her existing novels.

www.louiseburness.info

Printed in Great Britain
by Amazon

85706571R00108